Sophia Bennett

THE CASTLE

Chicken House

2 Palmer Street, Frome, Somerset BA11 1DS

Text © Sophia Bennett 2014
First published in Great Britain in 2014
The Chicken House
2 Palmer Street
Frome, Somerset, BA11 1DS
United Kingdom
www.doublecluck.com

Sophia Bennett has asserted her right under the Copyright, Designs and Patents Act 1988
to be identified as the author of this work.

Cover design and interior design by Steve Wells
Typeset by Dorchester Typesetting Group Ltd
Printed and bound in Great Britain by CPI Group (UK) Ltd, Croydon, CR0 4YY

The paper used in this Chicken House book is made from wood grown in
sustainable forests.

1 3 5 7 9 10 8 6 4 2

British Library Cataloguing in Publication data available.

ISBN 978-1-909489-78-3
eISBN 978-1-909489-79-0

To my father, Ray, who always knows the right way to go.

Prologue

Today, while nobody was watching, the prisoner gave me a special message for the girl. I must repeat it exactly, so I will say it many times in my head so I do not forget.

He did not tell me what they will do if they find her. He did not need to – I already know.

ONE

What is wrong with this picture?

It's Saturday afternoon. We're in the small, ancient church of St Thomas the Martyr in Winchelsea, where my granny does the flowers, and where I was christened fourteen years ago.

I'm in a satin dress. An old-fashioned bridesmaid's dress with a sash. It's apricot satin, apparently. Or peach. Some soft fruit or other. And it comes down to my ankles. Did I mention the sash? There are no words.

Sitting to my right are three tall blonde girls, also dressed à la fruit. Somehow, they look gorgeous. They're trying to pretend I'm not here. At the top of the aisle, my mother is

1

standing next to the blonde girls' father, who is Rupert, Mum's boyfriend. Fiancé. About-to-be-husband. She's looking lovingly into his eyes.

The vicar is saying, 'If anyone present knows a reason why these persons may not lawfully marry, they must declare it now.'

And about half the congregation are casting sideways glances in my direction. Because they know that I, for one, can think of one teeny little reason why these persons may not lawfully marry: my mother still happens to be married to my father. Which means she could end up in jail one day, when Dad comes home.

And THAT is what is wrong with this picture. Although the peach satin comes a close second.

But I promised I'd be good today. So I look up at the beautiful stained-glass window of a knight rising to heaven, which I know so well from endless Christmases and Sunday mornings spent in this place, and I keep my peace. If you can call it peace. Personally, that's not how I'd describe it.

Once the 'declare it now' moment has passed, a sigh of relief goes round the congregation: *The loopy daughter didn't mess it up for her mother.* The vicar smiles and carries on with the ceremony. Mum and Rupert are holding hands now. Eugh.

The tall boy on my right slips his hand reassuringly around mine. He knows how hard this is for me, and how brave I'm being. I think it's brave anyway. Maybe I'm just being stupid to go along with it all. This wedding is probably illegal (look up 'bigamy' in the dictionary: bad thing), but it's what Mum wants.

The boy is Luke McCrae, my best friend from Dad's old

army days. He looks pretty good in his dark suit, with his hair gently curling over his collar. He squeezes my hand gently, three times, while I hold my breath and say nothing. I'm counting up to a hundred in sevens in my head, to take my mind off things.

'Good girl,' he whispers, lifting his left arm out of its crutch to ruffle my hair.

Yes. Today I'm being a good girl. Mum thinks of herself as a recently bereaved widow, and that's tough. Rupert has indeed been very supportive – rushing over to be by her side the moment we got the news about the so-called bomb that supposedly killed my father in Baghdad.

Rupert's broody and good-looking, like a Brontë hero, and it isn't exactly Mum's fault that she let her hormones run away with her. We studied it in biology, but she just got antsy when I tried to explain it to her. She thinks this is true love. She wants a nice, romantic wedding and a honeymoon in the Caribbean. I want a quiet life.

'And do you, Isabelle Maria Henrietta, take this man, Rupert Simon . . .'

The hush of the congregation is suddenly shattered by very loud music. I recognise it straight away: Roxanne Wills singing 'Walk Away' – her club hit from a couple of years ago. It's coming from one of the front rows. The vicar looks up. We all glance round.

Walk away, uh-huh, don't look back
Walk away down a different track

We look up and down. The eight-year-old on the opposite aisle wiggles her hips to the music. From the front row, my grandmother's furious stare could cut the wedding cake all by itself.

Walk away, uh-huh, he's no good

Walk away like you know you should

It wails on and on and nobody stops it. The horrible truth sinks in. A certain bridesmaid realises that her phone is going off in her bag. When she looks down, she can actually see the bag vibrating at her feet. She simply can't be seen to lean forward and pick it up at this crucial moment, and so admit she was the one who chose this ringtone. The best she can do is to manoeuvre her peach satin scarf on top of it with her shoe, while trying to maintain a look of innocent bemusement like everyone else.

Eventually the vibrating stops and Roxanne Wills goes silent. Unlike Luke McCrae, who is sobbing by my side. No, wait – his shoulders are heaving, but that noise is actually suppressed giggles. Go, Luke. Way to be a friend.

'I can't believe you did that!' he mouths at me, while the vicar quickly recovers and gets on with the vows.

'I didn't! I didn't do anything!'

That's the whole problem, not that anyone will ever believe me. I was so busy stressing about Mum and the wedding and the dress (mine, not hers – Mum adores hers), and not saying anything and being good, that I didn't even think about turning my phone off. Besides, who would be calling me right now? Half my family are here; Dad's parents died years ago; and all my school friends know I'm busy at my mother's wedding, and so now is not a good time, actually.

As soon as the vows are over, Mum whips round and gives me a look that makes Granny's cake-knife stare seem positively friendly. I put on my *sorry, big-time accident, sorry* face. Honestly! I'm trying *so hard* today. Surely I deserve just a bit of credit?

Finally, the organ strikes up something old and loud while

Mum and Rupert head off towards the ancient tombs at the side of the church for the signing of the register. The congregation starts up a steady hum of its own, chatting about how lovely Mum looks in her vintage lace, and how well she's bearing up after . . . well . . . *you know* . . . And wasn't it dreadful when that phone went off? Talking of which, Luke leans across and surreptitiously pulls it out of my bag.

'D'you want me to check it for you?'

'No. *So* no. It's probably just someone trying to sell me insurance. Just turn it off. Please.'

He presses the button and holds it down. Just for a moment, I wonder if the call was from Dad. It's a hope I'm learning to crush, but every time something unusual happens I can't help wondering if it was Dad-related. I know he wasn't killed by that bomb, but I keep asking myself where he really is. Will he suddenly show up on our doorstep one day? Or randomly call me on a Saturday afternoon during Mum's wedding . . .?

No. He wouldn't do that – of course he wouldn't. But somebody did, and the timing was *weird*. It has to be a wind-up. I check around the church. Has somebody here called me deliberately to make Roxanne go off at precisely that moment?

The gorgeous blondes are chatting among themselves and paying me no attention (as usual). I don't think it was them. And I honestly can't imagine people like my Great-Uncle Alastair and my second cousin Emily hate me that much. Or know my ringtone. Or even my number. I can only assume it was a random joke.

Ha ha. *So* funny. Really loving my life right now.

TWO

'It wasn't my fault!' I repeated for the tenth time.

'Then whose fault was it?' Granny huffed. By now, we were back at her hotel for the reception. She and my grandad run a place called the Smugglers' Inn in Rye. In Georgian times real smugglers used the bar as their head-quarters, sitting with loaded pistols on the table as they made their plans to rob ships in the English Channel. Right now, if Granny had been standing there with a loaded pistol she couldn't have looked any more hostile.

'It was an accident,' I tried to explain. 'A coincidence . . . I don't know . . .' I still hadn't heard the message. I couldn't bear to listen.

Granny pursed her lips. 'Someone just happened to call during your mother's vows?'

'Yes!'

'And you just *happened* to have picked that ringtone?'

'Yes! Yes!' I could feel tears pricking and blinked them quickly away. That ringtone was special to me. It reminded me of Dad's last visit, when we danced round the kitchen to the song, shaking our booties and doing our diva faces. It had nothing to do with Mum, or this stupid wedding.

'Have you apologised to her, Peta?'

'Several times,' I muttered.

'Well, you might as well make yourself useful,' Granny decided. 'Go and find a tray of canapés in the kitchen. And when you're done, you can take round refills of champagne. We could do with some extra hands.'

I often helped out and usually I liked it, but today I didn't want to be The Girl Whose Father Died In A So-Called Bomb Last Year. It was the pity stares that killed me, but I found they were slightly easier to take from behind a tray of mini fruit tarts and sticky choux buns. That way, I could focus on the food and pretend I couldn't hear the repeated snatches of conversation as I went by:

'Poor Isabelle. She's been *so brave*. They say Peta never got over the shock of the news. She refuses to accept it, even now . . .'

'It happened a lot after 9/11, you know. Unless they see the body, some people just won't believe their loved one has gone. It's very sad. She's in therapy, of course.'

'Thank goodness. That ringtone! You can tell it was deliberate. She's quite a handful, I'm told . . .'

So not true! You'd think it would be good to have a daughter who's not grief-stricken the whole time. I wasn't 'a

7

handful' – just optimistic. I believed in my dad, and a long time ago, Mum used to, too.

I wasn't in denial about Dad being dead. He was a soldier for most of my life and I'd spent all that time hearing about friends' parents dying or being injured in a war zone. If Dad had been serving in Afghanistan when the bomb news came, I'd have believed it completely, but he was out of the army by then. He was working an IT adviser. How boring was that?

Also, Dad had a sixth sense for danger. He was much too clever to be caught out by a home-made device hidden under a vehicle, which is what they said had killed him. Goodness knows what was in that urn of ashes they sent us. My bet was stray dog and bits of old seat belt. When a big bomb goes off, there's not that much to scrape up so they gather what they can. People say I'm avoiding reality when it comes to what happened in Iraq, but believe me, I'm not. I've looked into it. A lot.

Out in the courtyard, seagulls wheeled overhead and an old school friend of Mum's lunged forward and grabbed a bun from my tray. I made a mental note not to come back to her with champagne refills: she seemed to have had quite a few already. She gave me the full-on pity stare.

'Poor, poor Peta,' she slurred, scrunching up her eyes in sympathy. 'You must be feeling so *awful*.'

'Well, I'm . . .'

'But that's the army for you. Terrible things happen in war.'

'Dad wasn't *in* the army when it happened. That's sort of why . . .'

'Aren't you lucky that your mum found happiness?'

'Erm . . .'

'You can see they're made for each other. Isabelle and

Rupert. Rupert and Isabelle. Isn't it wonderful? D'you think they'll have *children*, Peta darling? *Together?*

I took advantage of the temporary silence as she stuffed her mouth with pastry.

'Sorry. Somebody over there needs more cake. Got to go.'

The summer sun beat down. Soon it would be the school holidays. Just Mum, me, Rupert and the perfect blondes. I looked desperately around for a friendly face, and caught sight of Luke across the courtyard. He'd been captured by two of Rupert's elderly relatives, who were clearly commiserating with him about his crutches. He caught my eye and smiled.

I'd known Luke since our first year in primary, when we'd met at Buckingham Palace. Our dads were both getting medals that day – his for being a top bomb-disposal expert and mine, well, mine for doing lots of secret army stuff that nobody talked about. If Dad could defend his comrades through five ambushes behind enemy lines, the least I could manage was getting rid of the remaining six or seven pastries. I took a deep breath and upped the wattage of my smile.

'Can I tempt you?' I asked the elderlies, joining Luke and offering my tray around. For a moment, they were distracted by food, and admiring my dress, because they thought ankle-length peach satin was absolutely appropriate for a fourteen-year-old girl. As the pity stares began to emerge, it was Luke who rescued me.

'Dad!' he called out, grabbing my elbow and pulling me away.

His dad, not mine. I still got a strange, crazy pang of jealousy whenever I heard the word out loud. Sergeant McCrae and a few of Dad's other old army friends were sneaking inside. They were here today because they were friends of Rupert's too. It's beyond awkward when one of your dad's old officers starts dating your mother. It was good to see them, though.

'Luke!' Sergeant McCrae called back with a grin. 'Don't tell on us. Please?'

'Aw,' says one of the others, 'let him join us, Jock. Boy needs a break from the laydeez.'

No doubt they were heading for the Pool Room (snooker, not swimming, though guests at the inn were often confused). They'd be secretly off to drink whisky and smoke out of the window like naughty schoolboys. They'd want to avoid any talk of children, schools and wedding outfits, and reminisce instead about incredibly stupid things they had done in incredibly dangerous situations, usually in war zones. I'd been sitting at their feet listening to these conversations since I was tiny.

'Can I come too?' I asked eagerly.

Sergeant McCrae looked me up and down, taking in the tray, the full peach-satin scenario, the freshly straightened hair, the lip gloss Mum made me wear.

'That'll be grand, Peta,' he said. There was an awkwardness to his voice that was full of what happened to Dad. Not as bad as the pity stare, but close. And there was something else. It was to do with my dress and my hair and my all-round general girl-ness. 'Tell you what, we could do with some decent sandwiches. Why don't you see what you can rustle up for us?'

Rustle up?

For a moment, I stared back at him with my mouth wide open. *Rustle. Up?* This was the twenty-first century. Or had I just time-travelled back to when the smugglers used this place? Just because I was wearing lip gloss, it didn't mean I couldn't handle stories about near-death parachuting accidents, or the day Dad had to disguise himself as a bush and a pack of stray dogs peed on him, or Jock McCrae's famous party trick of using his prosthetic legs as pool cues. But he was already wheeling himself down the corridor without me.

Luke gave me a rueful smile and went off to join them. He knew it wasn't fair, but the chance of listening to some war stories was too good to miss.

That was it. Day over. Sorry, Dad, but there's only so much I can take. I bet *you'd* have struggled with those stray dogs if you'd been doing it in peach satin.

It was the stupid dress's fault. I hated dresses. I hated peach. I hated silk sashes and net petticoats and being a bridesmaid, when Mum shouldn't have been marrying at all. I dumped the tray in the kitchen and fled up the narrow back stairs of the inn, making for the top-floor flat where my grandparents lived.

Mum and I been staying here since the 'bomb' and I had Mum's old room, under the eaves. Its low, sloping walls were covered with pictures from her childhood. As I ripped the dress off and started digging around for my jeans, I checked out happy pictures of growing-up Mum with her pony, her little sister Eliza, her early, nerdy, spotty boyfriends, and then the confident, good-looking one, who was fifty times better than all the others put together, and whose straight eyebrows and slate-grey eyes matched the ones I saw in the mirror when I dragged on a T-shirt, rubbed off the lip gloss and mussed up my hair.

Mum and Dad fell for each other when they were teenagers and ran off to Brighton to get married, because they couldn't wait. Mum wore jeans and the wedding ring came from a stall at the Flea Market. I came along soon after and the three of us . . . we were It, the Unit, everything.

Dad was a hero. He'd fought in three wars, including one when he was not so much older than me, and won the Military Cross for what he did in those ambushes. It was hard not talking about him at school. 'What does your dad do?' 'He manages an office. What does yours do?' 'He's a soldier.' But what I really meant was, 'He saves the world. Like James Bond. Every day.'

How could Mum fall in love with Rupert? How could anyone do that twice? And having more *children* with him? His perfect daughters were bad enough: Damaris, Davina and Desdemona, collectively known as the Darling Ds. The thought of more of them made me shiver.

If Dad could see me now, those eyebrows would be frowning. I knew I should be sucking up more pity stares, not slumping to the floor with my head on my knees and tears streaming down my face. Worse still, I could hear Granny calling for the bridesmaids to come forward for more photos. People would be looking round to see where I was. They'd assume I was being 'a handful'. Maybe I was.

I reached across for my hideous peach satin bag, and got out my phone to listen to that message from the church at last. As I pressed the button to turn it back on, the door creaked and I leapt to my feet.

'Coming, Granny.'

But it wasn't Granny. It was Mum. Looking absolutely beautiful in her short lace dress and heels. And not incandescently angry any more. Just sad.

'Here you are!' she said. 'I've been looking for you. I'm about to get changed before we go, and I wanted a quick chat.'

I eyed her nervously. I'd apologised at least six times for the phone call. What else could I do?

'Don't worry,' she said, plonking herself down on the bed,

edging my sleeping cat along and patting the place next to her. 'I don't want to go away for two weeks and leave you like this.'

'Like what?' I perched uncomfortably between her and Lacy, the cat.

'All wound up and miserable. I just want you to know how much I love you, darling. And Rupe does too.'

Rupe. She called him 'Rupe'. I tried hard not to roll my eyes. Not hard enough, though.

'He does. Really,' Mum sighed. 'And most importantly, Dad loved you. More than you'll ever know. And, darling . . .' She bit her lip, working out what to say. 'I know this conversation is hard for us, but one day you'll learn to accept that he's gone. I know it doesn't feel real, but one day it will.'

I gritted my teeth. We hadn't talked about Dad properly for a while, what with the wedding and everything, and I really wished we weren't doing it now, just before she went away.

'He loved you so much. If there was any way for him to come back to you, he'd have done it by now. You must know that, precious girl.'

Her voice was soft and gentle, but the words still felt like sandpaper.

'I . . . I don't know,' I whispered. I had lots of reasons for believing that Dad was still out there, but . . . why didn't he come home?

'Listen,' she went on, 'he had his odd ways, and goodness knows we had our problems, but . . .'

'What problems?'

'Nothing for you to worry about. I just want you to know that it's going to be OK. I'll be away for a short time and then we can build our new life. You, me and Rupe. And you'll have

13

that beautiful bedroom in his house. And that wonderful new school to go to with the girls. Promise me you'll try.'

What she really meant was that we were moving in a few weeks, when the summer holidays started, and next term Rupert was going to send me to a posh boarding school in the country where his beautiful daughters went, and where *they were just average-looking*. (I'd checked their Interface pages and seen their friends.) I'd be the flat-chested certified nutcase, so that would be fun, and I wouldn't see my school friends from Rye again.

I stroked Lacy's soft fur and tried to keep my cool. After so many years of army life I was used to moving schools. All these things were going to happen regardless of what I did or thought. And if Mum was right about Dad not coming back, then what did it matter anyway?

'Sure,' I said. I bit back the *Whatever* that wanted to come next.

'Thank you.' She pulled me into her for a big, warm hug. 'That means so much to me, darling. I couldn't enjoy the trip if you weren't OK.'

She kindly avoided saying 'honeymoon' at least. She knew the word made me flinch. She was trying too.

Two minutes later, there was another knock on the door. It was Rupert, who looked relieved to see us hugging.

'Oh, good. I thought I might find you here, darling. Have you told Peta about the surprise?'

'What surprise?' I asked warily.

'Not yet,' Mum said, with a mildly annoyed head-shake at her new 'husband'. 'I was just getting there.'

'So?' I asked.

She smiled at me. 'We thought it might be lonely for you

while we were away. So we asked Luke and Sergeant McCrae if they'd stay on here for a few days so Luke can keep you company. Granny's giving them a free room.'

'Really?'

'Yes, really.'

'What about Luke's school?'

'He says he can do the homework online. He says he'll get more done here than at home.'

'So he knows about this?'

'Uh-huh.'

She was still smiling. Me not so much – I don't like secrets. However, this was a good one, no denying it. I gave Mum an extra hug, and felt even guiltier about the whole phone-in-church thing. Although that still wasn't my fault.

After they'd gone to get changed, my eye fell on my phone, on the floor in front of me. I still hadn't listened to that message.

Hope/don't hope/hope/don't hope.

Thinking about Dad was exhausting, especially when I needed him as much as I did today. As I picked the phone up, I said a little prayer. It had no words, but I knew what I wanted.

It wasn't Dad on my voicemail, though. It was hard to hear the message on the thin, crackly line, but it was someone I didn't recognise, with a quiet, musical voice. Young, and possibly Indian. A boy.

'Peta Jones?' it said. 'I have a message for you. The bad people are coming to get you. Please believe me. They are on their way. You must hide. Now. Do not call me.'

That was all.

As if the day hadn't been stressful enough already.

THREE

On Tuesday, Luke offered to pick me up after school and walk to my counsellor's consulting rooms with me. It was a long trek from Collingwood Academy to the Brightside Centre, and although he was brilliant on his crutches, they tired him out. However, he insisted. Luke was a gentleman that way.

Luke knew how I felt about my Tuesday sessions. I was supposed to 'open up' about 'being in denial' about Dad. Dr Benson, my counsellor, had no interest in *why* I didn't believe Dad was dead; he just wanted me to accept that he was. Usually, my time with him consisted of long silences, while he stared at me through his trendy red-rimmed glasses and I looked at all the pictures of him with his wife, three children and smug, smiling dog.

Luke was waiting at the gates when I came out of school. We set off down the road together, past small red-brick houses on one side and shaggy open fields on the other. As we walked along, he loped beside me with an easy, graceful stride.

'So you're going to tell Benson about the message?' he asked. Obviously, I'd told Luke all about it straight away on Saturday. He was the only person I'd mentioned it to.

'Yeah, but now he'll think I'm nutty with sprinkles on top.'

'A, he's paid to do that, and, B, it's hardly your fault if some sick idiot tried to wind you up.'

This was reassuringly true. In fact, I'd handled Saturday's message pretty well, I thought. It was obviously a hoax, so I'd deleted it from my phone and put it out of my mind. Well, mostly out of my mind. I only thought about it once or twice a day. I could still repeat it word for word, though, in my head. And I still had no idea who'd sent it.

At the bottom of the road, we stopped at the old-fashioned sweet shop where I always popped in to get supplies of Toxic Waste and Haribos, as my reward for after the session.

Sweet Sensations was full of people from Collingwood, despite the notice on the door saying maximum two school kids at a time. As we joined the queue to pay, Jason Ridgeway, a boy from my year, came in behind us. I sighed inwardly and put on my poker face.

'Hiya, Psycho,' he grinned at me.

I ignored him. Ever since the counselling started, Jason had found me very amusing. Was it him who'd left the voicemail? It was exactly the kind of thing he'd do – if he could think of it. But thinking up the nickname Psycho had been a major achievement for Jason.

Luke tensed beside me, but said nothing. Like me, he was trained to avoid confrontation. When you have a parent who can kill a man with a single blow, they tend to teach conflict-avoidance. Self-defence, yes, but mostly conflict-avoidance. Less chance of broken bones and jail.

I put our sweets on the counter. 'These, please.'

'Off to see the loony doctor then?' Jason did his googly eye impression, not that he had to try very hard. We looked quite similar, but if you wanted to cast a mildly insane-looking fourteen-year-old for a movie, you'd definitely pick him over me.

'Yeah. I keep getting this strange urge to cut people into tiny pieces,' I said casually, giving him a *what-can-you-do-about-it* shrug.

He took a step back, pretending to be terrified, and tripped over one of Luke's trailing crutches.

'Oi! Watch out!' he said crossly. 'Don't want to cause an accident. Kaboom!'

He laughed and winked at me. He did it every time – as if I hadn't got the bit about the bomb in Baghdad. Kaboom. Very funny.

'And we're the ones getting our heads examined,' I muttered to Luke as we left the shop. 'Although admittedly –' I gestured at his crutches – 'you need it.'

Luke was in counselling too, for his own interesting set of issues. When he found out that Sergeant McCrae had lost his legs in a minefield in Afghanistan, Luke had lost the feeling in his own. It still hadn't come back. Some people take bad news *way* too seriously.

'Whereas you, of course, are perfect,' he said.

'I'm glad you think so.'

We took a shortcut to Dr Benson's through the car park beside the railway station. It was lined with rows of empty tourist coaches, waiting for their passengers to finish their sightseeing trips in town.

'So, you know, I thought you'd like to see the real highlights of Rye,' I said, indicating the coaches and the railings beside the track.

He whistled. 'Wow.'

'Thank you.'

'No, look.'

A black Range Rover was drawing up just ahead of us. 'So?'

'It's been totally pimped,' Luke said, impressed. 'Blacked-out windows. Special paint job. Alloy wheels. It must be worth at least a hundred grand.'

'No way!'

'Way. At *least*.'

The car stopped and the nearest window rolled down on silent electric motors, to reveal a woman with a pale, oval face framed by long waves of dark hair. I was disappointed. After Luke's intro to the car, I'd been hoping for a pop star or a Manchester United player.

She leant over towards us. 'Hello? Can you help me?'

Luke went over. 'Sure.' He flashed the woman a grin. She was very attractive – rather like the Wicked Queen from an old picture book I had of Snow White. I couldn't help smiling when I saw that Luke's tongue was bright blue from the Toxic Waste already. Poor boy – he had no idea.

She looked at me in my crumpled blue blazer.

'I'm looking for Peta Jones,' she said. 'He goes to your

school. One of his friends pointed in this direction.'

I opened my mouth to speak. But . . . *his friends*? She must have meant *Peter* Jones, not Peta. There wasn't a Peter Jones at Collingwood. I shut my mouth again.

She looked at me, polite and hopeful. Luke gave me a quick glance. His eyes asked me if I wanted to make myself known to the nice lady in the very expensive car, who thought I was a boy. I shook my head fractionally. He turned back to her with a disarming, blue-tongued smile.

'Yeah,' he said, hardly missing a beat. 'Brown hair? Freckles? Squidgy nose?'

The lady nodded. I glared at Luke.

'You just missed him,' he said blithely. 'He's still in the sweet shop back there. He'll be out in a moment. Come on, Penelope.'

He grinned at me and loped off down the car park, while the pretty lady called her thanks. The Range Rover executed a smart turn and headed back the way it had come.

'Penelope? *Penelope?*'

'It was the first thing I could think of. It suits you, Penny.'

'It so doesn't. Oh, and squidgy nose?'

'I like your nose. It's cute as a button. So who d'you think they were?'

'No idea,' I said. 'Friends of Grandad's? Maybe I've won the lottery.' But my skin was prickling. 'You don't think . . .? No. Forget it.'

'Think what?' Luke asked, glancing round at the departing car.

Something ridiculous was bugging me. Very aware that I was on my way to counselling for being, as Jason so politely put it, psycho, I recited the words from the voicemail.

'"*The bad people are coming to get you.*" I'm crazy, right?'

'What? The girl who thinks her dead father gave her a cat?'

'Yes, crutch boy.'

He shrugged. 'Yeah, probably. Why don't you call that boy back? Find out what he was on about. I mean, it was a bit weird.'

Yes it was. I still had goosebumps on my arms from the Wicked Queen. I dug my phone out of my bag and checked the list of missed calls. Even though I'd deleted the message, the number was still there, so I rang it. After several seconds, a male voice answered.

'Uh-huh. Omar.' It was a lazy drawl, quite different from the urgent tones on the voicemail. The voice was deeper and more grown-up.

'Er, hello. This is, er . . . Did you call this number a few days ago?' I asked.

'Who, baby? I don't think so.'

'Are you sure? On Saturday? About two-fifteen.' (The time was etched on my heart. Painfully.)

'No . . .' he said. 'Ah, wait. Are you the chick from the party in can?'

'What?'

'Cannes, baby! In France? The blonde chick at the Crystal Ball? I thought I got your number wrong. You never called me back.'

He sounded sulky now. He was definitely, absolutely not the boy who'd left the message. Chick? Ball? What about hiding from the 'bad people'?

'No, that wasn't me.'

What an idiot. I ended the call. Two seconds later, my phone rang in my hand.

'Hello?'

'Hi, baby. So tell me, who are you really?'

21

His voice was syrup, sweet and flirty, like this was some kind of game. I didn't want this stranger calling me 'baby'. Or frankly anyone. I'd obviously made a big mistake and I didn't want to make it worse, so I switched the phone off and shoved it in my pocket.

'So?' Luke said.

'Wrong number. Don't tell anyone about this.'

Luke nodded without me needing to explain why. He knew there was only so much counselling I could take.

FOUR

Later, at the Smugglers' Inn, I popped my head round the bar and casually asked Grandad if he knew anyone with a Range Rover. He looked up from his glass-polishing and thought for a moment.

'Several people. Why?'

'Oh, nothing . . . Er, do any of them have a really posh black shiny one?'

Grandad suppressed a shudder. He disapproved of flash cars, flash boats and pretty much flash anything.

'Possibly. The Carsons who run the Three Bells had a new one last time I looked. Don't remember the colour.'

Then a guest asked him to recommend a pre-dinner

cocktail and he was too distracted to finish our conversation. I left him to it.

Why would the Carsons, or any of Grandad's friends, have remembered my name but forgotten I was a girl, and tried to meet me after school? It still bugged me, but as an explanation, that would have to do.

That night, just after midnight, my phone rang again.

The screen lit up the sloping ceiling above my head with a ghostly glow. When I saw the number I nearly didn't answer. I didn't want to hear that creepy syrup drawl.

'Peta? Peta Jones?'

But it was the first boy again, the one who had left the message.

'Ye-es?'

'It is you! They came, but you are safe!' His voice bubbled with delight. 'You hid, yes? As I told you?'

There was a long pause while I thought a lot of things.

One: it was late at night – this was a dream.

Two: if it wasn't, it was a seriously complicated wind-up.

Three: if this boy *was* winding me up, could he really have arranged for a Range Rover to stop me after school?

Four: what if it wasn't a wind-up?

Five: *what if it wasn't a wind-up?*

Six: Dad?

'Hello?' the boy said, checking I was still there. 'Are you safe?'

I looked around at my shadowy bedroom. 'I think so.'

'They did not find you!' He sounded gleeful.

I swallowed. The darkness seemed to buzz around me, like it was alive. 'Do they . . . Does one of them, um, have long, wavy hair?' *This is absurd, Peta! Cray. Zee.*

'That is her. Ingrid. The man is Marco.'

'They found me,' I whispered. 'But they thought I was a boy.'

'Aha!' he exclaimed. 'Your name . . . yes! They are *so stupid*. All the time they said, "Get the kid! We must get the kid!" And they did not think to check.'

Stupid is good, I thought. Liking stupid. 'But why would anybody want me?'

'It is because of your power.'

'My power? But I don't *have* any power.'

There was a slight pause. When the boy spoke again, there was a hint of doubt in his voice. 'But you must have a power. And besides –' he grew more confident – 'Mr Allud said so too, when he gave me your telephone number. He told me to tell you exactly – and I'm sorry, I forgot before – he said also to tell you "Never forget, you have the power." So you see, there must be one, no? Hello? Hello?'

'I'm still here,' I said quietly.

'I must go now. You must stay hiding. For two more days, I think. Be careful, Peta Jones – even Marco and Ingrid will not be so stupid a second time.'

'Wait! Who are you? Who is—?'

Click. My head was full of a thousand questions. I called him back instantly. He answered on the first ring.

'Do not call this number!' This time, he sounded terrified.

'But who are you? Who is this Mr Allud?'

'You must not call me, it is dangerous.'

'Then . . . how about the internet?' I suggested, thinking madly. 'What about Interface?'

'Ah. Interface.' I could feel him desperately considering. 'Yes. Perhaps. How can I find you?'

He knew my name already. I told him my school (the bad

guys knew that anyway) and my town (same story). I didn't know whether to trust him, but I had to talk to him again.

'I will contact you tomorrow,' he said. 'About midday.'

The line went dead.

FIVE

My chest felt tight and my heart was pounding. I got out of bed, pulled back the curtains and put my forehead to the cool glass of the attic window. Those phone calls were so weird they hardly seemed real. Now I needed to reassure myself that the Range Rover wasn't parked outside.

The front of the inn overlooked an ancient cobbled street, where no cars were allowed, but my room overlooked the back. The road opposite my window was full of parked cars, but they were all normal, small cars. The kind of thing that the people of Rye and our friendly tourists would drive. People who don't think too much about missing fathers and gangs of kidnappers on the loose. I watched them for a little while, taking in the ordinariness of each vehicle and telling my racing heart to slow down, and my imagination to stop over-reacting.

I turned back to the bed. Outside, the clouds shifted and a shaft of moonlight spilled across the room, illuminating the bedspread Granny made for Mum long ago, and Lacy, my cat, curled up at the end of it. The flat was quiet. My school uniform lay on the chair next to the door, with my blazer on a hanger hooked on the wardrobe, where Mum or Granny always put it for me when I left it lying around. The photos of Mum and her sister were all in their places, stuck to the sloping walls. Everything was normal and ordinary. Perhaps I *had* been dreaming.

Then Lacy gave a snort and stirred in her sleep, shifting into a new position. Her furry body took up the space where my feet should be. I stared at her in the moonlight.

Lacy had arrived on my birthday last year. After the bomb, my last birthday wasn't exactly the best. Normally, if Dad was home, he'd take me to the scariest theme park we could find, with the biggest rides, and we'd go on every one while Mum watched us through her fingers from the ground. If Dad was away, he would send me a hand-made card and a small present based on wherever he was working. He loved local research. So my shelves and drawers were full of Welsh dolls (training in the Brecon Beacons), a silver filigree prayer wheel (trekking in the Himalayas), and boxes made out of blue stone (serving in Helmand Province).

But after the 'bomb' there was nothing. No card. No parcel with my address hurriedly written in Dad's spidery writing. Nothing at all.

Mum had decided that an extra-good way to celebrate turning fourteen would be to go to the graveyard at Winchelsea Church and spend some time with his 'ashes'. *Way to go, Mum.* So we did, and it was horrible, but when we got back there was a cardboard box waiting for us on the steps leading up to the Smugglers' Inn. Inside it, shivering, was a tortoiseshell kitten with a luggage tag attached to her collar saying, 'PLEASE LOOK AFTER ME'.

Somebody had sent me a kitten. A stripy, grey *tortoiseshell* kitten, and I'd always specifically wanted a tortoiseshell. On my *birthday.*

Hello?

After a certain amount of arguing and crying (Mum did most of the crying) I was allowed to keep her. I called her Lacy after Ada Lovelace, the daughter of Lord Byron, who invented the first computer program in 1843. Dad would approve, I thought, being a maths geek who loved computers, and Lacy was obviously a present from him. I mean, your father goes missing in suspicious circumstances and a few months later a mystery kitten shows up *on your birthday*? And it's just a coincidence? Please.

So there was Lacy. And now there was this.

Never forget, you have the power. Those were the words Dad said to me every night he was home. Nobody else knew them, not even Mum.

Dad was away in Africa on a secret operation the day I was born. I came ten weeks early, tiny and purple. At the hospital, they said it was touch and go whether I'd make it. When Dad rang to see if we were OK, Mum asked him to choose my name.

Dad was always super-geeky about maths. It's his other

passion, apart from the army. I was born on the fifteenth of October, the tenth month of the year. He called me Peta, partly because it means 'rock' and rocks can be tough little survivors, but mainly because it signifies ten to the power of fifteen in maths. Just like 'kilo' means ten to the power of three – a thousand, and 'mega' means ten to the power of six – a million.

Mum was never sure about it, because of the whole sounding-like-a-boy thing. It has its advantages, though: there are three Savannahs in my class right now, but only one Peta. She should be grateful I wasn't born nine days earlier. I like my name, but Mega Jones? Painful.

So anyway, that is my power. 'Of fifteen.' It isn't the speed of light, or invisibility, or mind-reading: it's my name, and my birthday, and a little maths joke of my dad's. *Never forget, you have the power* was our secret code.

They were also the words Dad said to me on the phone from his last tour of Afghanistan, the two times he thought he was in real danger and might not be coming back. As well as being his goodnight, they were sort of like his goodbye.

He'd never said them from Baghdad, which was yet another reason I didn't believe the news about the bomb. However, if the boy on the phone was telling the truth just now, then somebody out there knew things that only my father knew, and was using his code for danger. Danger that didn't just affect Dad this time, but affected me too.

I went back to the window. Far below, a van drove slowly up the road, rumbling through the quiet of the night. The sound of the engine made my chest clench again, but it was a red post van, ordinary and normal. As it drove along, its headlights illuminated the parked cars ahead of it.

In one of them, a nondescript dark-coloured estate car parked right opposite the back of the hotel, a woman turned to look up at my window. I caught a glimpse of her pale oval face and her softly waving hair.

Ingrid, he'd called her. The Wicked Queen. Not so stupid a second time.

SIX

In the morning, Granny came to check I was ready for school. She found me sitting up in bed, clutching my knees, staring straight ahead of me. She folded her arms and pursed her lips.

'You're going to be late, young lady.'

I swallowed. 'Granny, can you look out of the window?' She did. 'Is there a dark car parked opposite? With someone inside?'

'No.'

'I think . . . someone might be watching me.'

She came and sat next to me. Her face looked tired and wrinkled.

'Oh, Peta.'

'This car stopped me yesterday on the way home from school. Then someone called me . . .'

'Really, dear. What would your mother say?'

'I'm not paranoid, Granny. It's—'

'Is it someone at school? Are you being bullied? Is that why you don't want to go? Or are you missing Isabelle? Let her enjoy the honeymoon. She deserves her special time, you know.'

'No! It's not that!'

Granny closed her eyes and did her *patiently listening to rubbish* face, which Mum had inherited so exactly.

'Tell me again.'

'That phone call in church was a warning. I got another one last night. I think it was from Dad. I—'

'Peta! Stop! Listen to yourself! The man is scattered in St Thomas's graveyard. I watched your mother do it and . . . I know he was a difficult man, but it broke my heart.'

Dad, difficult? But I didn't have time to argue. Someone was *trying to kidnap me*. How to convince her? I thought madly. I couldn't go outside with the Wicked Queen waiting for me.

'I don't feel well,' I moaned, with a bit of a pathetic cough.

'Oh, for goodness' sake! Stop play-acting and give your poor mother some peace!'

'I mean it! I hardly slept last night.' I hardly needed to act – I felt terrible.

Granny peered at my face and her expression softened a little.

'Well, you do look a bit . . . Those purple circles under your eyes . . . Promise me you'll stop playing those silly games till all hours.'

33

She meant Jelly Flop. It was the new craze at school and I was on Level 73. Yeah, I looked like this because I'd been squashing virtual jelly beans on my phone all night. Obviously.

'I'll give you one day,' she decided. 'One day only. No games, and lots of sleep. Promise me?'

'I promise. Thanks, Granny.'

One day. It was a start. As soon as she left me to get on with her chores, I sneaked downstairs and found Luke alone in his room, playing on his computer. I told him everything, including Granny's reaction.

'So? Why don't you just call that boy again?' he suggested. 'Get him to talk to her.'

'Because he sounded really frightened when he told me not to. I just . . . he's the only one who seems to know what's going on. I think I should do what he says.'

Plus Granny probably wouldn't believe him anyway. I mean, who would?

'OK,' Luke agreed reluctantly. 'And he's going to contact you later? By Interface?'

'That's what he said.'

'What are you going to do now?'

'Sleep.' Granny was right that I needed some. Luke had planned to get on with homework anyway, so I left him to it.

Back in my room, I checked out of my window again. No estate car now. But that didn't mean they weren't watching me somehow.

It was strange to be 'hiding' in one of the most famous landmarks in town. However, I felt safe enough here, with staff in all the corridors and Grandad working on admin tasks just outside my door. He looked like a friendly old hotel manager, which is what he was now, but he'd also spent thirty years in the army before he bought the Smugglers' Inn. He could do things with his Parker pen that would make your eyes pop. Literally. And I didn't fancy anybody's chances against him if he got hold of the heavy brass model of a smugglers' lamp that he used as a paperweight on his desk.

With the normal hotel sounds going on reassuringly around me, I finally managed to doze off. At lunchtime, with Grandad busy downstairs in the restaurant, I put my laptop on the bed and waited. After half an hour, I got a new Interface friend request from a boy called Omar Wahool. I accepted, and messaged Luke to tell him to come up. Soon after, Luke arrived and 'Omar' started a chat conversation with me.

Are you hiding?

Sort of.

Where are you?

Can't say.

There was a pause. Then:

That is good!

I could almost hear the delight in his voice again. He seemed to enjoy the game of lying low from these people, whoever they were. However, something bothered me.

Who's the other person I spoke to? I typed.

The other person?

I called you, and someone else answered. Also named Omar? He didn't know who I was.

Did you tell him?

No.

Good. He is – there was a long pause – my brother. He plays tricks. He is mean and stupid. You must not talk to him.

35

OK. Who told you about my power? This was what I really needed to know.

There was a long pause.

Mr Allud. He is a prisoner, the boy wrote.

A prisoner? What does he look like?

Very dirty. And very hairy. This place is not good

And then nothing. For a long time, Luke and I watched the screen and no further message came.

'Oh, great,' Luke sighed. 'Well, that was rubbish. All we know is there's a prisoner somewhere, we don't know where, called Mr Allud. Does that mean anything to you?'

'No.'

'Oh yeah,' Luke added snarkily, 'and there are two boys who call themselves Omar. That's helpful.'

'Actually, it is,' I said, thinking hard. 'Omar Wahool. We've got his Interface profile. That should tell us something.'

'Ah yes.' Luke's face lit up. 'You're right.'

Luke went off to get his laptop so we could work together. Meanwhile, I rescued the canister of Toxic Waste from my bag. I took a thoughtful mouthful and started exploring Interface.

Omar hadn't used his profile for a while – two years in fact, judging from his timeline. He listed his interests as 'Girls, parties, champagne, skiing, beach, adventure'. He went to school somewhere in Switzerland and many of his friends seemed to be princes, princesses and aristocrats from around the world. The photos were all of people making funny faces at parties, generally dressed in ball-type clothes or swimming costumes, and usually clutching champagne bottles. For his birthday, he'd been given a customised silver Ferrari.

He couldn't wait, he said, to learn to drive.

'How're you doing?' Luke asked a few minutes later, panting slightly from the stairs and hugging his laptop tightly under his arm. I should have offered to get it for him, but I was glad I hadn't – he'd have hated that.

'It's all a bit weird,' I said. I showed Luke the profile. 'The dad must be a millionaire. I mean, who gives their kid a Ferrari for their birthday?'

Luke looked wistful. 'Not mine.'

'I got a kitten. And it gets weirder. This profile hasn't been used for ages. He's got another one now, see?'

I clicked to a new page. New Omar was nineteen, and going to college in America. He was driving a blue Lamborghini now. Presumably he'd got his licence.

'How about you do a bit more research on Interface, and I look him up on Google?' Luke suggested.

'Fine.'

We worked away in silence, punctuated by tapping keyboards and the happy crunching of Toxic Waste. After about fifteen minutes, I shouted 'Aha!' and Luke stopped typing.

'OK, come on, Miss Clever-Clogs. What have you found?'

'You go first.'

'Fine. So Omar's dad is Emil Wahool. He was the Minister of Finance for a country called Marvalia, but he got booted out a couple of years ago. He's not a millionaire, he's a *billionaire*.'

'Oh, nice. Marvalia . . . Marvalia . . . It rings a bell.'

'They had a revolution.'

'Of *course* they did!' I said. 'I remember now. The Orange Revolution.'

'No.'

'Green? Purple? It was some colour . . .'

'Blue.'

'Yes! Exactly!'

Dad was home on leave when it started, before his last tour in Afghanistan and I remembered him watching on TV. Marvalia was a small country, but it had dominated the news. The people demonstrated for weeks. They poured into the streets every day, waving banners, blue paint on their faces. Students and workers, young men and women, facing down policemen with riot shields and tear gas, then soldiers with tanks. They were complaining about no food, no jobs, the universities being shut down, hundreds of people being thrown in prison and disappearing.

'You must remember it,' I said to Luke. 'They'd had this evil dictator for, like, thirty years, and in the end they kicked him out and took over. They've got a university professor in charge now. It was amazing.'

'Yeah, I vaguely remember,' Luke said, with the confused, lying look of someone who didn't remember at all.

How could anyone not remember the Blue Revolution? I Googled it on my laptop and brought up the famous video of a girl climbing on a tank and sitting there in a blue dress, with bright blue eyes and blue streaks in her hair, daring the soldiers to shoot her down. She was in a million photographs too. I pulled up one of them and showed Luke.

'Oh, *her*. Yeah. She was pretty.'

Yeah. Because that was *so* the point of the Blue Revolution.

And now one of the sons of the exiled Finance Minister was talking to me on the internet. Bizarre.

'So what about you?' Luke asked.

'Mmm?'

'What did you discover?'

'Oh. Well, Omar Wahool is not Omar Wahool.'

'Uh?' Luke's whole face was a question mark. It was very gratifying.

'There are three Wahool children: Omar, Maxim and a girl called Yasmin. It's obvious, really. The guy I spoke to that one time *I* made the call is the real Omar, the older boy. The stuff he said to me fits him perfectly: he was all parties and girls. The one who called *me* was totally different: he was all about warning me, and helping the prisoner. He's not Omar at all – I think he's Maxim.'

'Sorry?'

I grinned. 'He's the younger brother, pretending to be the older one. Maxim's sixteen. He's known as Max, by the way. He's using Omar's phone and his old Interface account to talk to me, instead of his own.'

'Why would he do that?'

'Because he's helping me? Because he doesn't want to get caught? Because he wants to get his big brother into trouble if anything goes wrong? Because he's really clever?' I suggested.

'Cool,' Luke said, grinning slowly. 'Not bad detective work, Miss Jones.'

I gave him a modest smile. 'It explains why I can't call him back.'

Luke hesitated for a moment. 'Any connection to your dad?'

I deflated a little. 'Can't think of one.' I'd tried to find something that connected the Wahools to Afghanistan or Baghdad, or Dad to them in some way, but there was nothing.

'So what now?' Luke asked.

That was a good question. Max Wahool had told me to hide from the 'bad people' and I couldn't keep doing it here:

Granny had made it clear she wouldn't let me. An idea had been forming. It seemed like the only sensible option.

'Find out where Mr Wahool's living now,' I instructed.

'But that could be anywhere!'

'You're brilliant, Luke. It won't take you long.'

'And then . . .?'

'I'll go and find him.'

'You'll *go and find him?* An ex-dictator?'

'He was only a friend of the ex-dictator. I won't go and find *him*, obviously – I'll find his son. The one who's helping me.'

And where I find Max, I find Dad, I thought to myself. But I didn't say that out loud. Even Luke's belief in me had its limits.

'He could be in South America, Peta, or China or Russia.'

'He could be in London. You never know.'

'*Honestly!* What are the chances? You can be so . . .'

It took him eleven minutes. Luke was brilliant on computers. I knew he'd be quick.

'I don't believe it!' he said, looking up from the screen. 'Wahool *does* have a house in London.'

'Told you so.'

'You're weird.'

'It's just logic. London's home to lots of dodgy rich people. It's on the news all the time.'

'If you say so. But listen, he probably won't be there. He's bought himself a place in Miami too. And another one in the Cayman Islands, and an island off the coast of Italy.'

'An *island*?'

'Literally. A whole island. It's not big, but I bet it's mega.' Luke started trying to show me pictures, but I didn't care.

'Tell me about the house in London.'

He sighed. 'He won't be there, I promise you.'

'Tell me.'

'It cost fifty million pounds last year.'

'Fifty *million?*'

'That's why it made the news.' He scrolled back through his search results as I leant over to look. 'It's on some square. Eden, I think. Don't go there, Peta, it's pointless.'

'I'll be back before you know it,' I said, straightening up. 'I'll slip out from school tomorrow. You'll hardly know I've gone.'

'Peta! No!'

'Tell Granny I've run off to see a boy band. If the worst comes to the worst, tell her I'm staying with my Auntie Eliza. But leave it a couple of days, OK? Give me a chance to find something out first.'

He tried some more to stop me, but it was his own fault – he'd found the house for me. At last, there was something I could do. For the first time since Mum scattered those *stupid* ashes, I felt as if I was getting closer to the truth.

SEVEN

I'd run away to my Auntie Eliza's before, just after Christmas, when Mum announced her engagement to 'Rupe'. I'd spent three days in her flat near the O2 in London while she baked me brownies and listened to how upset I was. Not my proudest moment. I still had the old backpack I'd used – I'd kicked it under the bed when I got back, and not thought about it since.

I pulled the backpack out now and looked it over. It was small and covered in a pattern of garden birds, but comfortable to wear, and waterproof. It would do for a day out in London tomorrow, looking up the Wahool house and going to Auntie Eliza's to spend the night.

Two days, Max Wahool had said. Two days of hiding. And meanwhile Dad was out there, and in trouble. If I could, I would go to him, just as I knew he'd have come for me. Besides, anything was better than sitting here, with the Wicked Queen outside my window.

As I packed, it was as if Dad was in the room with me. I used to watch him get ready before he went on tour, or even if it was just us going camping, and he was always very precise about packing. All soldiers are. I think it's the first thing they teach them in the army. Dad could fit the most enormous amount of stuff in the tiniest space, and it would never, ever get wet. Paper (you always took a pen and paper) went in sealed plastic pouches from the kitchen. Pills (you always took headache pills, so you could concentrate) went in pouches of their own. To go to Auntie Eliza's, I'd swiped a range of Mum's painkillers from the bathroom cabinet. They were still in their pouch at the bottom of the backpack.

Even though I'd only be away for one night, or two at the most, I packed the old, familiar things in the old, familiar way. Thin layers to wear – rolled, not folded. Trousers with zip-up pockets, for keeping things safe. Trainers. A windproof jacket. A hat for disguise. (This was my idea, not Dad's, but it seemed sensible in the circumstances.) Torch. Chocolate. (This actually was Dad's idea. Things tend to go wrong when you run out of energy.) Phone charger. Water. Photo of me with Mum and Dad at Buckingham Palace, a bit crumpled because it went with me everywhere.

The bag was still only two-thirds full. Lacy watched me from my bed as I considered what to add.

'What?' I asked.

If a pet can look sceptical, Lacy did. Disloyal cat.

Or maybe she was just being sensible. I caught sight of

43

myself in the wardrobe mirror, clutching the photo frame. What was I *doing?* My mother's boyfriend wanted to send me to boarding school and I'd convinced myself some 'bad people' were trying to kidnap me. Maybe Granny was right. If Dr Benson could see me now, he'd have a field day.

I decided to go downstairs and have a proper chat to Granny. Maybe she could help me sort things out in my head. Also, she'd never forgive me if I ran away during Mum's 'special time' with Rupert. Some things you can't undo.

It was dinner time and the inn was humming with activity. Chefs clattered in the kitchen; waiters moved swiftly through swinging doors, bearing multiple plates of food stacked up their arms, like jugglers, while diners laughed loudly in the restaurant, and louder still in the bar. It was hard to track Granny down. Eventually someone told me she was signing in a new guest. I found her in Reception.

'Ah, Peta darling, do come and meet Mr Bellacqua. He's come all the way from Rome.'

A square-jawed man with a head of dark curls glanced up from the paperwork he was signing.

'Bellacqua. Like the—' He cocked his head and smiled at me. His brown eyes caught mine and held them. He knew me. And because of that, I knew him.

'—pop star,' I finished lamely.

'Oh yes?' he asked.

Yes. There was a famous pop star called Giovanni Bellacqua who was in all the charts right now with a beach song. That must be where he'd got the fake name from.

Marco, the Range Rover's driver. I'd seen him before, in profile, sitting next to the Wicked Queen. I felt dizzy.

'He's writing a travel piece about the best hotels on the

south coast,' Granny told me happily. 'I hope he'll be nice about us. I've given him the Flaskers Suite.'

She smiled at him coquettishly. My grandmother was flirting – actively flirting – with the man who'd been sent to get me. She was booking him into a bedroom two floors below mine.

I pictured how the conversation would go:

'He's not a travel writer, Granny, he's trying to kidnap me.'

Big sigh. 'Don't be silly, Peta darling. Why would he do that?'

'Because of my power.'

'What do you mean, you stupid, deluded girl?'

'I don't know. It's got something to do with Dad.'

'Hello? 999? Can I have the nearest mental institution, please?'

'Hi,' I said. 'Pleased to meet you.'

'You too.' He held out his hand. I shook it. 'Peta, is it? What an interesting name.'

'Yeah. Some people mistake it for a boy's name.'

He stared at me hard after that. I turned on my heel and went back upstairs.

Back in my room, I was cool and calm. I added some fresh underwear and a few more practical things, ready for tomorrow. On my laptop, I looked up train times to London and the best way of getting to the Wahool house by Tube. It was in Eaton Square, not Eden. It looked pretty central on the map.

An image flashed across my mind of a policeman going through my computer history later, putting together a picture of what I'd done. Well, this should give him a good indication. For good measure, I wrote an email to Mum, which they could find in my drafts folder if they looked.

'I love you. It's OK. This is not about you. Peta xxx'

Then I added, 'PS, I hope you had a great holiday', because even though that wasn't strictly true (I liked to imagine Rupert having food poisoning for most of it), it was the right thing to do.

Lacy watched me unwaveringly, her sceptical expression never changing. What girl pictures *policemen* going through her stuff and leaves messages accordingly?

One whose would-be kidnapper is unpacking in the Flaskers Suite.

Once Granny and Grandad were in bed, I crept to the main door of the flat and locked it from the inside. The door handle rattled twice in the night, as far as I could tell. Knowing Grandad was there was a big help, but even so, I didn't sleep. I didn't really expect to.

EIGHT

The next morning, as soon as I heard Granny and Grandad moving about, I got up and checked the contents of my bag. Everything was ready. I'd expected to feel exhausted after last night, but in fact I was buzzing. I just wanted to get to London as fast as I could.

I skipped breakfast and pretended I couldn't find my homework, making myself so late that Grandad had to drive me to school. Marco/Giovanni watched us leave from behind his paper in Reception. I gave him a little wave. He didn't wave back.

Grandad complained about my inefficiency the whole way, but got me to Collingwood door-to-door, safe and sound. I hesitated before heading through the gates. Soon I'd have to come back out again and head for the railway station. I wasn't looking forward to walking through that coach park. Even though I was planning to get changed at school, it would be quite easy to spot me if someone happened to be, say, watching out for me from a dark estate car parked nearby.

Today, there was a big coach parked in front of the school gates. Even that made me shiver a bit.

My phone rang and I fished it out of my bag. Luke.

'Hi.'

'You didn't say goodbye!' he complained.

'Kind of in a rush . . .'

I was lying. I hate goodbyes. I've done too many of them in a lifetime of moving schools. I'm great at hellos, though.

'I wanted to tell you, I did some more research last night,' he said. 'Have you got a moment?'

I lurked near the coach. Lots of Year 7s milled around me, waiting to get on it. Tragically, I was only slightly taller than most of them, and shorter than the tallest boys.

'Sure.'

'I found another article about that house,' Luke said. 'You've got to hear this.'

The coach door opened. A nervous young teacher stood on the steps, muttering stuff about the Houses of Parliament, and had they brought their fact sheets? Oh – a day trip to London. Lucky them.

'It's got an underground swimming pool,' Luke went on, 'and a cinema and two kitchens.'

'Two kitchens? What on earth do they need two kitchens for?' I tried to focus on what he was saying. But my plan was rapidly changing.

'No idea,' Luke said.

The nervous teacher got out of the way so the Year 7s could start boarding. He had that frightened look of supply staff and didn't know anybody's name. Ideal. A better plan was forming. In fact, it was beautiful.

'Sorry, gotta go,' I said, grinning down the phone. 'Send me the link.'

'OK. Catch you later. Call me from the train.'

No, I thought to myself, *not necessarily.*

The whole thing felt as if it was meant to be. Free trip to London. No worries about getting to the station. Nice, comfy ride . . . It had to be worth a try.

I slotted in among the jostling crowd and climbed up the steps of the coach. The supply teacher happily waved me through, though some of the Year 7s gave me strange looks as I headed down the aisle.

'Special project,' I muttered. They shrugged and left me to it. Sometimes it helps to have a reputation for being odd.

I walked right down to the back and checked out of the window. There *was* a dark estate car parked further along the road.

Sorry, Queenie. Bye.

By the time the rest of the teachers arrived, I was sitting in the corner, head down, checking my phone. Nobody bothered me.

The next two and a half hours were so much better than if I'd caught the train. The coach wound its way past the open marshes and the wind farm by the sea, and on through little villages and larger towns, then up the motorway.

I used some of the time to check out the details of the Wahool house. According to the article Luke sent me, one of the rooms was set up as a nail bar and another was purely for wrapping presents. So the people of Marvalia were starving and the Wahools had a *present-wrapping room*? No wonder there was a revolution.

I got to Level 74 on Jelly Flop and caught up on some more sleep. Luke sent me a couple of messages. I told him I'd call him later. Didn't want the Year 7s overhearing my conversation. I was pretty sure Dad would approve of my super-sneaky spy approach.

Eventually, the coach hit the slow, busy streets of London. It followed the bank of the River Thames before dumping us near the Houses of Parliament. The supply teacher tried to count us off, but it was easy to dodge behind someone and avoid him. I milled about on the pavement with the Year 7s, waiting for the chance to get away.

Big Ben loomed over us as we walked beside the grand, ornate buildings, until we came to the open space of Parliament Square. Last time I came here with Dad (research trip) the place was full of anti-war protesters with sleeping bags and banners. Even though they were protesting against the war he was engaged in, Dad admired them for fighting for their cause. Today, the square was smart and green and empty. I kind of missed the mess.

By the time we reached the House of Commons, I was starting to get more strange looks from the Year 7s. A large group of tourists walked towards us, following a guide with a Japanese flag.

One minute I was there, and the next, I wasn't.

If anyone had looked closely at the Japanese tourists, they might have noticed a pair of school shoes among all the walking boots and trainers heading across the square towards Green Park. A brown head among the black ones; a Colling-

50

wood school blazer quickly disappearing into a backpack; a school tie stuffed into a pocket.

The sky was blue and I was on my own. It was a beautiful day.

According to Google Maps, Eaton Square was a twenty-minute walk away. I even got to go past Buckingham Palace. It reminded me of the day Dad got his medal from the Queen. He'd looked so smart in his dress uniform. Mum wore a navy suit and looked très chic. I wore something purple with a short skirt and looked hideous.

When I got there, Eaton Square was not what I expected. For a start, it was more of a rectangle. It was even bigger and grander than I'd pictured, with two long terraces of creamy-white houses down each side and railed-off gardens in the middle. The whole effect was green and cream and space and trees and money. OK, so if I had fifty million, I might consider wrapping my presents here.

Judging from the pictures on the web, the Wahool house was at the far end. It was taller than some of the others: five storeys of glistening windows, with a balcony above the front door and steps leading down to a basement.

It wasn't hard to find but, annoyingly, a yellow furniture van was parked right outside. There was a ramp leading up to it and the shutter was open, which meant it was being used. I didn't want to be spotted by anyone coming in or out of the house, so I quickly crossed the road and crouched behind a jeep parked next to the gardens. I still had a pretty good view.

A burly man in a yellow T-shirt and sand-coloured shorts emerged from the van and disappeared into the basement. I ducked further behind the jeep, but he didn't even glance in my direction. The place went quiet again. I got my phone and turned it to silent. Now was not the time for Roxanne Wills to go off in my bag.

I stared up at the gleaming windows, willing someone to look out – some face to give me a clue as to who was inside. But the house was dark behind the shining glass.

After another five minutes, a different man came up the basement stairs, struggling with an old-fashioned upright trunk. He put it on a trolley and wheeled it up the ramp into the van. He was straining under the weight of it. Were the Wahools moving out? Or just going on holiday? Either way, these were clearly not people who stuffed their clothes into the nearest rucksack and hoped for the best.

However, one other thing seemed certain: for the moment, at least, the family was here. Of all the places they could have been, I was right – this was this one.

Was there a cell in the basement, I wondered, near the underground swimming pool? After one simple coach ride, could I really be so close? *Dad? Are you a prisoner behind those walls?*

I shivered. The air seemed to shimmer. The house, so close, seemed impossibly distant and impregnable. It was eerily quiet. Apart from the removal guys, there didn't seem to be anyone about. The only sounds were birdsong and passing traffic, and a pneumatic drill going off somewhere in the distance. A black cat jumped on to a nearby wall, curled its tail neatly around its paws and watched me.

I couldn't stop thinking that Max Wahool could be inside right now, which meant Dad was there too. I couldn't imagine how, or why. Or rather, I could imagine a million scenarios, but none of them made sense.

My muscles were cramping from all that crouching by the jeep. There's only so long a girl can pretend to tie her non-existent shoelaces. Even the removal guys seemed to have given up for a while. I straightened up and checked my watch: 12.15. Perhaps they'd gone for lunch. It seemed amazing that they should leave the van open like that, shutter up, with the ramp leading into it, but they had.

Rather like an invitation.

I got a prickle down the back of my neck.

The house looked impregnable, but the van was wide open. This was the school coach story all over again, but scarier. I could hear Luke in my head, screaming at me not to, but the thing was . . . maths.

The statistical probability of me making it into the van, finding out something useful about the Wahools and getting out safely was, oh, about ten per cent. Or maybe five. Or – the more I thought about it – one. But the family was moving, it seemed, and the chance of me ever seeing Dad again if I didn't do *something*, now, was zero. Absolute zero. That's how it felt to me. And I was the only one who cared enough to try.

This was my chance. The only one I'd get. So I ran.

NINE

I was panting by the time I got inside, and I instantly knew I'd made a mistake. The van was half empty. There was a clothes rail to one side, next to the trunk, and some antique chairs and tables held in place with ropes and blankets near the back. What could I possibly learn from trunks and clothes rails? But beyond them I could just make out one other thing: an ornate writing desk with lots of drawers. Drawers could be full of papers. I ran over to it as fast as I could.

Only one drawer opened and it was empty. I tried the others. Maybe I'd find a letter mentioning Dad, or a photo, or something connecting them, or . . . But even as I desperately tried each new drawer, the possibilities seemed increasingly unlikely. *You have the power to be way over-optimistic, Peta Jones.* Anyway, the other drawers didn't even budge. Of course they didn't budge. Why had I ever thought this was a good plan? Oh, wait – I never had.

That's when I heard voices coming up the basement steps. The removal men, both of them, this time. Perfect. It was as if they'd been waiting specially for this moment.

My eye fell on the nearby clothes rail, packed with garment bags. It felt as though the beating of my heart was powerful enough to catapult me through it. I ducked behind the bags and rearranged them in a solid mass in front of me. Thank God the Wahool family had loads and loads of clothes.

'You seen what's in this one?' the first voice said in an Australian accent, tramping up the ramp into the back of the van.

'No.'

'Basketballs. Dozens of 'em, all blown up.'

'What does he need them there for? Don't they sell basketballs in Italy?'

'No idea. Guy inside said they were signed or something. How much more've we got to go?'

'Three more boxes? Then the cases and the shopping bags. That's about it.'

'Won't take long.'

The men arranged their boxes in the middle of the van and disappeared again. Somehow, they hadn't heard my heart pounding.

I could have gone at that moment. Should have done. But I was busy trying to think of excuses. What would I say if they caught me? I'd tell them I lived nearby. I'd say I was curious. I'd say my cat had jumped inside and I'd come in looking for him.

But before I could move, I heard more steps on the ramp. This was someone new, and big. The van shook as he entered. I could smell his aftershave – it was strong, like lemons.

I made a tiny gap between the clothes bags to peep through. Despite the thud of the new man's walk, he wasn't bulky like a rugby player; he was like the men in Dad's old regiment who were experts in judo and karate. His body was lean under his business suit, but solid muscle, and his head was shaved. You could just tell he could beat you in a fight (not only me – obviously he'd beat *me* – but even someone tall, and mean, and trained). He radiated calm efficiency. This was not a man you made excuses to.

Holding a shallow black box in one hand, he approached the desk. He opened the one drawer that *would* open, felt around for a minute and took out a key. The key opened the central drawer. He put the box inside, locked the drawer and replaced the key in its hiding place. Then he left. Outside, I heard him call sharply to the removal men.

'One of you's always looking after the van, right?' He sounded brisk, commanding.

'Yup,' an Australian voice assured him.

Really? They so *weren't.*

'Good. Keep it that way.'

'Sure thing. No problem, mate.'

Oh, great. So *now* they were turning all conscientious. I waited for a few more minutes, then peeped through the clothes to see if they were still outside. Even if they were, I'd use the cat excuse on them and run. It was better than staying here.

At that moment, a car pulled up behind the van. A Range Rover. Dark, with blacked-out windows. I peered into the light and adjusted my vision. The driver's door opened and a woman got out.

Ingrid – the Wicked Queen. Right here. Right now. Right in front of me.

My heart beat so fast I thought it might blow itself up.

Stupid idiot, Peta Jones. You went straight to them.

As she locked the Range Rover with a quiet beep, I heard somebody call sharply across to her: it was Muscle Man. 'So you're back. Where's Marco?'

'I left him there,' she answered. Her accent was clipped and sounded German now she wasn't trying to hide it. I watched her through the garment bags.

'Does he have the kid yet?' Muscle Man asked, coming into view.

'No. He's staying down there to get her. I'm bringing the car back because he said it was too con . . . con . . . It stood out too much.'

'Conspicuous,' Muscle Man said. 'Yes, I can see that.' He sounded unimpressed by her grasp of English, and also her grasp of kidnapping.

'Anyway, Marco will finish the job tonight,' she said crossly. 'He has the equipment.'

'Good,' Muscle Man said. 'The boss is waiting. He'll join us later with Miss Yasmin. Madam is still in Paris, shopping.' He almost spat out the word 'shopping'. Obviously that wasn't something he was very impressed by, either. 'So – Southampton docks, nine-thirty tomorrow. Marco must have the kid by then.'

'Oh, he'll have her. Alive and kicking.'

He laughed at that. A short, sharp, satisfied laugh.

'How's the princess?' Ingrid asked. 'Is she ready?'

'Magnificent,' he said. 'The best in her class. She's every-thing he wanted and more, they tell me. And yes, she's ready.'

They walked out of sight, but as they did so, the removal men came back with more bags and boxes. They made a couple more trips while I hid as far into the shadows as I could.

I waited for everything to go quiet again. I was ready to run as soon as the coast was clear.

What I *wasn't* ready for was for one of the removal guys to come back, pull down the shutter and lock me in the dark.

I wasn't ready for the engine to start up and the van to move off, with me inside it.

I wasn't ready for that at all.

TEN

The engine rumbled and the van shook and rattled like an orchestra of loud banging things. Inside, I was exploring fear in a totally new way.

They had me! Without even trying, they had me! And worst of all, I'd done it to myself. I actually had negative power. *Stupid, crazy, stupid girl.*

As the van drove slowly through the city streets, all I could think about was that when we came to a halt and that shutter went up again, I'd be caught like a mouse in a trap. *Alive and kicking. Hahaha.*

I kicked out in frustration and my foot caught the box of basketballs. Flinching in pain, I heard something rattle on the floor beside me. My phone had fallen out of my pocket. My phone! As soon as I found it and pressed the button, the glow of its screen reassured me a little. At least I had light. And I could call for help. I was about to call Luke when I noticed I already had a text. Actually, three.

Where r u? School called. Your gran's gone nuclear.

Seriously P. Call me. Ru ok?

Peta dear. It's Granny. You're not in trouble, but please call.

It's when they tell you you're not in trouble that you know how bad it really is.

I found Luke's number. He answered after a few rings.

'Hello? Hello?'

'Hi, Luke! It's me!'

'Peta? Are you *crackle crackle*? Did *crackle* message?'

I shouted that I was LOCKED IN A MOVING LORRY. But it was hopeless. The signal was terrible and the very loud rattling around me meant he could hardly make out a word I said.

'*Where* did you say? Are you *crackle*?' I assumed he meant 'OK'.

'No! Really not!' I shouted.

'What?'

In the end, I decided it would be easier just to text him. So I sat on a box and wrote him a long text about the house, and the van, and Southampton docks, and the fact that I had accidentally got myself kidnapped, and asking him to get the police to look out for a big yellow—

And that's when my phone died. Bam. No warning.
No battery.
No light.
No text.
No way.
All because I'd played too much Jelly Flop on the coach.
Granny was right about my dangerous addiction.
Alive and kicking. Hahaha.

I sat there with my head in my hands, reliving all the
moments when I could have told Luke what I was doing, or
– you know – *not* climbed into the back of a van containing
the possessions of a very rich man who was trying to kidnap
me, or just done something, anything, that wasn't spon-
taneous and stupid.

This wasn't like getting a detention in school, or the
'Death Dive' rollercoaster, or even lying in bed listening to
the rattle of the flat's front door. This level of fear was so
strong it sounded like an electric wire humming above my
head.

Dad would know what to do. He was trained for this stuff.
He'd have fought his way out by now, using his martial arts
training. Or he'd have found some hidden exit from the van
that I'd missed.

I was not trained. I was desperate. At some stage, those
men were going to reach their destination and unpack this
van, piece by piece. They might just notice that one of the
objects was a terrified, hungry girl.

One thing I discovered, though: as long as they haven't
actually got you in their grasp, your brain doesn't stop working. However scared you are, you keep thinking. After all –
there's nothing else you can do.

The darkness wasn't total – a few rays of sunlight made their way through a small gap at the edge of the shutter. As my eyes grew accustomed to the light, I ran them over the outline of each object near me, calculating its size and weight and the chances of me fitting into it, or under it, or behind it while the van was unloaded. My head was a whirr of *That? No. That? No. That? No.* for five minutes. And then, *That? Maybe.*

The big heavy trunk. I'd seen one like that in a film once. They called it a steamer trunk. The heroine was a Victorian heiress, and she'd used it like a travelling wardrobe. It had a cupboard in the top half for dresses, with drawers underneath for her gloves and underwear. I crawled over and pulled tentatively at the top half of this one. It opened. The van braked sharply and several dresses fell out on top of me. Beads and feathers scratched my face and got in my eyes. I pulled the dresses out properly and examined the space behind them.

It might be big enough. Just.

The van drove on for hours. When it finally stopped, I was curled up in my hiding place, ready, but the men didn't even open up the back. They just pulled at the shutter to check it was locked, and walked away.

The rays of light filtering through the gaps in the shutters grew dimmer, and eventually it was dark. I heard other lorries pull up nearby, and other lorry drivers wish each other goodnight. Looked as though the Australians weren't coming back for a while.

I risked coming out of my hiding place. As it grew cold, I put on the trousers and trainers from my backpack, a few more top layers, and the windproof jacket. Dad had been right about packing warm. I ate half the chocolate, which wasn't enough, and tried not to think too much about needing the loo. I found a fur coat in one of the garment bags and used it as a makeshift mattress. In the morning they would come back and they *would* unload the van, but until then there wasn't much I could do. I tried not to think too much about anything.

ELEVEN

The van set off about an hour after it got light. I had already replaced the fur coat and curled up in my hiding place. Soon, I could hear seagulls and smell the salty sea air. We must be close to the docks by now.

After a short drive, the men parked up again. With a shudder and a loud rattle, the shutter went up and the interior was flooded with light. Bumping and thumping, the men let down the ramp and began unloading. Some things they carried. For others, they used a trolley with squeaky wheels. Every squeak made my heart race. Every thump was a clue about what they were doing. I knew the contents of the van by heart now, and pictured every move, waiting for them to come for me.

They took the heavy desk off with a lot of grunting and swearing. They carried off the small antiques and wheeled the clothes rail down the ramp. Then they put the old steamer trunk on to the trolley and wheeled that off too.

'That everything?' someone called to them.

'Yeah. Truck's empty. Wanna sign this?'

Made it! Oh my God, I made it. If I hadn't been such an idiot to get here in the first place, Dad would be so proud of me.

The smell of the sea was stronger now: briny and sharp. There was the sound of flapping, and a sing-song noise of metal cables hitting each other in the breeze. Boat sounds. They reminded me of the harbour at home. Thinking about them took my mind off my aching arms and legs. There isn't much space for a curled-up girl in the wardrobe of a steamer trunk. If I'd grown another few centimetres, I wouldn't have made it.

I heard the van start up and drive off. As soon as every-thing quietened down, I'd sneak out of my hiding place and slip away.

'Oi! Lads! Over here. This lot.'

But not yet.

Oh, I ached. By now, every bit of me ached and my muscles were screaming. When I'd climbed inside the trunk, I'd left a couple of beaded party dresses inside and draped them over me. Now they scratched and tickled my face. But that was nothing compared to the pain in my arms and legs, which were folded up around me and were agony with cramp. And *that* was nothing compared to my back, which was bent double and pressed up against my backpack. Every bone in my spine was complaining. And all the bits in between. I hadn't been to the loo since yesterday morning and my bladder had a special pain all of its own.

Someone put the trunk on a trolley. Bump. Bump. Bump. Quite a lot of swearing.

'What on earth does she keep in here? Bloody diamonds?'

'Probably. Wouldn't put it past her.'

'Don't diss the family, OK? Shut it.'

Bump. Bump. Bump. Up a ramp. Down a ramp. Bang, rattle, clatter. Bump. Bump. BUMP.

'Oi! Careful! That's an antique! Louis Vooton.'

'She can keep it. Bloody furniture.'

'I *said*, don't diss the family. Got it? Anyway, you can leave it there for now. I've got special instructions for this lot.'

I pictured a container ship. An old, rusty hull. The furniture loaded inside. A huge trap door closing . . .

Crazy.

Stupid.

Crazy.

Girl.

Suddenly, there were voices close to me.

'Mr Paoli, Miss Herscht, this is the Captain.'

A man's voice said hello in an accent I didn't recognise. Then there were footsteps. One person left, the others stayed.

'So,' the man's voice resumed, 'you have been on a mission for the boss, I gather.'

'Yes.' It was Marco speaking. Even in that one word, he sounded beyond irritated.

'And? Do we have the special cargo to deliver?'

'No.'

'I need to know the truth,' the captain insisted, quiet and steady. 'There are . . . certain places it can be stored. For safety. In case there's an inspection.'

'No, we don't have it,' a clipped and irritated voice repeated. Ingrid. 'We didn't get it, OK?'

'How unfortunate.'

'Yes.'

'The boss will not be pleased.'

'Yes. We know.'

I could almost feel their frustration through the walls of the trunk. More footsteps. It went quiet outside, but I kept still and silent in my tiny hiding space. *You have the power. You have the power. You at least have the power to be totally still for one more minute, Peta. And another. And one more.*

It helped that my fear and pain were mixed with pride. OK, so their cargo would rather be ANYWHERE ELSE THAN HERE RIGHT NOW, but it was curled up under their noses and they were 'so stupid'. Oh how Max Wahool would laugh if he knew.

Then someone came to pick up the trunk and take it wherever it was going. It was heavier than they expected and as they lifted it, it slipped sideways, falling sharply. I fell with it, banging my head hard against the side of the wardrobe as it landed.

Blackness. Silence. Nothing.

TWELVE

When I came to, my head felt as though an army of removal men had spent the day stamping on it. It hurt even more than my muscles had been hurting before, and I didn't think that was possible. Now I thought about my arms and legs, they still hurt. Everything hurt.

It was dark. I tried to move and couldn't – my limbs were pinned fast. In my growing panic, it took a while for my aching brain to realise that I wasn't chained up or buried alive – I was still tucked inside the trunk. I couldn't stay here any longer. My muscles had to stretch or they'd explode.

Pushing myself hard against the wardrobe door, I tumbled

out, taking one of the dresses with me. I lay on the floor with my eyes tight shut, too scared to see where they'd imprisoned me.

More silence.

A soft and eerie silence. And something fuzzy under my cheek. As I gingerly opened one eye, the room seemed out of focus. Then I slowly realised it was because everything was beige. Beige carpet, beige wood, beige padding on the walls and ceiling. Only the desk, the trunk and the clothes rail stood out as being different, grouped together in one corner.

Slowly, very slowly, I sat up and looked around. The room was full of bright light, like something out of a sci-fi film. I half expected to find myself in some strange mental health facility or, to be honest, a spaceship – I was still very woozy – but instead I saw an empty bedroom. A big one, with floor-to-ceiling windows. Okaaay. Not expecting that. Really not expecting that.

I must have sat there for five minutes, suppressing the urge to groan, while my muscles tried to remember how to work again, and my head tried to stop hurting quite so much. When I thought I could move without being sick, I crawled over to the nearest wall and touched it. It was padded with the softest leather. That's why it looked so strange. It was like being captured inside a vast beige quilted handbag, flooded with light.

Fighting the urge to throw up, I crawled across to the wall of windows to see what was outside. I lay flat on the carpet and peered out. What I saw didn't make sense for a moment. I squeezed my eyes shut, then looked again.

Blue sky, everywhere, and sun blazing down. No buildings. No streets. Just sea, as far as the horizon, and boats. This enormous bedroom was on a *boat*. And it must have put to sea ages ago, because there was no sign of Southampton anywhere.

There was a balcony outside the window with two sun loungers on it, and below that I could just about make out the front of the boat – far away, and elegantly pointed, white and sleek and *huge*.

I looked back. The main feature here was the bed, draped in pale gold silk. Above it were two familiar-looking pictures of yellow sunflowers and blue irises. Opposite was a vast flat-screen TV, set into the padded leather, with two pale wood doors either side of it. One of them, I thought, must lead to a bathroom. Which is when I realised that I still desperately needed the loo.

That gave me the energy to move, and move quickly. The first door I tried led on to a large empty corridor and I had to suppress a shriek as I shut it fast. It took a moment to get my breath back. Behind the second door, though, was a room lined entirely in white marble, with copper taps and a copper bath. And a burnished copper toilet, ready and waiting.

After that, I began to feel better. The bathroom was silent, except for the distant hum of the engines, which I hadn't really noticed before. I sat where I was for a while and started to think.

Was this a cruise ship? No – too small. But it was still very much bigger than any boat I'd ever been on, except the ferry to France. And the bedroom was grander than any room I'd been in in my life, apart from the trip to Buckingham Palace. I thought about the leather padding, the silk on the bed. Also those pictures of sunflowers and irises, which really seemed very familiar. A thought occurred to me. I risked going back into the main room, tiptoeing across the thick, soft carpet, where I checked out the paintings.

Both were real, not posters. Both were signed with the word *Vincent*. A helpful little plaque set into the frame said *Van Gogh*. I swallowed. I was in a floating art gallery.

This was no ferry. This was the kind of boat that sheikhs and Russian billionaires used. Pop stars tweeted pictures of themselves on balconies like the one outside when they went on holiday. I'd managed to get myself accidentally kidnapped on to a *superyacht*.

Luke *seriously* had to know about this.

Yeah, and how was I going to tell him? Semaphore?

Minor detail: at least three people on this boat wanted me *alive and kicking*. The captain had places he could put me where no one could ever find me – I'd heard him say so. This place was *amazing*, but about as safe as the back of that van, which was NOT AT ALL.

However, nobody, it seemed, knew I was here yet. Before they found me, there had to be a way of contacting Luke, or someone, and telling them where I was. I looked around and the place was bristling with technology. There were two phones by the bed – one big, one small – and a bank of polished steel remotes with helpful labels saying things like *lights*, *curtains*, *sound*. But I didn't dare touch any of them, in case they alerted someone that the room was being used.

I tried my mobile again. Still as dead as ever. I did find a charger in one of the bedside drawers, but the lead didn't fit. I was on a boat that could probably send signals to Mars, and I couldn't even send a text.

So no Luke, no coastguard. No rescue.

On my own, surrounded by bad guys and water.

Stupid. Crazy. Stupid. Girl.

I imagined calling Mum in Barbados: *Er, right, so I'm on*

this superyacht and . . . I tried to turn it into a joke, but it wasn't funny.

Why did I have to climb into that STUPID VAN? Was Dad a prisoner in that house in London all along? If so, I was moving further away from him every minute.

Sorry, Dad. I didn't mean to mess up like this.

There was nothing to do but hide. They'd catch me, probably, but I had to put off the moment for as long as I could.

Outside the cabin door a noise started up, loud and harsh. It startled me so much it took a while to realise it was a vacuum cleaner. Someone was moving up and down the corridor with it. Couldn't go out there.

I looked round the room again. No *way* was I going back in that trunk. Not for now, anyway – my muscles simply couldn't take it. I examined the room more carefully. *Think, Peta, think.* The wall opposite the windows was covered in panels of padded leather. The nearest panel had a handle in it. Creeping across, I turned the handle and pushed.

I was looking into a small, dark room: a closet, lined in pale, polished wood. It had rails for suits or dresses, and box-shaped shelves for dozens of shoes. There were already two silk robes hanging from padded hangers on one of the rails. I saw something embroidered on the pocket of the nearest one. I looked more closely. It said *Princess Nazia*.

Oh, great, so the princess was coming and this was her cabin, and she could be here at any moment, maybe with Vacuum Person hot on her heels. I didn't know if I was too scared to cry, or just too tired.

The closet also contained a long wooden box – slightly coffin-like, but big enough for a small, frightened girl. I opened it up. It was full of four identical beige cashmere blankets. It wasn't perfect, but I could take some of the blankets out and wedge the lid open with something so I could breathe. Anything was better than the trunk.

I had to lie on my side and curl my arms around my knees to fit inside, but it wasn't as bad as before. Trying to ignore the darkness in this room, and memories of every horror movie I'd ever seen involving coffins – which was many, none of which ended well – I focused on controlling the shaking.

Don't think about the bad stuff, Peta. Think about something good, something far away from here.

I tried doing times tables in my head, but the numbers wouldn't work. According to Dad, captured soldiers learnt to recite long texts from memory to stop themselves going mad. I couldn't remember anything except nursery rhymes. So, huddled up in my coffin, I quietly hummed 'Incy Wincy Spider' to myself.

Up the water spout . . . washed poor Incy out . . . dried up all the rain . . . up the spout again . . .

Over and over.

THIRTEEN

I must have slept. When I woke up I was sore and stiff, but not as badly as before. I decided to risk peeping into the main cabin to see what was happening.

It was still empty. By now, the beige had turned to pink. Out at sea, the sun was slowly sinking to the horizon.

My stomach rumbled. On top of being super-scared, furious with myself and freaked-out by all the beigeness, I was also starving. I finished the chocolate and three dead Haribos I found at the bottom of the backpack. They hardly helped. I sat for hours in the closet but nobody came: no princess, not even a cleaner.

Eventually the outside lights on the boat were turned off

and stars filled the sky. I thought about Granny. She must be frantic by now. She'd have called the police. Worse – she had probably called Mum.

I pictured the scene. Mum would be on her way home, maybe on some emergency flight, clinging to 'Rupe' for comfort. Meanwhile, the police would check the CCTV cameras at Rye station to see which train I'd caught, and there would be no sign of me. Even if a Year 7 came forward to say they'd seen me on the coach, they might trace me as far as the Houses of Parliament and then . . . *poof!* Gone.

Back at the inn, there would be the message for Mum on my laptop – *I love you. It's OK. It's not about you.* That had seemed so reassuring when I wrote it, but what would she think when she got back and read 'It's not about you'? Rude.

I desperately racked my brains for something I might have said or done that would lead the police to me. There was my research into the Wahools, and Luke would tell them about the house on Eaton Square, and maybe even about Max. But none of them knew about the van. Would anyone think, 'Ah – Mr Wahool's yacht left Southampton this morning, let's see if she's secretly on it'?

No, they wouldn't. They would think I'd just run away from home, because I'd done it before. And the police didn't waste too much time looking for runaways.

Stupid stupid stupid girl.

I'd run out of chocolate, ideas and hope. All the time, the boat ploughed on through the waves. When I stole a look through the windows again, we were still in the middle of the ocean. It felt as if the journey would never end.

By 3.15 in the morning, the aching hollow in my stomach became even worse than the terror of being caught. I was on a *superyacht*, for goodness' sake. The boat must be groaning with food, and surely everyone would be in their cabins, asleep, by now? I just had to find something to eat. If I got caught, I got caught, but my stomach was close to not caring any more.

I climbed out of the blanket box, putting on the darkest layers I had, and my windproof jacket, so that from far away I might look like one of the crew. Possibly. From a distance. Well, it was worth a try. Noiselessly, I went into the bedroom and opened the cabin door. All I could hear in the silence was that steady hum of the engines and my own pulse throbbing in my ears.

The corridor ahead of me was long and wide, thickly carpeted and dimly lit by glowing glass panels set into the ceiling. It was just like how I pictured a posh hotel.

OK. Imagine you're in a posh hotel, Peta. A friendly, posh hotel, where as long as you're very quiet, nobody will catch you alive and kicking. *Then you can breathe.*

It helped. I crept along quickly, listening for danger. On the left was a doorway set into the wall, with a button beside it. A lift. This boat had an actual lift! Presumably that's how they'd brought up the furniture, with me in it. On the right was a small gym (naturally – superyacht) and a room crammed with Panama hats and Gucci deck shoes in different shades of white and cream. Beyond that was a dining room (superyacht), but no kitchen, or food.

The final door opened on to a large, deserted sitting area, facing the back of the boat. Enormous white leather sofas and low glass tables were scattered around. Crouching, I ran past them and ducked down near the glass wall at the back. Outside, I could see a deck with a large dark shadowy rectangle on it. The rectangle rippled in the moonlight. I had to double-check. Yes, it really *was* a swimming pool.

Suddenly, I spotted movement on a lower deck. I pulled back. Several metres below me, a blond-haired crewman was patrolling the boat, looking out to sea. He hadn't seen me, but I realised it was time to stay away from the windows. Keeping low, I returned to my hunt for food.

A long, sinuous piece of furniture ran along the far wall of the saloon, glimmering reddish-orange in the moonlight. Copper. There was a lot of copper on this boat, I realised. Behind it, mirror-backed cabinets stocked bottles of every possible kind of alcohol.

Yes!

It was a cocktail bar. When you live in a hotel, you learn a few things, and one is that where there is a bar, there is bar-food. One of my Saturday jobs at the inn was to stock the bar shelves with snacks. My stomach rumbled at the very thought as I ran round behind this one, crouched down and checked it out.

Perfect!

From the back, it looked achingly familiar. Shelf after shelf, neatly arranged with tempting-looking foil packets of crisps and nuts of every sort. By now, I'd half expected that if I found anything at all, it would be caviar or quails' eggs or something weird and over the top, but even billionaires liked crisps and nuts, it seemed. I could have cried with happiness.

OK, so I did. For a few moments, I admit I cried with happiness. I was tempted to scoop up an armful of packets to take with me, but people would notice that. Instead, I lifted two from the back of each row. Eight rows. Sixteen packets. Once I'd carefully rearranged the rest, you'd hardly know they were gone.

*

Ten minutes later, back in the closet, and full to the brim with peanuts and salted almonds, I felt better. *Much* better.

When we were out camping, Dad always made sure we sat down to eat our rations long before I ever thought we needed to. But Dad said food can make an enormous difference to your mood. It's one of the reasons the enemy starve you if they capture you – to make you too depressed to resist or escape. I should have packed more chocolate, but peanuts and salted almonds TOTALLY ROCK.

I rethought my situation. Here I was, on a *superyacht*, surrounded by famous art works, great daytime views and now, night-time access to unlimited bar snacks. Marco and Ingrid were having to explain how they'd let a fourteen-year-old girl slip through their clutches, and meanwhile, the girl in question was getting ready to snuggle under a cashmere blanket, a couple of decks away.

Yeah. Take that, kidnapper dudes.

FOURTEEN

The next day, the yacht sailed on, and the seas grew more stormy. With nothing to read, no internet, and not daring to turn the TV on, I discovered that even a superyacht can get a little boring after a while. Very boring, in fact.

I thought about what I would do when the boat landed. Find Max, find Dad, escape. Somehow. I had no idea how. Max Wahool would help me. I'd just have to make it up as I went along.

I became obsessed with watching the ever-changing sky, which was the only thing that *did* change around here. At sunset, I was sitting on the bed, admiring the way the sinking sun created a pale gold ribbon of light under the glowering clouds, when out of nowhere, a crewman appeared outside the window. He had bright white teeth to match his white sailing jacket, and wore sunglasses despite the gloomy weather. Behind them, he was staring right at me.

I froze. No breath to scream, no time to hide. He grinned and adjusted his shades to a nattier angle. Then he walked away. For a moment, I was rooted to the spot, before scooting – too late – to the blanket box. I waited in the stuffy darkness as the seconds ticked by, but there were no shouts, no running feet. Nobody came barging through the cabin door, searching for a stowaway.

Back in my hiding place, still gasping for breath, I tried to make sense of it all. It was as if the crewman had just been admiring his own reflection. Yes! He had! The windows must be mirrored on the outside. Even if they walked by, nobody could see me. Privacy glass. I liked it. I liked it very much.

I'd also learnt another thing. I'd been worrying that at any time the princess might come and find me in her cabin. Now, though, I knew I didn't need to worry – about the princess anyway. There was no princess.

Or rather, there was. The crewman's jacket had said *Princess Nazia* in smart blue letters, matching letters on the silk robes in the closet. *Princess Nazia* was the yacht. And she *was* magnificent: the best in her class.

The *Princess* sailed on for another day. I spent most of it sitting by the window, staring out at the stormy skies. By now I assumed we must be heading for one of Mr Wahool's properties in Miami or the Caymans. Where else could possibly be this far away?

The following morning, though, when I woke up

something was different. It took me a long time to work out what it was, but the hum from the engines had changed: it was lower and slower. The permanent vibrations I'd been feeling through the floor were almost gone. I wondered whether the boat had stopped, but then it pitched and rolled as it went over a wave.

I peered out cautiously into the bedroom: still empty. Outside, the sea was calm and the sky was a piercing blue. There was land ahead at last. Scrubby green hills with white houses on them and, near the waterline, white blocks of flats. This wasn't how I'd pictured Miami.

I could just about make out the crew calling instructions to each other as the *Princess* navigated a careful course between dozens of other boats. The place was packed with them, heading to and from the shore and lined up in neat rows. The *Princess* was bigger than all of them, and every single person on every other boat turned to check her out. She must look good, I guessed: sleek and elegant, but most of all, absolutely huge. From my hiding place near the top, it was like looking down on toy boats in the water.

It was time to hide again. At first I tucked myself up in the too-small steamer trunk, waiting for someone to come and unload the furniture, but when the pain got too much, I stumbled back to the closet and hid in the blanket box, where I must have fallen asleep.

When I woke up, the vibrations were back and the engine hum was higher. We were moving again. I risked a peek through the closet door into the room beyond. Still empty. We were sailing along the coast now, past other yachts decked out in fairy lights. I had no idea what we'd just been up to in the port.

*

That night, I found out. Not intentionally.

I was crouching down behind the bar, getting more snack supplies. It was two-thirty a.m. The saloon door opened and someone switched the lights on. I froze to the spot.

'You want a drink?' a man's voice said. Steps moved across the carpet towards my hiding place.

'No, Papa.' A girl.

The steps stopped. 'What makes you so sad, my angel? When I saw you on deck, I thought your little heart was going to break.'

'No, I'm fine, really,' she lied. I know when a teenage girl is lying to one of her parents. So this must be Yasmin Wahool. Oh my God. The Wahools were on the yacht now. 'I was just thinking about . . . my party.'

'It will be magnificent,' the man said. Emil Wahool. Ex-Finance Minister of Marvalia. The man who was holding my father prisoner. Standing only a few metres away from me. He resumed his steps and the floor shook as he got closer. 'You will be sixteen. My little girl, sixteen. We will celebrate.'

In ten seconds he would find me, maybe seven. I looked around for somewhere better to hide and spotted a tall kitchen bin under the sink. In one quick movement I pulled it forward and crouched in its place. Any barman would notice it wasn't in position. I held my breath and listened to my own heartbeat while I hoped Mr Wahool wasn't overly familiar with bars.

White trousers appeared at the far end, and bare feet in white leather slippers. He selected a glass and a bottle and poured himself a drink. Whisky. I could smell it from here. Despite holding eight snack packets, I didn't rustle. Amazing how long a girl can hold one breath.

'Ice,' he said. 'Do you know where they keep the ice?'

I did. The fridge was right next to me.

'No,' Yasmin answered, in a not-interested voice.

'Aah. Don't worry. This is good.'

He walked away again. I breathed slowly and deeply. *Thump, thump, thump.* My heart, pounding.

'About the party, Papa . . .' Yasmin said.

'Ah yes! I have a present for you. Something special for your birthday. I was going to give it to you on the island, but tonight will do. You need something to make you smile.'

He pressed a buzzer and a minute later someone coughed politely from the doorway.

'Sir?'

'Get me Dixon. Tell him to fetch the box he's been looking after for me.'

'Now, sir?' asked an English voice.

'Yes, now. Is there a problem?' Mr Wahool's voice was suddenly sharp and threatening.

'No, sir. Of course, sir. I'll get him straight away.'

The door closed. Mr Wahool sighed.

'Some of the new servants have no manners,' he said. 'I'm sorry, my angel.'

It was two-thirty in the morning and somebody was being woken up so they could fetch a *box*? Uh-oh: *the box he's been looking after for me.* That could be the box in the desk in my cabin. Maybe Mr Dixon was Muscle Man, and he could be heading there right now. I rapidly thought through the room. I'd tried to be careful: clothes in backpack; backpack in blanket box; blanket box shut; bathroom in immaculate condition. Had I forgotten anything? I didn't think so.

Yasmin began to speak.

'Yes, Papa, but about this party . . . I had a new idea about the theme.'

'You did? But I thought we agreed: Pirates of the Mediterranean.'

'But that isn't even, like, a film or anything.'

'No. It is "like" history. It is learning. The castle was built to defend the coast from pirates. And the Grandfather has approved the theme. He finds it . . . amusing.'

'Sure, Papa. But it's not the Grandfather's party, it's mine.'

Yasmin sounded sulky. Mr Wahool padded over to her and made little clucking noises to reassure her.

'I know! We will call it Pirates and Princesses. That is good, no? Girls will like it. Every girl wants to be a princess.'

'No, they don't. That's so lame. It's like a six-year-old's party.' There was a pause, then her voice changed and sounded more caressing. 'It's just . . . I was thinking . . . as the castle's in Italy, Papa, it might be nice to have the theme of *Roman Holiday*. It's so much more stylish and—'

'Hmm. *Roman Holiday*. Let me think. Yes. I see what you mean. The Emperor Tiberius had a palace on Capri. We could do things with togas and grapes and so on. The Grandfather would enjoy it.'

'I wasn't thinking that kind of Roman,' Yasmin said crossly. 'I was thinking of Audrey Hepburn. You know? The film? She was a princess in that, actually, but she was pretending to be a normal girl. It's my favourite movie at the moment and—'

'No, not that,' her father cut her off. 'The Grandfather doesn't approve of Hollywood. No, we'll go with togas. It's historical. Your mother can be a Roman queen.'

'But, Papa! I don't want a toga party for my sixteenth birthday! It's such a cliché!'

She was right. But her father wasn't listening.

'It's decided,' he said. 'The Grandfather will be delighted.

You are very honoured that he is coming to your party. And soon . . . well, soon there will be lots more parties, I promise you, my angel. Parties like the old days.'

'I hated the old days!'

'Don't say such things!' Mr Wahool's voice rasped, but at the sound of a subtle knock, it turned instantly to velvet. 'Ah! Here he is. Come in, Mr Dixon.'

'Good evening, sir. I have what you requested.'

I smelled it straight away. Even at three-thirty in the morning, he was wearing lemon scented aftershave. Muscle Man walked across the room. I shrank further into the shadows.

'Open the box,' Mr Wahool instructed.

There was a rattle, a click, a pause.

'Oh wow,' Yasmin said flatly. 'Diamonds.' I had never heard anyone say that word with so little interest. She wasn't even trying.

'Two hundred and eighty-nine, to be exact,' her father said proudly. 'It's a historic piece, made for one of Queen Victoria's granddaughters. It was recently sold at auction by a duchess. I had the stones reset, of course, to suit you, my little princess. A special present from your papa for your birthday. Isn't it lovely?'

'Lovely,' she said. The same way I'd say 'lovely' if you asked me to admire Jason Ridgeway's googly-eye impression.

'Put it on.'

There was a bit of fiddling.

'It's exquisite,' Muscle Man said in a deep, respectful voice, like he used the word 'exquisite' a lot, and meant it, which I doubted. 'Perhaps you'd like to see for yourself, Miss Yasmin?'

He must have indicated the mirrors behind the bar,

because Yasmin walked over towards where I was hiding. She remained on the far side of the copper counter, staring at herself in the mirror with serious dark eyes. I watched her reflection. If she'd glanced down she might have seen my eyes glinting in the darkness. But instead she focused on the total bling area around her neck.

There were so many big diamonds they looked fake to me. I was more interested in her face, which was bare of make-up, tousle-haired, very beautiful and quite miserable.

'Thank you, Papa,' she sighed.

She turned away, glittering in the light. I almost felt sorry for her.

So we'd been picking up passengers today, and that made things more complicated, but much more interesting. I'd learnt more in those few minutes than in all my other days on the boat.

Yasmin said she was tired and went off to bed, and her father soon followed. I waited long enough to let Muscle Man put the diamonds back in their place, heard him take the lift down to another floor, then crept silently back to my cabin. (I was starting to think of it as 'my' cabin now.) I practically fell inside and sank down with my back to the door.

Made it, Dad. Not sure how, but somehow I made it.

Those white leather slippers . . . They'd come so close I could almost have touched them. That sour whisky smell . . . If Mr Wahool had glanced down even once, I'd be in some dark hole at the bottom of the boat by now, locked up where no one would ever find me. And yet here I was. I'd never felt so alive. I felt sharp and bright, like diamonds.

I ate two packets of pistachios to celebrate, and thought about our new destination.

Italy. It was obviously a lot further away by boat than I thought. Luke said that Mr Wahool had bought an island there: *'I bet it's mega.'* Well, if this boat was anything to go by, it would be.

Was I wrong about Dad being in London? Could he perhaps be in this castle they mentioned? Was he a prisoner, like the Count of Monte Cristo, maybe? Dad and I read that story years ago.

Yeah, right, Peta. Your supposedly dead dad is really being held captive on a MEDITERRANEAN ISLAND and he's going to come back as some kind of fake aristocrat and get his revenge. Because that's how life works. IN YOUR STUPID, CRAZY HEAD.

One thing I was sure of: wherever he was, Dad was not bits of ash and bone, sunk by the rain into the scrubby grass around Winchelsea Church. I'd often wondered if he was in a monastery in Tibet or Bhutan or somewhere, leading some kind of spiritual life. Maybe he'd lost his memory. Maybe Dad had no idea he even had a family. Of course, that wouldn't explain me finding the kitten, but then nothing made sense about Dad . . . nothing at all. If he could be in Tibet, then why couldn't he be on this island?

I wasn't properly crazy yet, I realised, but I was pretty close. This whole 'hiding out on the blingiest yacht on the ocean' thing wasn't helping.

FIFTEEN

When I woke up the next morning, I looked out for the Wahools. I noticed Yasmin sunbathing on a spot near the front of the yacht, and I occasionally caught sight of Mr Wahool doing tours of the deck or talking to the crew, but I didn't see any other passengers. It seemed as if Yasmin and her father had been the only ones to join the boat.

When I'd given up on scanning the decks, I reconsidered the antique desk. It sat there in the cabin, big and dark and ugly. It was the reason I'd got caught in the van, because I'd spent too long trying out its stupid locked drawers. But what I'd forgotten since then was that Muscle Man had shown me how to open those drawers. Maybe they *did* contain some information about the castle or Dad. Or just *something* to explain what was going on.

Muscle Man had produced a key from the one drawer that would open. There had to be a secret compartment in there somewhere. I opened the drawer again and felt around as carefully as I could. Eventually, by pressing every spot on the wood, centimetre by centimetre, I felt the shelf above the drawer give way to the pressure from my finger. A little box dropped down on smooth, oiled hinges. The key was inside, small and silver. I tried it in the drawer that held the diamonds. It worked: there was the box. But that was locked with a key I didn't have. I put it back again with a sigh.

Afterwards, I opened all the drawers one by one. Most were empty, or contained loose bills for work to the house in Eaton Square, generally for many thousands of pounds. I read each piece of paper and put it back exactly as I found it. Nothing remotely mentioned Dad, or a man called 'Mr Allud'.

There was one paper I rather liked, though. It wasn't a bill, but a proposed list of costs for Yasmin's birthday party. They included fifty thousand euros for flowers, twenty thousand for food, a hundred thousand for champagne, the same again for musical fireworks, and a *million* for 'entertainment' (unspecified, but several famous pop stars were mentioned, with question marks after their names). When Mr Wahool said 'celebrate', he wasn't joking.

There was also, I was pleased to see, a chocolate fountain. Because you can't have a decent party without a chocolate fountain, can you? That was priced at two thousand euros, but I knew of several places near Rye where you could get one much cheaper. Although not, admittedly, musical fireworks or Rose Ireland and her backing band.

In one of the bottom drawers there was also a sample invitation for the party itself. It was being held at 'Castello Rodolfo, Isola Sirena, Italy' on the twenty-first of July. So in about two weeks the castle would presumably be full of teenagers in fancy dress, drinking champagne (maybe that was legal for teenagers in Italy? Or maybe the people on the island just didn't care?), listening to music and lounging by the chocolate fountain, talking about their Ferraris, taking pictures of themselves and posting them on Interface. I popped the invitation into my backpack as a weird souvenir. I needed some sort of proof that I'd ever been in this place.

The day wore on. I got bolder and madder. Some of the excitement from not being caught last night still hadn't worn off. While I pictured the party at the castle, I couldn't resist trying on some of Yasmin's dresses. I swapped my trousers and vest top for a series of frothy cocktail dresses, posing in front of the full-length mirror near the window and admiring myself in the beads and feathers. Or sort of 'admiring'. Yasmin Wahool was much taller than me, and bigger in the chest department. Also the bottom department. Most of the dresses were probably designed to skim her thighs, but they came down to my knees.

I ignored this, and my dirty, messy hair and freckles, and danced around barefoot to music in my head. Despite me, the dresses moved with their own innate grace. They were possibly even worth the thousands of pounds it said on the store labels that were still hanging from some of them.

It was getting dark. I was in a yellow fringed number that said 'Crow Lamogi' on the label, when I heard footsteps in the corridor outside.

No? Really? *Now?*

As the door flew open, I disappeared behind a curtain, which was the closest thing to me. *Seriously, Peta, WHAT WERE YOU THINKING?* I had no idea if they'd seen me. Thank God I'd kicked my normal clothes into the closet. All I could do was hold my breath and wait.

'It's OK,' a voice said. Yasmin. 'This is my mother's room. They're using it to store some stuff from the London house. No one comes here.'

I sensed that my bare toes were peeking out beyond the hem of the curtain. Slowly, carefully, I scrunched them in.

'Somebody's been here,' a deeper voice said. My heart was pumping.

'Really?' Yasmin asked.

The other person laughed. 'Look at this!'

If I looked at the window, I could just about see their reflections. Yasmin was with a young man, wearing the crew uniform of navy and white. He was thin, with the beginnings of a beard, and he was holding up an empty cashew nut packet. Oh no. I'd been eating the last of them as I pranced around in the dress.

'Huh, servants stealing,' Yasmin grumbled. 'They do it all the time. So . . .' her voice became low and seductive, '. . . you saw me last night. Why did you want to see me again?'

She didn't care about the nuts: she was flirting with this man. She was prettier than ever when she flirted. She looked safe. And happy. So did he.

'I want to see you all the time,' he said. 'Why d'you think I got the job on this boat? I hate the sea!'

'You must be a very good liar.' Still flirting. She moved closer. She was only wearing a simple vest and shorts, with bare feet and no make-up, but she looked a million times more amazing than I did in her dresses.

'I'm an *excellent* liar,' he laughed. 'For you. But however well I lie, I'm not going to see you tonight. We're having a party in the mess. They'll notice if I'm gone.'

'A party? The crew aren't supposed to have parties. Not when we're on board.' She sounded piqued. When she wasn't focused on him, there was a touch of the princess about her.

'Shhh,' he giggled. 'Don't tell anyone. But it's the last night of our maiden voyage. We have to celebrate.'

'And you'll be celebrating without me.'

She pouted. It worked. He lifted her face up towards his and kissed it.

'I'm only here because of you, and you know it. There's something I wanted to give you.'

He pulled a slim box out of his pocket and put it in her hands. She waited while he opened the lid, and gasped slightly at what was inside. Whatever it was, it was way more precious to Yasmin than two hundred and eighty-nine diamonds.

He took out a slim gold chain with some sort of charm on it. She lifted her long hair and turned round so he could put it on for her. Then she ran over to the mirror to admire herself. He followed and, stuck behind my curtain, I couldn't see even their reflections from here.

'It's beautiful, Nico. I'll wear it all the time,' she said.

'Don't! Your father will guess.'

'He won't. I'll tell Papa that Mama gave it to me, and Mama that Papa did. They never talk to each other, so they'll never know. You're the only one who's ever cared about me, Nico. I wish . . .'

'Well, we can't. Your dad would never let us.'

She sighed. 'I know. But I won't take this off, I promise.'

He moved in closer and I guessed he was giving her a hug. Then I heard a slurping sort of noise and realised it was more than a hug. I waited. Places I'd rather be right now . . . plenty of places.

'When will I see you?' she asked eventually.

'Whenever you come to the boat.'

'I'll come every day.'

'Don't make it too obvious.'

'It's Papa's new toy!' she said. 'He'd be surprised if I *didn't* come. But when can I see you alone?'

'I don't know,' he said. 'I'm sorry, baby.'

Eugh. He called her 'baby'. She seemed to sob into his chest, and then there was more slurping. I took my mind off it by admiring the lights on the distant coastline.

After a couple more minutes he left, and soon afterwards, checking that the corridor was empty, so did she. I sank to the floor in a puddle of relief.

So I wasn't the only girl on this yacht with a secret life. Interesting.

SIXTEEN

At lunchtime the next day, the engines slowed again. This time, there were more footsteps on deck and in the corridors, more instructions. The atmosphere was different. I sensed the *Princess Nazia* had finally reached her destination.

Like yesterday, the yacht was sailing in a calm crystal sea, under a cloudless sky. The distant coastline was rugged and hilly. Was this Italy? I wanted to look at it more closely, but before we got too close I had no choice but to tuck myself up in the trunk again, draping the yellow dress over me and hoping my cramping muscles wouldn't give me away.

I clutched my chest to my knees in the hot, stuffy

darkness, singing pop songs silently to myself – every lyric I could remember – and wondered if I was getting closer to Dad, or further away.

It felt like hours before the *Princess* finally came to a stop. There were toots from boats around her, and orders barked sharply to the crew. Then came the unloading. That took hours too. Inside the trunk, my muscles were screaming. The pain seemed to come on quicker this time, because they knew what to expect.

Someone put the trunk on a set of wheels and pushed it along the corridor to the lift. Once it reached the waterline, the trunk was lifted, heaved and swung in the air until I felt dizzy. It was dumped and bumped and raced through the water on a speedboat, engine churning through the waves. Bump. Bump. Bump. Voices around me, speaking a language I didn't recognise.

We stopped. The trunk was lifted out amidst lots of swearing. I could tell they were swearing, even if I didn't know the language. And I could guess roughly what they were saying: 'Blimey, this is heavy. What does she keep in this thing? Bloody diamonds?'

Actually, no, I could have told them. *They keep the diamonds in the desk.*

Another heave, a groan, a thud. The trunk hit the ground and suddenly, the wardrobe door swung open and bright daylight nearly blinded me. I stifled a scream.

More swearing. I caught a brief glimpse of a tanned and grizzled face as a man bore down on me, but he was looking elsewhere, shouting at someone. He banged the door shut.

Oh my God. He banged the door shut. If he'd glanced down even for a second, he'd have seen my elbows and knees poking out from behind the yellow dress. I held my breath, certain he must sense my terror – smell it, even. But he didn't. He just lit a cigarette – its pungent fumes hit my nose from the moment he took his first puff – and argued with the other men on the dock,

I was swayed around one more time, and a diesel engine coughed into life, rattling me to the bone. The trunk was on the back of a truck, which set off up a steep track. The wardrobe door opened again as we rounded a bend, and this time I managed to pull it shut, gripping at the inner catch with my fingernails. But not before I'd glimpsed where we were heading. At the top of a hill, the massive stone walls of a castle rose up and up and up and up, to towers so high I couldn't see the tops.

Castello Rodolfo. It was like something out of a fairy tale. Or a nightmare. My cramping muscles told me definitely nightmare.

We rattled and bashed, bashed and rattled up the track, and all the time the air inside the trunk got hotter and hotter, and the walls burnt under the heat of the sun. I thought about castles. There were a few around Rye, and one even in the town, but they were small or in ruins. This one was solid, and vast, and high: just the sort of place you'd use to defend the coast from pirates. Then I got too hot to think about it any more. My throat hurt. Muscles ached in places that hadn't ached before.

It was hard to concentrate on anything except the burning sun, but I suddenly remembered Auntie Eliza and her yoga lessons. She'd made me go with her that time I ran away. They were learning to meditate. You had to lie flat on the floor of the studio and imagine that you were in a beautiful, exotic place where you felt really happy. Ironically, here I was on an island off the coast of Italy, and my happy place was an old studio in east London. A cool, fresh studio, with the sound of the yoga teacher's soothing voice in the background. You had to focus on relaxing every muscle in your body, one by one, while she talked you through it. Your right foot is . . . relaxed, your right ankle is . . . relaxed.

Bump, rattle, bump. But the yoga teacher's voice was really working. It was weird, but when we got to the top of the track and the truck drove down a short piece of smooth road and came to a halt, I was kind of disappointed. I still had 'my right ear' and 'my forehead' to do. And I'd been enjoying the studio's air conditioning. Dad always told me that survival is ninety-five per cent in your head, and now I was starting to see what he meant.

The trunk was carried inside, where the air smelled cool and musty, like old stone. Two people were arguing nearby and their voices echoed off the walls. They were quarrelling, I eventually realised, about how they were going to carry the trunk up several flights of stairs and down several corridors. They never really agreed how to do it, and kept up the argument all the way. But luckily it never occurred to them to open the wardrobe door and see what was inside to make it so heavy. Instead, they bumped and swayed me for several minutes, until finally, a female voice gave an order, and they put me down and there was silence.

After counting to two hundred in my head, I risked opening the wardrobe door a crack and peeped round the yellow dress. All I could see was painted roses and a high ceiling. I opened the door some more. Nobody screamed or called for security. I was alone.

Off the boat. On dry land. Scared. Strangely excited.

I pushed the trunk door fully open and tipped myself out. Once again, I landed on the floor with a thud and a crunch. Sitting painfully upright, I looked around.

Another bedroom. I'd landed next to the clothes rail and on top of one of the shopping bags, near a huge four-poster bed that was hung with white lace and scattered with dozens of cushions. Beyond the bed, a tall, open window, framed by rose-pink shutters, looked out on to the bright blue sky. Way above me, the ceiling was painted with flying cherubs and hung with a crystal chandelier. On a desk in one corner, a rose-pink iPod sat on a speaker, next to a matching tablet and desktop monitor. Even the air smelled of roses.

This is the bit where Julie Andrews comes in and tells you you're the Princess of Marvalia.

In a MOVIE, Peta. Right now, what would probably happen would be some hulking great delivery man would appear with another load of shopping bags, find me sitting here and hand me over to Muscle Man. Or, just as bad, Yasmin would arrive – I guessed this was her room – and wonder what this smelly, dirty schoolgirl was doing here. (I hadn't dared wash on the yacht in case they noticed the messy towels.)

But they weren't here yet. I'd got this far. I just had work out how to stay ahead.

Stretching my sore muscles, I straightened out the shopping bag I'd landed on (Chanel, enormous), grabbed my backpack and ran for the window, which was framed with real roses, growing up the wall outside. Looking out, I tried to work out exactly where I was.

And it was heaven.

It just *was* heaven. The castle was very high up, at one end of the Isola Sirena. It wasn't a large island – just the castle, on a hill, and down to the right the jetty where I'd landed, some scrubland dotted with blue and yellow wildflowers, a few ruins and an abandoned shack. You could probably explore it in a day. Ahead, the sea glittered under the blazing sun. Boats dotted the water, all tiny compared with the massive *Princess Nazia*, the size of a small island herself, moored a short way out to sea. Further away over to the left was a strip of land that looked like the mainland. Close enough to see, but much too far away to swim.

I looked down to where a series of neat green lawns led down to an infinity pool. Everything within the castle grounds was fresh and immaculate, apart from the wing to my left, where building works were going on. Opposite them, a tower on the right wing soared towards the sky, topped off with picture-perfect ramparts and parapets, just like the ones from my storybooks.

A gull flew by and I watched it land on the tower. As it did so, a security guard in bulky black body armour emerged from a door in the ramparts, pulling his black baseball cap low over his eyes to protect them from the sun. It was only as he turned away that I noticed the gun tucked into a holster on his belt.

So that was nice.

Heaven was patrolled by armed guards. Real guards with real guns. This *so* wasn't a movie with Julie Andrews. I wanted my mum, and I wanted to go home.

A splash from below distracted me. Someone had dived into the swimming pool and was carving through the water like a professional athlete. His tan was emphasised by a small pair of red trunks. I watched him as he executed a perfect turn.

Footsteps in the corridor.

Stop admiring the swimmer, you IDIOT. Hide.

There was a small pink silk-covered armchair in front of the window. I ducked behind it instinctively, still thinking about the boy in the pool. He looked about the right age to be one of Mr Wahool's sons. Which son? The creepy one, Omar, with the honey voice – or the younger one, Max, my friend, the one person in this place who could help me?

A moment later the bedroom door burst open and some-one moved through it at speed. She raced up to the window, right beside where I was crouching, and yelled out:

'Max! Get out of the pool! Max! We're back! Maxi!'

It was Yasmin. Her brother obviously didn't hear her, because she groaned in frustration. Then she moved back into the room and called out:

'Amina! Amina!'

There was a pause. Someone must have arrived in the room, because Yasmin started giving out instructions.

'Find me a bikini. Three, so I can choose. And a kaftan. I'm off to the pool. God, it's been tiring today.' *Yeah. Getting off a superyacht. Try doing it in a trunk, Yasmin.* 'I'm going to relax for a bit and then we're having dinner on the boat, so Papa can show the boys. Find me something from Dior. There's a blue dress I brought from Paris that should do. Oh God, I'm *so tired*. Where's Omar?'

She yawned loudly. A quiet voice muttered something about Omar going to see the *Princess*. Then the servant moved around, opening and closing drawers.

The chair I was hiding behind was so small and inadequate it was almost funny. If they weren't so busy finding bikinis, they would spot me in an instant. But I was too busy thinking about what Yasmin had just said to be properly terrified this time. Meanwhile, she changed quickly and soon the room was empty again.

Alone, undiscovered, I breathed in the scented air. In that one shouted sentence through the window, Yasmin had changed everything for me.

It *was* Max in the pool.

I'd found Max! He must have called me from this castle. And where the boy was, the prisoner was. I'd accidentally ended up in the perfect place.

Dad, I'm here, I whispered. *I'm coming. Wait for me.*

SEVENTEEN

It took me five minutes to find Max's room, dashing across the corridor in the eerie silence, heart racing. There were four bedrooms on this corridor – all of them enormous – but only one of them had an almost life-size photograph opposite the door of a dark-haired boy on a polo pony smiling to camera, with a caption saying *Max Wahool* underneath.

OK, so he wasn't exactly shy, but if you look that good on a polo pony, life-size photos must be tempting.

The rest of the room was the opposite of Yasmin's. This one was pure boy, apart from the fact that it was insanely tidy. It had everything Luke could possibly have wanted – two huge TV screens, a stack of gaming equipment and a walk-in wardrobe full of (I checked) immaculate polo shirts and designer jeans. There was also a vast double bed, a futuristic leather armchair that swivelled, five electric guitars on stands, and a punch bag hanging from the ceiling near the window. So he could punch something while he admired the view. Kind of weird. Presumably it kept him fit, though. Which he was, from what I'd seen in the pool just now. Very.

It was the swivel chair that attracted my attention – much more promising than the fancy little armchair I'd crouched behind in Yasmin's room. This one had a deep leather seat and a broad back, wide enough to hide a polo pony from view. I shoved my backpack under the bed, dashed across to the chair and sank down in its comfy seat, moving it with my feet so it faced away from the door. My plan was to swivel round when Max came in, like someone from a Bond movie. Except it would make me look like the villain, but whatever. I sat in position and waited.

And waited. Thirty long minutes ticked by. I used the time to stretch out my aching muscles. Eventually, there were footsteps in the corridor and the door opened. A young man's voice shouted out, 'Amina! Amina!'

Hell. That servant girl would be here in a minute. Didn't anyone in this place spend any time alone? I hunkered down where I was. *Another bad choice of hiding place, Peta. Seriously bad choice.*

'Sir?'

It wasn't a girl who answered, though. This time, it was a boy.

'Not you,' Max said, irritated. 'I called for Amina. I want Amina.'

'Can *I* help you, sir?' the boy insisted. Odd. His voice sounded familiar. 'Amina is busy. Miss Yasmin has asked—'

'I don't care about my sister! I don't care about *you*! I want Amina. Tell my sister I want her now. Do it.'

The boy disappeared. Max opened another door and I heard the sound of a shower running. Meanwhile, I sat where I was and thought about those voices. One was quiet and musical, the other harsh and cruel. But they were the wrong way round.

Max wasn't the boy who'd called me.

Somehow, I'd made a terrible mistake.

As I hunched in my stupid swivel chair, the sound of the shower stopped. Max could emerge at any moment. I sat there, frozen. The bathroom door opened and the harsh voice snapped, 'Ah, Amina! Good. You're here.'

'Master Max,' the girl said obediently. Once again, I hadn't heard her come in.

'Tidy the bathroom. Lay out my clothes. The blue linen for tonight, I think. No, the silk. Do it!'

While she worked, I listened to Max's fists rhythmically hitting the punch bag. *Smack. Smack. Smack.* I moved the chair around, microscopic centimetre by centimetre, using my toes, so it was still facing away from them both.

'Your clothes are ready, sir,' the girl said. Her voice was hardly more than a whisper.

He moved over to inspect them. 'What's this?' he called out.

'Shirt. Sir.'

'The *linen* one. Did I ask for the linen? No! It was the silk.'

The sharp sound of a slap. A hard one. She gasped and he grunted with the effort of hitting her. I bit my lip. This wasn't my secret friend. This boy *so* wasn't my friend.

'Get me the silk,' he said icily.

The girl ran past him to get the new shirt. On her way

104

back, eager to stay as far away from him as possible, she passed around the front of the swivel chair. Her leg brushed mine; she glanced around and gasped again.

The shock on her face matched the shock I felt seeing her.

She only looked about ten, with a black scarf over her hair, a red mark on her cheek where he'd hit her, and big dark eyes staring at me. Then, in a single moment, those eyes went blank. Her face was a mask – you'd never know she'd seen anything at all. She went over to Max and handed him the shirt.

'Now go,' he spat. 'I don't know why I ask for you, you lazy dumbskull.'

She almost ran from the room. I stayed motionless while he went back to the bathroom, humming. My mind was racing. What if he found me? Should I try and hit him with something? Or go for his nose, or eyes? Those were the vulnerable places. But Dad said never to take on someone stronger than you in a fight if you could possibly avoid it. Cheat or run away, he said. I wanted to run, but where?

Here was it. Max had always been it. Max Wahool was where I'd been running to.

Without warning, the chair swivelled round, flinging me sideways. *Hell!* But to my amazement, I was facing the little girl again. She must have come back silently. She brought her finger to her lips.

Very confused, but so glad she wasn't Max, I gave her a nervous smile. She pointed at the wall opposite and made a motion for me to follow her. I stared back, more confused than ever. She glared at me, angry now, and motioned again. The wall was blank. What did she mean? With no idea what we were doing, I eased myself out of the chair and followed. When we got to the wall, she put her palm up against it and pressed.

And the wall gave way.

A tiny, invisible door opened in front of us – just high enough for a child to pass through – leading to a black hole. The girl moved quickly into the dark. Nearby, the bathroom door opened with a click.

I have never followed a small, angry stranger so fast in my life.

EIGHTEEN

She pushed the door shut behind me, put her cheek to it and listened. I waited, heart racing, blood singing. She turned back briefly with her finger to her lips again, and I nodded. *Got the message. Not exactly going to draw attention to myself here.*

We crouched in the near-darkness, catching our breath. The hidden space wasn't as pitch-black as I had thought. A shaft of light from somewhere further along the passage made it possible to see that we were in a low, narrow tunnel, cut into the super-thick castle walls.

Before I had time to think, the girl set off down the tunnel at speed and I had trouble keeping up with her. The ceiling was so low I had to crouch. On either side of me, the damp walls brushed my shoulders and banged my elbows, while the ceiling kept scraping the top of my back. Sometimes it was easier to crawl, but the rough ground cut and scratched my knees.

The girl kept going, and I was glad to get as far away from Max as possible, even like this. It was never entirely dark, and never entirely light. The air smelled of dirt and mould. The ground under us was a mixture of earth and stone, and small, hard, knobbly things that felt a lot like mouse poo. And possibly rat poo. And things that crunched underfoot like dead bugs. There were spiders, by the way, *everywhere*.

I didn't dare ask where we were going, and I didn't think she would answer anyway. Whenever two paths met, she knew instantly which one to take and I just had to follow. On we continued, launching ourselves down narrow spiral stairs. This was where the light was coming from: there was a window high in the stairwell, several floors up. After several more passages and another staircase, she eventually stopped next to a door-shaped crack of light in the wall. She felt for a handle and pulled it hard, and we were through.

We were in a large room with a ceiling of vaulted stone, like a church. No windows. It felt as though we were underground. At either end, there were two huge stone fireplaces, big enough to roast an ox. This place was unreal! Honestly, you could stick a school tour in here and tell them it was from the Middle Ages and they'd definitely believe you. However, these kitchens also had a bank of modern, steel ovens in the middle, lots of steel worktops round the edge, and several men in white jackets stomping around, swearing loudly.

While they were busy with steaming pots and spitting pans, the girl grabbed my hand and pulled me quickly past them, out through the nearest door and into a cold, damp corridor. She went so fast we almost ran into someone.

'*Mannaggia!*'

A man bustled past us in chef's whites, carrying a pyramid of buns topped with spun sugar. I paused for a moment to admire it. A *croquembouche* – a speciality of the chef at the Smugglers' Inn. Mum had one as her wedding cake. But the girl yanked me out of my mini-reverie, bowing low and mumbling apologies.

A moment later, she brought me to a cold room lit only by a small window high up in the thick stone wall. In the middle was a wooden table, and on its surface something large and delicate glistened in the dim light.

It was a boat. A pale and ghostly boat, as tall as me, and made of ice. It looked as though it should have been a pirate ship or a galleon, but actually it was a big, modern yacht. I checked out the many decks, the graceful shape. Then I did a double-take. There, at the front, was my old cabin on the *Princess Nazia*, with the balcony outside it. They had reproduced the whole boat, perfectly, in ice.

The little girl saw the wonder on my face and nodded gravely. Then her face became a question. She pointed at the ice boat, then at me.

'Yes,' I whispered, nodding. 'That's how I got here.'

She held out her hand, not pulling me this time.

'English girl. *Ayo.* Come.'

I followed her down a series of passages lined with little storage rooms. The further we went, the more damp and dirty the rooms became. Some were full of kitchen supplies like tinned food and bags of potatoes. Others held mops and tools. A couple contained people dressed in tattered clothes, working under the harsh light of bare bulbs, or resting on mattresses on the floor. It felt a million miles away from the bedrooms upstairs.

In the furthest room, at the end of the longest passage, a teenage boy sat cross-legged on a mat, sewing a pair of trousers. Reaching his open door, the girl stopped and waited on the threshold. The room was about half the size of the bathroom on the yacht, with bare walls covered in rough plaster. The boy looked up from his task and his face dropped in shock at the sight of me. So did his needle.

'You!' He scrambled to his feet, staring at me as if I was primed to explode. 'You!'

He had the voice I recognised from those phone calls, and Max's bedroom upstairs. He was thin and scraggy, with wild black hair and dark eyes. He was dressed in a threadbare pair of shorts, which were practically falling apart. His skin was scarred. He looked as if he'd never been fed properly in his life, or told to comb his hair. He looked like the most pitiable, unloved creature in the world.

As the girl shut the door behind us, his face broke into a pillarbox smile, showing all his teeth.

'Welcome to my castle, Peta Jones!'

NINETEEN

'Y ou? You?' I couldn't help echoing his original words. 'You're the boy?'

I stood there, staring.

'Come in, please. Sit. I beg you.' He indicated the filthy mat as if it was a sofa at Buckingham Palace. His smile had returned. He looked surprised, but pleased to see me – delighted, even.

I was in shock.

'You *are* the boy. The one who helped me . . . But how did you know it was me?'

'From your computer picture,' he said. 'I do not understand why you are here. But it is good to see you.'

'It's good to see you too,' I lied.

It would have been so good to see him if he'd been the boy in the swimming pool. If he'd been the fit, powerful one, acting as if he owned the place. True, this boy also acted as if he owned the place, but he *so* didn't.

All this time – in the furniture van, on the boat, in the rose-scented bedroom – I'd been relying on Max, the son of the family, to get me out of trouble. He was my secret weapon, my back-up plan. And all this time, the truth was that Max was an evil bully who made my flesh crawl, and my only 'friend' lived in a filthy cellar room lit by a single bulb. I thought Max would save me, but this boy and girl looked as if they needed saving more than I did.

I sank down on to his ragged old mat, and stared hard at the floor.

'Don't cry, Peta Jones. You have only just arrived!'

'I'm not crying. I'm just . . . It's been a long journey.'

'I'm sure you are tired. I am sorry; where are my manners? Have you eaten? Have you had anything to drink?'

I shook my head. The boy barked orders to the little girl, who quickly left the room.

'My sister will come back soon. Don't worry.'

I looked up and he smiled again. Generous. Relaxed. Or, rather, almost relaxed. He had the face of a happy boy, but the wrinkled eyes of a tired old man.

'Amina is your sister?' I asked.

'Ah, you know her name!' he said softly. 'Yes, she is my Amina.'

'How old is she?'

'She is young. Only twelve, I think.'

'You *think*?'

A shadow of embarrassment fell across his face. Why

didn't he know?

'She looks younger,' I said.

He dipped his head. 'Yes. She is still a child.' The wrinkles around his eyes deepened and he looked really ancient, suddenly, although he couldn't have been that much older than me. But he shook himself out of it. 'How did you get here, Peta Jones?' he asked. 'Why did you come? Did I not tell you to hide?'

'I didn't know "here" existed,' I said hotly. 'And I didn't exactly mean to come.'

I explained about going to the house in Eaton Square, and the van, and finding myself on the boat. His eyes widened with surprise, but the more I explained, the more laughter started to flicker there. 'Bad things' happening to me were funny, it seemed. In fact, he was exactly how I'd imagined him all this time. Or his face was, anyway: bright and confident. His thin, ragged body told a totally different story.

A few minutes later, Amina returned, clutching her dark skirt up to her chest and revealing a pair of old black trousers underneath. She knelt carefully on the floor and laid the skirt down. Out of it tumbled pears, grapes, a bag of soft white balls that looked like marshmallows, more nuts (I smiled gratefully at these, like everything else, but to be honest I was a bit sick of nuts), and a couple of fat, glistening pastry cones. She also held a cup of pink liquid, which she handed ceremoniously to me. I took a big gulp. My mouth filled with a sharp, bitter taste. Then something sweet: sugar. I stared at the glass again: it was pink lemonade.

After everything that had just happened, the shock of its loveliness was almost overwhelming. I wanted to cry again. I wanted to hug her. I wasn't sure how she'd take it, though, so

I settled for a shaky grin.

'Peta,' I said, pointing at myself. 'Peta Jones. Thank you.'

'Amina,' she said with a shy smile, bowing. I bowed back. Then I turned to her brother.

'I don't know your name,' I said, feeling rude for not asking before. And guilty for not caring before. But any boy who can summon up pink lemonade at a moment's notice needs a proper introduction.

'Karim.'

'Thank you too, Karim.'

He shrugged, as if providing food and drink to strange girls who showed up out of nowhere was all in a day's work for 'his' castle.

'Carry on, please,' he said, once we were all sitting down again. 'You were telling me the interesting story of your adventures on the new vessel. It is a vessel, yes?'

'I think so.' Were yachts vessels? His grasp of vocab was better than mine.

'Very good. Continue. You had got to the part where you went looking for food.'

Soon I was deep into the story of my adventures behind the bar. Amina gasped at all the scary bits and grinned at all the good bits. Despite her unwillingness to speak it, she understood English as perfectly as her brother. I told them about how I hid as Yasmin and her father argued about the birthday party.

'They don't seem a very happy family,' I said.

'No,' Karim agreed. 'They are not.'

'Mr Wahool kept talking about his *own* father,' I said. 'Like he was in charge.'

Karim looked surprised at this. 'The master's father is dead.'

114

'But . . . but, he kept saying "the Grandfather".'

Brother and sister exchanged glances and giggled nervously.

'The Grandfather is what we call the great leader,' he explained. 'The President of Marvalia. He was our ruler for many, many years, until a bad thing happened.'

'D'you mean the Blue Revolution? That was a good thing, wasn't it?'

'Not for the Grandfather,' Karim said flatly. 'He was a rich man. A powerful man. He lived in the Great Palace. It had a thousand rooms. His throne was made of copper.'

'He had a *throne*?'

Amina joined in. 'In the Great Palace, all the floors were made of copper, polished to shine like gold. He had a hundred slaves to shine them.'

'Why copper?' I asked. 'There was lots of copper on the *Princess Nazia* too.'

'It is the metal of Marvalia,' Karim explained. 'There are many copper mines. Mr Johnson told me that nowadays everyone in the world needs copper for electricity. Copper is very valuable. It is why the Grandfather is so rich. And the master too. He owned many of the copper mines. He is very angry to see them used by the people now, with nobody paying him taxes.'

'I bet he is,' I grunted.

Wait. The other thing. Amina had said something odd. Or had I misunderstood?

'The Grandfather had *slaves*? They still had them in Marvalia?'

Amina cast her eyes down. Karim swallowed, before nodding silently.

Something began to dawn on me.

'And . . . Mr Wahool – he had slaves too?'

No answer.

'And . . . you?'

They didn't need to say anything. I'd heard that slap on Amina's cheek. I saw how these people lived.

I hadn't found Dad. I'd found slave children, living in squalor under a massive castle filled with spoiled and psychotic teenagers and patrolled by armed guards. And there was nothing, nothing I could do.

I smiled weakly. They smiled weakly back. An awkward silence hung in the stuffy room, like hope dying.

A bell jingled outside and suddenly the corridor was filled with the sound of running footsteps. Karim announced that he and Amina must go too. They were needed by the family. Just like that, they were gone. I was alone.

I looked down at what Amina had brought for me. She might be a slave, but she had provided the best selection of food I'd seen in days. While she and her brother were away, I worked my way ravenously through everything, including the nuts. It turned out the small white lumps were soft, fresh cheese. The pastries were stale, but full of vanilla cream. Some of the fruit was old and turning brown, but I was so hungry that it all tasted good.

Karim came back, clutching some things in a bundle of cloth, just as I was finishing the last pastry. He moved a couple of loose stones out of the wall and tucked the bundle away in a secret hiding place.

'Usually, we are very busy in the evening,' he said. 'There is always a celebration of some sort, but tonight it is on the vessel. And we are not invited to the vessel!'

He was clearly thrilled *not* to be going aboard the *Princess*

Nazia, and given the way he and his sister were treated by the family, I could understand it.

'I expect you are worried about the prisoner,' he added, suddenly serious. 'Mr Allud. You are concerned for him, yes?'

I caught my breath. *Yes!* I'd been so shocked and confused that I'd forgotten, for a moment, that it was Karim who had given me Dad's message.

'Of course! Where is he?'

'In a place beneath the kitchens. He is very . . . You are crying again, Peta Jones. You really are a tearful girl. I did not expect this. Because you are also brave – you have come to find him. Do not cry. It is all right. Really. It is all right.'

'I'm sorry.' Dad was here! He really was. My tears were pure relief. 'And who . . . who is looking after him?'

'I am, Peta Jones. And sometimes my sister. We bring the prisoners food. We tend to their wounds when they are not cared for by the guards. It is not a healthy place down there. They are dirty. They get diseases. And . . . other things.'

There were other prisoners? And *wounds*? There was so much I needed to know, and could hardly bear to ask. 'But . . . Mr Allud . . . What do you know about him?'

Karim sighed and came over to sit near me.

'He came here many months ago. One day I saw the guards dragging him from his computer. They took him to a special room and asked him questions. They did not . . . look after him. For a long time, he stayed in that place. Then they moved him to the dungeons.'

'This place has dungeons?'

'Yes. He was there for a long time. But recently they took him back to . . . the room where they do these things. The master asked Mr Allud about 'the power of Peta' but he did not reply. Then they told him they were sending some people

117

to go and get the kid – which was you – and when they brought you here, they would kill you.'

'Kill me?' I whispered. 'You said "kill" me? Can they do that?'

'Yes, they can.' He shrugged, as if that was a fairly typical conversation here at the castle. 'After that, Mr Allud asked me to telephone you and give you the message. Later,' he went on, 'I heard Marco and Ingrid boasting to their friends that they would bring you back on the super-boat, and they would get a free ride.' He seemed very proud of himself. 'That is how I knew how long you must hide.'

'Yes,' I said. 'I see.' My voice was shaky. My brain was still processing *kill you*, and *Yes, they can*.

'That message . . .' Karim went on. 'I still do not understand. Mr Allud said you have a power. The master said so too. What is your power, Peta Jones?'

'I don't have one. It's just my name.'

'Please?'

Really? I had to go into this now? *Really?* But Karim looked so curious and confused.

'Peta means ten to the power of fifteen,' I sighed.

He frowned at me, puzzled. 'That is all? It is a big number? Ten times fifteen?'

'Not ten *times* fifteen. Ten times ten, fifteen times over. It's called a quadrillion sometimes.'

'That is a very big number,' he said, nodding gravely. 'But I do not understand why the master should want to know it.'

I agreed. Overall, Karim seemed disappointed by my answer, and so was I.

Silence. That awkward silence again. He broke it with a smile: 'Well, now you know everything about Mr Allud.'

He was wrong.

I still didn't really know anything about this man with a name I didn't recognise – except that he had suffered and suffered while they 'didn't look after him' in 'the room where they do these things', and that for some reason connected to him, a bunch of strangers now wanted me dead. I knew he cared about me, though, and of course my heart told me he was Dad, Dad, Dad.

TWENTY

We were all talked out. Karim could tell I was preoccupied and went back to his sewing task. Meanwhile, I tried to make sense of what he'd said. Why would Dad have been working in this place? And why did Mr Wahool care about the power thing? But none of that mattered. Dad was very close, and from everything Karim had said, he needed me even more than I thought.

Amina came back from her chores and settled down to join us. She'd been pressing and hanging Yasmin's new clothes and she looked exhausted.

'Look, you've both helped me enough already,' I said. 'Just tell me where the . . . dungeons are and I'll get there somehow.

Don't worry about me.'

I was half hoping Karim would offer to take me there anyway, but that didn't happen.

'You are a very stupid, brave girl,' he said, shaking his head at me and half smiling.

'No, really. Just tell me where to go.'

'No. It is dangerous. The guards. Your face and hands . . . Perhaps . . . Let me think about this. It would take time . . .'

'I don't *have* any time,' I shouted, louder than I meant to. I made Amina jump, but this was unbearable. 'You don't understand. I have to go now. Mr Allud's in trouble. I have to get to him as fast as I—'

'*You* do not understand,' Karim interrupted, staring at me with a stern expression that reminded me of Granny on a bad day.

I turned to Amina. Maybe the little sister would be easier to persuade. But as I opened my mouth, she gave me a kick to the ribs so hard she sent me sprawling against the wall.

Hello?

I stared back, astonished.

The door flew open and she didn't even glance at me. Her face did that mask thing as she looked up at whoever was standing in the open doorway. From the other side, a high-pitched woman's voice addressed the brother and sister briefly. Karim got up and followed her outside, closing the door behind him.

I struggled to catch my breath.

'Did she see me?' I asked Amina.

'No. My brother has gone to read for her. He will be back soon.'

She didn't apologise for kicking me out of sight, and I didn't need her to. Karim, though, when he came back, was very apologetic.

'The others who live down here – they are not bad people, but they are afraid of the master. If he asks them a question about you, they will tell him what they know. It is not safe for you here tonight. You must return to the tunnels, I think.'

I nodded. Mouse poo. Spiders. All on my own. Fantastic. But it didn't look much better for Karim and his sister in the cellars. Here it was cold and bare, and the stale air smelled of old sweat. Amina had no one to tuck her in and wish her goodnight. I wondered if such a person had ever existed.

It was getting late. Karim checked that the path was clear and took me back, past the storerooms, where he picked up a thin woollen blanket for me to use, and through the almost-empty kitchens, where a solitary chef kept his back to us as he wiped his work area clean. We reached the door to the tunnels.

'But what if someone comes in?' I whispered. 'A guard? A servant?'

He shook his head.

'They do not come here. They cannot. Only Amina and I can fit inside. There is a story that a rich woman made these passages many centuries ago, because she did not like to meet her servants in corridors. She employed only children and monkeys.'

'Monkeys?'

'That is the story. I don't know if it is true. I am sorry you must stay here.'

'It's OK. There are loads of smugglers' tunnels in Rye, where I come from. I'm used to them.'

He looked surprised. 'We have smugglers' tunnels too,' he said, showing off, I thought. 'I am glad you are used to them.

I must go to my prayers now. Goodnight.'

He bowed and left. It was dark, and once again, I was alone.

I hadn't told the entire truth about the smugglers' tunnels at home. They did exist – some even led from the Smugglers' Inn – but most of them had disappeared long ago, and I'd never been inside one. The pictures I'd seen were of broad, stone-lined spaces, tall and wide enough for two men to pass through, and well lit by burning torches set into the wall.

Not like this.

I looked around to get my bearings, but the dim moon-light penetrating through the nearest stairwell hardly made it as far as this low, cold, narrow passage. I couldn't stay here. And not just because of the new and unwelcome image of sharing it with thousand-year-old monkey poo. It was at the heart of the maze of tunnels, and somewhere beneath me were the dungeons.

Dad was *here*. If Karim wouldn't help me, I'd just have to find him by myself.

Further along, at least three other passages led off the main tunnel, into deeper darkness. I remembered I'd left my back-pack under Max's bed. Oh hell. All alone in the darkness I really missed that bag, and especially MY FAVOURITE TORCH, which I'd packed in the front pocket.

Too late to worry about that now. Dad never had much time for people who let fear stop them from doing something perfectly simple and straightforward. This was only crawling in the dark. How hard could it be?

You know those horror movies where you're screaming at the girl, 'Don't go there!'? It was like that. I wasn't sure if I was more terrified of what I might find, or what would happen if

I got lost. I moved along on my hands and knees, using the fear to push me forward. I tried each tunnel in turn, and other passages beyond that led further into the dark, trying not to think too much where I was going, ignoring the impression that the tunnels were closing in, and that the darkness was like a living thing, waiting for me.

But however long I looked, however sore and bloody my knees became, however much I scraped my elbows on the narrow walls, I couldn't find a staircase leading downwards – only up, or round in circles.

After what felt like hours, I ended up back where I'd started, and the constant dread had left my throat dry and my muscles exhausted. I decided to leave it until morning, when at least I'd have enough light to see where I was going. I lay down and huddled under the thin blanket as best I could.

Karim had said he was going to his prayers. I tried to think of some, but all that would come was *You have the power*. Yeah, right. *You have the power to be utterly depressed, Peta Jones*.

Back at the inn, Granny would be comforting Mum, dragged home from her ruined honeymoon. Luke would be back at his house, worried too.

And Dad? Dad was in the darkness somewhere down below. Alive, but perhaps barely. And just out of reach.

We tend to their wounds . . .

Tiny feet skittered along at super-speed a few centimetres from my shivering body. Mice. Probably. A spider landed from out of nowhere on my cheek, just below my left eye, and crawled across my face until my stiff and tired fingers finally managed to flick it away. Fabulous.

TWENTY-ONE

Amina woke me with a shake.

'Come! Come!' she said, frowning at me.

'Why? What time is it?'

I'd been dreaming about finding Dad in Winchelsea Church, and eating iced buns and *croquembouche*. I looked at my watch in the light of her torch. Ten past four. I stumbled groggily to my feet.

'*Ayo*. Come.'

A clock in the kitchen said ten past five. Of course, the time was different here. Ten past five was still a bad time to be awake, but not quite so horrific. And it was good to be back in the light.

Being careful to avoid the only chef at work this early in the morning, we crept along to Karim's cellar room. He was dressed and busily making something in a bowl. The harsh light of the bulb cast strong shadows on his skin. He had an elegant face, I realised – fine features under his shock of black hair. The muscles on his arms looked powerful.

'Hi. Is that breakfast?' I asked, thinking how starving I was again.

He looked up, grinned and shook his head.

'Good morning, Peta Jones. No, it is not food. It is for later. Wait two minutes, please.'

Amina and I watched as he poured dark brown liquid from a teapot on to a fine, dark, reddish powder in the bowl. At first, he looked like a wise guru as he sat cross-legged and stirred, but the longer he did it, the more I wondered if he really knew what he was doing. He didn't seem sure how much liquid to add, testing the consistency of the mush in the bowl with a quizzical expression. He saw me looking at him and shrugged.

'I have not done this before. Nor have I often watched the women do it. Amina?'

He asked his sister something in their language, and she giggled and went over to the bowl, poking at the sludge with the spoon and making faces at it.

'Amina knows, but she does not remember. This will have to do. Ah, I forgot to tell you last night. A bad thing has happened.'

Another bad thing? He seemed very fond of bad things. 'What?'

'Your bag. Amina found it in the young master's room and I burnt it.'

I gasped. 'My backpack? You burnt my backpack?'

'Bad,' Amina echoed, shaking her head.

Yeah. Bad. Absolutely. I stared open-mouthed at her brother.

'I am sorry. Also the jacket. And the photograph,' he continued.

I pictured them. My school blazer, with the Collingwood Academy crest on it. The photograph that showed Dad and me together. *Hell*. Karim was right: they were a dead give-away. If the guards had found the bag here, they'd have started hunting for me straight away. I nodded grudgingly.

Karim brightened. 'But there is this.' Going to the hole in the wall, he extracted the little bundle I'd seen him hide yesterday and handed it to me. Inside were my phone, the torch and some other bits and pieces from the bag.

'You are happy, Peta Jones?'

'Yes!' I found myself hugging the useless phone like a long-lost teddy bear.

'And now you must dress.' He indicated a pile of old, dark rags in the corner, and left the room briefly while Amina helped me put them on. They were held together with patches, but made of softest cotton and very clean. Consisting of a mismatched shirt, tunic and trousers, they covered every part of me, from neck to ankle. As a finishing touch, Amina added a scarf, winding it over my hair and around my neck.

When Karim returned, he laughed.

'You look different, Peta Jones.'

'Better?'

'Different is good. Now – breakfast. You are hungry, yes?'

We hid back inside the tunnel door and feasted on hot bread rolls scavenged from the kitchens.

'Soon, Amina and I must work,' Karim announced

through a mouthful of bread. 'You will stay here. At twelve o'clock, I will meet you in this place.' He tapped the ground in front of us. There he was again, handing out instructions like some sort of maharaja.

'Look,' I pleaded with him. 'Why don't you take me to the prisoner now?'

'I can't,' he said, shrugging.

'Why? It's quiet. There's no one around.'

He shook his head. 'It is the wrong time. It is impossible. You will stay here. Promise me.'

'But—'

'Promise me!' His eyes blazed.

He was impossible. What had happened to the person I spoke to on the phone? The one who loved the game, and danger? Now that I actually wanted to meet the prisoner, Karim seemed to be finding any excuse not to take me to him. Perhaps he was scared of what would happen if we were caught. Being a slave would do that to you, I supposed. I could understand it, but it was a shame.

'Sure, I promise,' I said meekly. I was a much better liar than Yasmin Wahool. He didn't need to know what my plans were.

He looked relieved. 'That is good. I will see you at twelve o'clock.'

'Got it.'

He headed back out into the kitchens, looking furtive. Amina went the other way, up into the main living quarters.

As soon they were out of sight, I changed my watch to Italian time, before hiding it under my ragged sleeve. Ten to six – plenty of time for what I had in mind. Then I slipped back out into the kitchens too. No way was I staying in a cold, damp stairwell all morning. I had things to do, places to

128

go. People to find.

Karim had looked very shifty as he headed off just now, and that made me curious. Maybe the stairway to the dungeons wasn't in the tunnel system after all.

TWENTY-TWO

This corner of the main kitchen was mostly used for storage. Crouching behind a stack of empty crates, I watched Karim on the far side of the room as he took some scraps from a bin of leftovers and put them into bowls on a tray. He added four golden croissants from a cooling rack and set off down a corridor next to one of the walk-in fireplaces.

A couple of kitchen workers entered the room, shrugging on white jackets and switching on more lights. The day was starting. When their backs were turned, I ran down Karim's corridor and ducked into the first doorway I found, which was an empty laundry room.

Five minutes later, he walked back past my hiding place. I held my breath and shrank into the shadows. As soon as he was gone, I headed off into the dark, retracing his steps.

The corridor led to a long, deep spiral staircase that wound down, down, down into the depths of the castle – so far down these levels must have been cut into the rock. This was not like the side of the island I'd seen from Yasmin's bedroom window, which was all gentle slopes and scented flowers. The sound of crashing waves penetrated through rough-hewn slits for windows. I sensed steep, jagged cliffs outside, and a raging sea far below. Inside was blackness, dripping water, bad smells and danger. The lower I went, the more the air smelled of blocked-up drains and stale sweat. The stones oozed slime, and the stairs were dangerous and slippery. It felt as though I was finally heading in the right direction.

At the bottom, I made out another dingy corridor heading off round a corner, where a buzzing ceiling light flickered intermittently. Pausing on the last step, I crouched down and peeked forward just enough to see what was there.

The corridor wasn't long. In the uncertain yellow light I could just make out two men sitting at a small metal table at the far end. Dressed in heavy jackets against the cold, they were busy eating the croissants and talking to each other, but if either of them looked up, they would see me. Behind them were three doors – one at the end and one on each side of the table – all very solid and guarded and shut.

I sat back on the stairs. I was really here at last. It was scarily, in fact, how I had pictured it in my worst nightmares. After all this time, Dad must be behind one of those doors – so close that if only my own heart would stop beating so loud, I felt sure I would hear his.

But first I had to get past the guards. Every cell in my body wanted to fly down the corridor, defeat them or slip past them somehow, and break into his cell. A part of my brain even started telling me I had a chance. But I wasn't Buffy, or Katniss Everdeen. I might be ten metres away . . . He was *right there*. But the two large men were closer.

While I rapidly thought of, and rejected, a dozen mad ideas, the reality of the situation sank into my bones. It was maths again. Unlike the furniture van – which had been a stupid enough idea in itself – this time I couldn't even see a one per cent chance of getting past those guards. I'd be found out, I'd be killed, or worse – they'd take me to *the room where they do these things*. And I really didn't want to go there.

When it came down to it, I was as bad as Karim. I could hear Dad's voice in my head, like he was talking to me through the walls of his cell.

You have the power to stay alive, Peta. You have the power to hide. Do it, quickly.

So I retreated pathetically back up the stairs. This was NOT what I'd come for. Armies hate retreating. So do teenage girls.

Back near the kitchen doorway, I crouched in the shadows for a long time, trying to calm my ragged breathing and hating myself for giving up. I hated Karim too: if only he'd helped me, I was sure we could have found a way. Somehow, I still would. I would not cry. I *would not cry*. I would hide in the tunnels again. I would think. I would fix this. Because right now Dad needed me, and frankly, I needed him.

I stayed too long.

In the kitchens, several chefs were at work by now, chopping, whizzing and slinging heavy pans on to fierce blue flames. There wasn't a quiet moment for me to run back to my hiding place, and the more I watched, the busier the place became. Servants in uniform arrived, grabbing plates of food and loading them on to large silver trays. I couldn't stay in this passage forever. I waited until I thought everyone was distracted, then pulled my scarf over my head and, crouching low, made a dash for the tunnel door.

I'd almost reached the packing cases when a hand grabbed my elbow and held me hard.

'*Oui!* You!'

I thought my heart would explode. The hand spun me round. An arm in a white chef's jacket dragged me across the room.

'*Tu vois ça?* Take it!'

Why was he shouting at me in French? I didn't dare look at his face. He was pointing at an enormous tray on a nearby table, loaded with crystal jugs of red and yellow juices.

'*Vite! Vite!* Quickly!'

Oh my God. He wasn't capturing me: he had no idea who I was. He was just looking for another pair of hands.

Before he could look at me any more closely, I picked up the tray, which was so heavy I could hardly hold it, and followed him to the outer passageway. A crocodile of waiters and waitresses was heading off, loaded with trays of food and drink.

'*Allez!* Go!'

Still in shock, I went. I didn't exactly have a choice.

With me at the back, the crocodile wound its way up a brick flight of stairs into the main part of the castle. Bending low under the weight of my tray, I followed the line of servants down a white-painted passageway and out on to the terrace, where bright light and warm air hit me like a camera flash.

The crocodile stopped. I blinked in the light. After just one day I'd forgotten sun could be this bright. To our left was the building site, covered in scaffolding. Straight ahead, on a rose-covered terrace, two white-clothed tables groaned under huge arrangements of exotic flowers. One of the tables was set for four people to eat breakfast. The other was for serving food and looked as sumptuously laden as a banquet at the Ritz. Behind the banquet table, a butler-looking type barked orders.

'The guests are on their way. Speed it up! You – put the cold meats there. You – arrange the seafood platter. You – go back. No, wait! Help set the table first. Quickly!'

The last 'you' was me.

Absurdly, amazingly . . . luckily . . . the butler didn't seem to know or care who I was either. I put down my tray and used my shaking hands to pull my scarf down as low as possible over my face. I was almost too scared to think, but if I did as I was told, maybe nobody would notice me.

Set the table. Oh my God – I could do this.

I never thought that helping Granny out with banquets at the Smugglers' Inn would one day keep me alive. There were four places laid out on this table, but two waiters were hurriedly dumping trays with plates, glasses and cutlery for five more. Other servants were drawing up five extra chairs, so I just had to lay a place setting in front of each chair. I could even copy what was already there. Big plate, small plate, glass, coffee cup, knife, spoon, knife . . .

WHAT WAS I DOING? Mr Wahool wanted to kill me and I was *laying his breakfast table*?

Well, yes, I was. Quite efficiently, as it happened. Until one of the servants looked more closely under my scarf and asked what I was doing there, when I would faint.

The fear of being out in the open was so powerful I could actually hear it, like a buzzer inside my head. However, like last night in the tunnels, I used it to keep going. Also, it's amazing the power it gives you when nobody knows who you are.

'He's here!'

The servants snapped to attention. I snapped too, in a head-down, don't-look-at-me sort of way. Out of the corner of my eye I could just make out a large figure, in a linen suit and white leather shoes, stomping across the terrace. I nearly fainted, but not quite.

I hadn't seen Mr Wahool close to before – well, apart from his feet and trousers anyway. I glanced up enough to see that he was short and portly, with thick grey-black hair, blotchy skin and bushy eyebrows framing narrow, pudgy eyes. His natural expression was a scowl. It was clear Yasmin didn't get her looks from him.

'Coffee,' he barked as he marched towards the table. 'And get the boy to bring my tablet.'

He sat down, still scowling. Everyone got back to work. I couldn't stop my hands shaking violently as, at the other end, I finished the last setting. As soon as that was done, I melted behind a stack of building materials at the edge of the terrace. Nobody seemed to notice me disappear. The trouble was, I had no idea where to go.

A group of young people was approaching from the same direction as Mr Wahool, laughing and chatting. There were five girls and a boy, all looking slightly dishevelled. The boy in the middle looked like an older, less mean-looking version of Max.

'Good morning, Papa,' he said, stretching in the sun, revealing a tanned stomach under a too-short T-shirt.

Mr Wahool's scowl lifted slightly. 'Omar . . . come. Join me.'

'These are some chicks from last night's party, Papa. They stayed over. Not a problem, right?'

'Not at all,' his father said, waving a hand to indicate a total lack of inconvenience. Behind him, the butler-type looked on impassively. So did the row of servants next to him, who had been busting a gut for the last fifteen minutes to create extra food and places.

'Your boat's so cool, Mr Wahool,' the prettiest girl gushed, sitting down near him and picking some strawberries from a dish that was quickly offered to her. 'It's, like, really, really . . . big.'

'Yes,' he nodded graciously. 'Yes, she is.'

The others joined them at the table, waiters arriving like magnets to pour coffee and offer them food. The nearest girl to me was less than two paces away from the stack of stone and spare scaffolding poles that were hiding me, but nobody even glanced up to see who was serving them, never mind the frightened eyes beyond. If you want to hide from rich people in this place, put on a uniform.

'My uncle's got a cool boat,' a girl in a crumpled party dress observed, letting a waitress fill her glass with fruit juice, 'but it hasn't got a pool. I say there's kind of no point without a pool, right?'

'Absolutely,' Omar agreed. 'My sister seems to live in that pool. But I like the jet skis. Wanna jet-ski later?'

As the girls all cooed their agreement, a thin, muscled arm appeared from behind Mr Wahool's shoulder and a bony hand put a black tablet on the table beside him. The big man took it with a grunt.

I gasped. Karim. Where had he materialised from?

Unlike the others, Karim missed nothing. As he straightened up, his eyes caught mine almost instantly and widened in shock. A short, silent exchange took place, made up of furious glances.

What are you doing here?

Sorry! Not my idea!

This is a bad thing.

You think I don't know that?

He nudged his head very slightly. *Follow me.*

He moved quickly past the table, skirting round my pillar and grabbing my hand as he headed through the nearest open doorway to the house. His grip was so tight I thought my hand might break.

The doorway led to an empty sitting room. Karim rushed me through it, towards a blank section of wall at the back. I knew what was coming. He pushed at an invisible door in the silk wallpaper and it swung into the semi-darkness. Gratefully, I ducked into the tunnel beyond and Karim followed close behind me, pushing the door tightly shut.

We crouched next to each other in the narrow passage, not speaking for a while. I felt sick and dizzy. His chest rose and fell with the beating of his heart. His eyes blazed into me with a thousand questions.

'I got caught in the kitchens,' I whispered. 'Sorry.'

His eyes were a big 'How?' but I couldn't bring myself to answer. He shook his head angrily.

'Stay here,' he commanded, before heading off again.

I nodded guiltily. *Not going anywhere.*

TWENTY-THREE

For a long time I didn't move. I never, ever wanted to go through that again. Every time I thought back to what had just happened, my whole body juddered with the shock. So I tried not to think about it. Instead, I thought about the dungeons, and those thoughts weren't pretty either.

It was all very well to imagine that I'd find a clever way to get past those guards, but I'd just proved that the longer I stayed in this place, the more dangerous things got – for me, for Dad, for everyone. Maybe it was time to call in people who actually knew what they were doing. The more I thought about it, the more certain I became.

Slowly, the pain in my muscles from the surge of adrenaline

died down. My brain stopped feeling quite so fried. I realised it was actually quite pleasant in this tunnel – not like the ones downstairs. It was warmer here, and much lighter. I looked around to see why. As well as sunlight from a nearby stairwell, there were shafts of light pouring in at regular intervals down the passage, so I crawled along to see where they came from.

It turned out that at this level there were little grilles set into the wall, so the servants in the tunnel could see into each room, and even hear what was going on. Perhaps that's how they'd know that someone wanted them.

The first grille I came to overlooked a home cinema (naturally: billionaire's castle). I crawled round a corner and found myself peering into a quiet, book-lined library, where golden sunlight spilled on to the carpet. Karim had said not to move, but at least in these tunnels I was safe, and I had nothing else to do. I crawled around for ages, exploring the whole ground floor. With the grilles and the light from the stairwells, it was easy not to get lost, and in my new clothes I was more protected from scratches and unidentified dried-up poo-like objects. I still managed to crawl into several spiders' webs, but after a while I got used to scraping them off my face.

As the morning wore on, the air grew heavy with heat. There was the sound of a helicopter arriving. Its whirring blades made me feel restless. I checked my watch: still more than an hour before my meeting with Karim.

Actually, there *was* something I could do. I could make that call for help. My heart beat faster at the thought of entering one of those rooms to find a phone, but if I hesitated any longer, the chance might not come again.

I crawled back towards the library, but the sound of classical music coming from inside warned me it was being used. Never mind: I soon found another room, which was empty and quiet. Peering through the grille, I could see that it was a study, whose walls were lined in leather, like the yacht, and hung with paintings and maps. Against one wall was a large antique desk with a bank of computer and printer equipment on it – and not one, but three golden handsets. Perfect!

Holding my breath, I found the crack of light that marked the secret door, felt around until my hand found the thin rope handle . . . and pulled. The door swung open and I was through.

I paused on the thick carpet for a few moments, adjusting to the light and the gentle noises from the open window. Birdsong. The sound of sweeping from the terrace. The hiss of automatic sprinklers on the lawn. Inside, there was only the sound of my rapid breathing. The smell of leather and cigar smoke hung in the air.

I didn't have much time, so I ran over to the desk and crouched behind its heavy mass, grabbing the nearest handset as I went. The keypad was framed with diamonds. So didn't care.

Police. Call the police, Peta. Except, I suddenly remembered that the emergency number is different in Italy. I tried 999, just in case, which didn't work, and 111, which seemed likely, but didn't either. I even tried 911, which I remembered from American TV programmes. Nothing

Stop panicking. Don't breathe so hard. Think.

I decided to call a number I knew. My first thought was Luke, but he'd be in school by now. So Mum, then. Explaining everything to her would be harder, but at least I'd hear her voice. Actually, I could hardly bear to think how much I wanted to hear her voice.

I dialled the number. Still no connection. *Really?* Then I remembered about the international code. What was the code to England from Italy? Oh, this was *ridiculous.*

I spent a couple of minutes crouching behind the desk, hating myself. Really hating myself. This was the girl who couldn't even call the police on a diamond-studded golden phone. I was *that good.*

Looking at the handset, it occurred to me that it might already have foreign phone numbers programmed into it. I scrolled through, looking for something promising. One of the names said 'Eaton Square'. I checked its number, memorised the code at the beginning and tried it with Mum's mobile number. Worked first time.

OH YEAH, KIDNAPPER DUDES.

When it kicked in, that ringtone was the sweetest sound I'd ever heard. It was a bit faint and tinny – but then, the signal was coming from hundreds of miles away. From home.

Pick up, Mum! After what seemed like an age, someone finally answered.

'Hello? Can I help you?'

A man's voice, not Mum's. Not Grandad's or Rupert's either.

'Hello?' he repeated. His voice changed. 'Peta? Is that you?'

I was about to tell him, when my skin prickled. It was something in the way he said my name.

Why was a stranger answering Mum's phone?

I rang off, dropping the handset like it had scalded me. For a moment, I just stared at it, shaking. However, back in the near-silence of the room, my heartbeat slowed and I started to regret being so hasty. Perhaps Mum was too upset to speak. Perhaps it was a policeman, helping out.

I stood up and put the phone back in its place, unsure whether to call again. As I considered what to do, my eye briefly fell on a painting on the wall next to the secret door. It was a series of swirling shapes in blue and yellow, and if you looked at them closely, you realised it was a woman reading a book. I squinted at the signature, painted in red and under-lined, at the top.

Picasso.

I gulped. Still not used to the whole art-gallery thing.

'And you are?'

I spun round. The study door was open and a man was standing there.

Hell. Hell. *Hell.*

He was wide, very wide, and even in this heat, when every-one else was in holiday clothes, he looked as if he was dressed for a business meeting in London. His eyes were beady and hard, and staring straight at me. Fear sang through my blood, like electricity.

'Yes?' he persisted.

I realised I hadn't answered his question.

'My name is Amina,' I mumbled, staring at the floor.

'Well, get the hell out of here. We're having a meeting.'

I nodded, heading for the secret door as fast as I could, bowing and scraping as I went. Oh God. I could hardly catch my breath. Oh God. Oh hell. Oh *hell.*

Two seconds later, Mr Wahool came in. 'I apologise for the delay,' he announced. 'I trust—'

'One of your servants was just here,' the man interrupted. The grille muffled his voice a little, but I could still make out every word. His accent was cut-glass English – posher than Rupert's, even. 'I thought you said we wouldn't be disturbed.'

'We won't be. Who was it?'

'Small girl. Aneena?'

'I see. Amina!' Mr Wahool called. 'Amina!'

I stayed exactly where I was, flattened against the tunnel wall, still trying to breathe.

'She is gone,' Mr Wahool sighed after a pause. 'We are alone now. It is good of you to come.'

'It is good of you to offer to pay me so much money,' the man laughed. 'Are you sure you can afford it?'

'Of course.' Mr Wahool sounded offended.

I slumped, silently, to the tunnel floor.

'I heard you had some problems with one of your men.'

'You hear too much,' Mr Wahool said stiffly. 'The money is quite safe.'

'Good. Because that many helicopters are rather expensive. I can get the missiles for less than I said, because there's a glut at the moment, but the copters don't come cheap. And if you want them in situ, that means transports too.'

'I know,' Mr Wahool replied. 'It is all arranged.'

'You've got people to fire these things? Fly them?'

'That does not concern you.'

'It does, actually. This kit is high-tech these days. You can't use children to operate it. Which reminds me . . .' The wide man gave a short bark of laughter. 'I hear you've got them as well. In your guest accommodation. Is that true?'

'As I say –' Mr Wahool sighed – 'you hear too much. If we *do* have such people, I can assure you they are not children, they are enemies of the state. And they will not be my guests for long.'

When the wide man said 'children', I assumed he meant Karim and Amina. But it sounded as though Mr Wahool was referring to other prisoners, and the 'guest accommodation' was the dungeons. Ha ha.

'Now, business,' the wide man said. 'I've seen your list. You've seen my prices. I can do you a deal on the small arms and ammunition . . . Nice Picasso, by the way. Is that Marie-Thérèse?'

'It is. I got her at auction last month. Delightful, isn't she?'

They talked for a while. Art and money and bullets and guns. Mr Wahool was planning something big. And expensive. And explosive. He sounded as excited by the guns and missiles as he had about the diamonds for his daughter. Eventually, he offered to continue the conversation in his wine cellar, and the wide man agreed. They walked outside.

Note to Peta: stop wandering around like some kind of visitor. You are a fugitive from a man who keeps children in 'guest accommodation' and is BUYING MISSILES.

I sat there shaking for a while. Why wasn't I dead yet? *How* wasn't I dead yet? I kept on doing crazy things and it was a miracle I'd survived this long.

TWENTY-FOUR

There were still twenty minutes to go until I could meet up with Karim. As I crawled towards our meeting point, I heard the faint sound of classical music again. It was just the kind of soothing distraction I needed.

The music was violins and piano, played on CD. Lots of sweeping, emotional phrases that suited my shaky mood. Peering through the grille, I saw that the library was occupied by two people playing chess at a small table near the window. The man facing me had a sharp nose in a handsome face. Opposite him, the other player sat with his back to me, concentrating on a game. There was no mistaking his matted hair, his ragged shorts and a body so thin you could see his bones through his shirt.

Karim?

Here I was, desperately trying to get help, nearly getting caught, nowhere closer to seeing Dad or saving him, and Karim was *playing chess*?

I watched the game, slowly boiling with anger. The older man moved a white piece. Karim moved a black one. The man touched Karim's hand before he let go of the piece, and seemed to question him. Karim laughed and changed his mind. The man nodded approvingly. And I boiled and boiled inside.

Couldn't he have given up his chess game for just one day?

When the game finished, Karim got up and turned the music off.

'Some great moves there,' the man said. 'You get better every week, son. Keep it up.'

'Thank you, Mr Johnson, sir.'

'And how's your writing coming on?'

'It is slow, sir, but I practise when I can.'

'Don't forget to call by the guardhouse later. Get them to give you more paper. Tell them I sent you.'

'I will, sir.'

The man was obviously kind. How could I resent this boy spending time with the one person who was good to him? I might be desperate, but was I so selfish that I'd deny him even that?

Yes, I decided. With my father in the dungeons far below us, yes, I was.

At midday precisely, I was waiting for Karim further down the passageway, exactly where he'd left me. He greeted me with a smile of relief. I was too furious to say hello, but he didn't seem to notice.

'It is good to see you here,' he said. 'You are hungry?'

I nodded reluctantly. These days, I was always hungry.

'You need food. Perhaps that is why you look so sad. Now why are you smiling?'

Yes, I was angry, but his eternal enthusiasm was hard to resist. 'My dad taught me that hunger makes you feel bad,' I told him. 'Who taught you?'

He grinned and patted his flat stomach. 'My tummy taught me! That is who! Come, let us steal some rice.'

If nothing else, he was stopping me from starving. We crawled back to the kitchens and I copied as he took a bowl from a cupboard near the tunnel entrance, sliding it into the top of a vast pot of steaming rice on one of the stoves. The rice was topped off with a spoonful of simmering vegetables. We hurried on through, clutching our bowls to our chests, until we were seated in his room at the end of the cellar passageway.

'It is not a banquet,' he grinned, 'but they understand that we must eat.'

When he'd finished most of his rice, he leant forward.

'Now, we must talk. The plan for tonight, when I take you to Mr Allud . . . We must be careful.'

'Wait – so you're still taking me?' I asked, pausing mid-mouthful.

'Of course.' He looked surprised.

'But I thought . . . when you wouldn't help me . . .'

Karim frowned at me, confused. 'When?'

'This morning. When you wouldn't show me to the dungeons.'

'Ah!' His frown lifted. 'This morning was a bad time. There are guards, and in the morning they are alert. In the evening, though, they drink and play cards. Then we have a chance. You will bring the food to the prisoners with me. Amina sometimes does this, and if the guards are busy, they will not look at you too closely – only your hands, holding the dishes.'

I looked down. Next to Karim's golden fingers my pale-skinned hands seemed to glow like moons. That, more than anything, had worried me while I was laying the table outside.

'But how can I hide them? Gloves?'

He shook his head and pointed to the bowl of mush that he'd been working on when I first saw him today.

'Henna, to dye your skin. It is not perfect, but it will be good enough at night. I think it will be ready now.'

He reached across for the bowl and peered at it. The mush had half dried into a reddish-brown mound of goo. I remembered how carefully he had tried to prepare it this morning, not sure of what he was doing. He'd probably never had to work out how to dye pale skin before.

'You did this . . . for me?'

'You need it. And you will need to cover your head very much. Maybe a bigger shawl. And walk like Amina. Have you seen her walk? And—'

But I was just staring at him.

My backpack . . .

The blazer he burnt, with my school crest on it. The photograph, showing me with Dad . . .

The henna for my hands and face . . .

Ever since I had arrived, this boy had been planning, watching, waiting, keeping me safe. He wasn't scared: he was kind of awesome.

'I bet you're very good at chess,' I said.

He looked startled. 'I am still learning. How did you know?'

'I watched you today. Through the grille to the library.'

'Oh! I am sorry about that. It is my time to play chess with Mr Johnson. He is Mr Wahool's security adviser. If I had stayed with you, he would have asked why if I had not come. I—'

'Don't worry, I get it now.'

He'd thought it all out. Planned ahead. Every detail. Maybe things weren't as hopeless as I thought.

TWENTY-FIVE

Amina arrived with a bowl of rice and wolfed it down, saying little, looking miserable and exhausted. Karim explained that the castle went quiet at this time of day, when the sun outside was super-hot. Building works stopped for a few hours. The family went into their rooms for long siestas. The servants sneaked a bit of nap time. The slaves kept themselves very quiet, so nobody would give them anything else to do.

I turned my back to give Karim and Amina privacy while they went into separate corners of the room to pray. Then Karim loosened the stone in the wall, bringing out a book and pencil from their hiding place. He practised writing, while I lay down and Amina started to spread the henna goo on my forehead, smoothing it on with a lolly stick and her strong, rough fingers, muttering almost under her breath to her brother. She hadn't said a word to me since she'd arrived.

I assumed she was telling Karim about her morning. It obviously hadn't been good, from the frown on her face and the low, fearful tone of her muttering. Karim looked up from his writing, first confused, then angry, then . . . something else. He was staring at me, I realised, and even though I was covered in goo and probably pretty funny to look at right now, he wasn't smiling.

'When I left you, did you enter any rooms in the castle?' he asked me. His voice was quiet and tense.

'Yes. How did you know? Did Amina see me? I thought nobody had, apart from—' *Apart from the man who sold guns like they were sweets.* Maybe I should have mentioned him. 'Why?' I asked, seeing the scared look on Amina's face, and the stony look on her brother's.

'A visitor saw a girl in the special study of Mr Wahool. We are not allowed in that room. The master has said Amina must be punished.'

I scrabbled to my feet, almost knocking the henna bowl out of Amina's hands. She wouldn't look at me.

'No! But they can't! It wasn't her! We must stop them!'

'There is nothing we can do.'

I saw Amina's frightened eyes and felt ashamed. Her lips trembled as she focused on the henna bowl, trying not to cry. She didn't want to blame me, I could tell. Through all the kicking and shoving and general life-saving I owed her so much, and now . . . this.

'I'm so, so sorry, Amina.'

She nodded and said nothing.

'Look, I'll own up,' I sighed, sinking down again. It was the only solution. 'I'll tell them that I'm here.'

'And they will kill you,' Karim huffed, swatting the idea away like a fly.

He wouldn't let me consider it. For now, all I could do was apologise, which I did, over and over, while Amina replaced the henna I'd caused to fly everywhere, and put more on my eyes and cheeks.

'It's not your fault, Peta Jones,' Karim sighed. *'Insha'Allah.* All will be well. It is always worse before a beating. Please, ignore our rude sadness.'

But I couldn't ignore it. All I seemed to do was get them into trouble. I couldn't even cry, because it would make tear tracks in my new henna face pack.

'I . . . I was trying to call for help,' I muttered, not that my pathetic excuse made any difference.

'Who did you speak to?' Karim asked sharply, sounding alarmed.

'Nobody. Not really. I tried to call Mum, but a man answered. I panicked. I—'

He groaned. 'You must not do this. They talk about your mother in the guardhouse – they are paying someone close to her to find news of you.'

They were armed. They were everywhere. Suddenly it hit me what a terrible mistake I'd made.

'They'll see the castle's number on her mobile . . .'

Karim paused, thinking. 'Did you say anything?'

'No. I put the phone down.'

'Perhaps . . . perhaps if they check, they will think that one of their own people called from here. They are stupid sometimes.'

I nodded. They weren't always stupid. The wide man

152

wasn't stupid. But their stupidity was our best hope.

You have the power to totally mess things up, Peta Jones.

For a while, there was silence, while Amina finished smearing the henna on my chin and neck, and started on my hands. In the end, Karim spoke up again. Anything, I sensed, to distract his sister from what they had planned for her.

'Tonight we will be visiting three prisoners, Peta Jones. They are called "One", "Two" and "Three" by the guards. "One" is the girl, Parissa. The young man is "Two". His name is Sammy, and he is sick. They are both from Marvalia, from the Blue Revolution. The Grandfather hates them. So does the master. Mr Allud is "Three". We are not allowed to talk to them, but I do so quietly when the guards are busy and not listening.'

I nodded. So Dad was a number.

Karim must have noticed my bite my lip. 'Tell me about this man,' he said softly. 'Why have you come so far to see him?'

Hadn't I said? I must have been so busy explaining *how* I'd got here that I never told them *why*.

'My father was a soldier,' I began. It was weird, lying there with my eyes closed, but it made the memories so vivid. 'One of the best in the army. His job was to go behind enemy lines and report what was happening there. But when the last war finished, the army binned him. Made him redundant, I mean. Dad wasn't happy about it, but I was kind of OK with it. It meant he was coming home for good.'

'And Mr Allud . . .?' Karim prompted.

'I'm getting there. A few weeks before he was due to come back from Afghanistan, Dad said he'd found a new job as an IT adviser, working for a big company in Iraq. Mum said the job was very well paid and we needed the money. But Dad never did anything for the money, he wasn't like that. And he hated big companies. Anyway, he went to Iraq to do this stupid IT job – supposedly – and someone put a bomb under his car – supposedly – and it blew up –' Amina gasped – 'and I haven't seen him since.'

'Ah!' Karim said, sounding like he'd just spotted a clever move on the chess board. 'So you think the bomb was a trick? And Mr Allud is your father? Yes?'

I opened my eyes to check his face. He'd got it exactly, of course, but even he looked unconvinced.

'Most people say I'm in this thing called denial,' I admitted, 'but my friend Luke believes me. At least, I think he does.'

'Who is Luke?'

'Oh, he's my Crazy Psycho Mirror Twin.'

'Excuse me?'

I explained about Luke losing the feeling in his legs when he got the news about Sergeant McCrae. 'He believes too deeply what people tell him, and I don't believe it enough, I suppose . . . I was just starting to, but then I got your message.'

'*Never forget, you have the power,*' Karim muttered, nodding to himself. 'Mr Allud made me learn it very specially.'

'I don't know why Dad would be here, but that's something only my dad would say.'

'You are a crazy girl, Peta Jones!' he grinned. 'You pin your hopes on very little things!'

I couldn't help smiling. Six words. That's what had brought me here.

'Yeah, maybe I do.'

154

TWENTY-SIX

Karim and Amina left me lying flat on my back while they went off to their chores and the henna worked on my skin. I stayed very still, but though I was worn out with guilt about Amina's beating and my nerves about tonight, there was no way I could sleep if I was going to be visiting the dungeons so soon . . .

What felt like five minutes later, I woke up feeling cold and stiff. I was still alone in the cellar room, but there was movement and talking in the corridor outside. I checked my watch: it was nearly seven in the evening. I'd slept for four hours straight.

Karim and Amina were probably still upstairs. I shifted

myself into the corner behind the door, in case anyone should open it without warning, and used Amina's abandoned lolly stick to scrape some of the henna goo off my hand. The skin underneath was orangey-red. Not exactly golden, like Amina's, but nor was it the pale whitish-pink of a wanted English girl. The henna had worked well enough, so I scraped it off the rest of me, tipping it as best I could into the bowl. I wiped my face and hands with a cloth. Still no sign of Karim and Amina. I tried to calm my nerves.

Suddenly there was a shout outside. Shock, and panic, and running feet. Silence. Stomping boots. More silence, and then a cry I'll never forget. A girl's cry. Two more of them, and by now I was panicking so much myself I could hardly think. The boots stomped away. Sandaled footsteps scurried along and died down.

When the corridor had been silent again for a while, I risked opening the door and running towards the place where I'd heard the cry. There was a small room near the kitchens, whose door was half open. A woman in a black scarf like mine was coming out of it. I nipped into the nearest cupboard and shut myself in as she walked by. Once she'd gone, I went back.

Inside the room, a tap dripped relentlessly into an old-fashioned sink. Amina lay with her chest resting on a sack of potatoes, moaning gently, while Karim crouched next to her, holding a damp cloth to her forehead. He looked up as I came in.

'I heard . . . What happened?' I panted.

'Master Max found out about the beating,' he said in a low, precise voice. 'He asked to do it. It is incorrect for the family to intervene in such matters, but . . .'

But nobody says no to the masters. I pictured Max

accompanying the guards down here. Tall, fit Max, who had a punch bag in his bedroom . . .

'Was it bad?'

Don't be an idiot, Peta. Of course it was bad.

'A kind lady has bathed the wounds,' Karim said dully. 'My sister must rest now.'

I went over and lifted Amina's damp tunic as carefully as I could, but she still flinched with pain. There were three long, angry red marks criss-crossing each other along her back. They went from shoulder to waist.

I wanted to throw up, but I had to focus and make this better. Even Karim looked used up by sadness. It was time I actually helped these people. I owed them.

I remembered a bonfire night long ago. They boy next to me was hit by a stray firework that burnt half his face. The shock of that night felt similar to this, and most of the crowd had panicked, but Dad had stepped in, cool and certain. Dad was never flustered or upset. Not when there were practical things to do.

'Ice,' I said, swallowing the bile in my throat and turning to Karim sharply. 'Go and get some. Wrap it in a cloth. Oh, and Karim . . .'

'Yes?'

'Chocolate.'

'Chocolate?'

'Yes. It's got some . . . I can't remember . . . ingredient that makes you feel better. Can you get some of that too? What she really needs is painkillers, though. Maybe we could . . .'

I was thinking about raiding one of the bathroom cabinets upstairs, then I remembered the cache of pills from my backpack. Karim ran to get them and I looked through the packets while he went off for the other things. There were three packets and, like Goldilocks and the Three Bears, one set looked too weak, one looked too strong (I was worried they would knock Amina out completely) and the other looked just right.

I gave her a couple of pills with some water, bathed the wounds again, and held her hand. All the time, I sang to her:

'Incy wincy spider climbed up the water spout . . .'

It was the only song I could think of, and it had worked for me, a little, on the boat. Amina turned to me and smiled slightly.

'It will get better,' she said.

'Yes, it will,' I assured her, stroking her hair. 'It will get better soon.'

Karim rushed back bearing ice cubes in a plastic bag and a few squares of thin dark cooking chocolate. Only then did I notice that he was walking oddly, hobbling a little.

'Are you OK?'

'I am well, Peta Jones,' he replied stiffly. But he wasn't.

'What happened?'

Eventually he admitted that he had stepped forward, unable to help himself when Amina cried out. He'd received four lashes.

I bathed those too, despite his protests, wiping my tears away when he wasn't looking, and made him take two pills. Then I shoved the packet up my sleeve in case he needed more later.

'What about your chores?' I asked.

Karim gestured towards his sister and shrugged, wincing as his shoulders moved. 'Tonight we do not need to work. Because of . . . this. Miss Yasmin gave the order. She is upset. She blames her brother.'

158

'Oh. Good.'

'She is very annoyed. She had a dress for this evening that it is difficult to put on without assistance. Another servant had to help her.'

'Poor Yasmin,' I said, poker-faced.

'Indeed,' he answered, with just a flicker of mischief in his eyes.

TWENTY-SEVEN

We made Amina as comfortable as we could on a mat in her own cellar room, and Karim focused on getting me ready for the visit to the dungeons. My excitement was laced with more guilt than ever.

'Do not blame yourself,' he instructed briskly. 'What is done is done. Now, when you walk, you must do . . . like this,' and he demonstrated limping and hobbling, as if I was an old lady in a great deal of pain. So I did. I pretended to be his sister, with my scarf pulled low over my head and my hennaed hands held close to my chest.

'That is good,' he said. 'Now, come. We will collect the food and you follow close behind me. Go to Parissa and

Sammy first: prisoners One and Two. While I talk to the guards, you will slip quietly into the other cell. I will distract them for as long as I can. When I say goodnight, you must come immediately.'

'Goodnight?'

'Yes. That is the signal. Bow low, and be quiet, so they do not notice from which cell you came.'

In the kitchens, we collected a tray of food: three red bowls with plastic lids, and two plates stacked using metal catering covers like the kind the chefs used at the Smugglers' Inn to keep food warm. Karim had fitted the tray with a long piece of string, tied through the handles so he could hang it round his neck, which made it easier to carry as we walked. Every step clearly hurt him, so I quickly took the tray from him. He didn't want me to, but even he had to recognise that he couldn't always be the gentleman.

He led me down the passageway at the far end of the kitchens and we started to descend the spiral staircase. Halfway down, he turned back to me.

'Remember, you do not speak much English. You are shy. Only signs.'

The distant sound of harsh voices punctured the air. For a moment, I wondered if they were interrogating someone (*Dad! Wait! I'm coming!*), but when we rounded the corner into the corridor the two guards were sitting at the small metal table, as before. This time, they were playing cards, smoking and drinking from a tall bottle of bright yellow liquid on the table beside them. They were shouting at each other, slamming cards down on the table. When we arrived, they held up their hands and called to Karim.

'Ah! *Cena!* Dinner time! *Vieni qui.*'

Karim took the tray from me and carried it over to the

table. I stayed in the shadows, head bowed. It helped that the light was low and flickering. It helped too that I was supposed to be recovering from a beating: it gave me an excuse for bending down.

'The chef made special soup for number Two,' Karim said to the guards. 'I will wait while my sister gives it to him. And I have something to show you.'

'Is it a trick?'

I froze. Were the guards on to me already?

'One of the best,' Karim said, sounding quite relaxed. 'While you eat, I will show you. I have been practising. Sister, come.'

I hobbled forward. Karim picked up the abandoned pack of cards. Oh – they meant a *card* trick. While Karim shuffled the pack, I picked up the three soup bowls in a stack. The guard nearest me took a large old-fashioned key from a ring that hung on a hook nearby and unlocked the door at the end of the corridor. While he was up, he unlocked the one to the right too. That must be the one that led to Mr Allud's cell. (*Dad! Just two minutes more . . .*)

My heart pounded in my chest as I walked through the first door and into a small bare cell. Two faces looked up at me. Both had filthy, matted hair and looked dirty, hungry, freezing and desperate. The only furniture was a long wooden bench, and the young man was lying on it with his head in the girl's lap. Their wrists and ankles were attached by long chains to iron rings cemented into the stone.

With shaking hands, I put the stack of bowls down by the door and carried two of them over. All the time, the shivering girl didn't take her eyes off me. She'd noticed straight away that I wasn't Amina, and she stared at me, confused. Her eyes were piercing blue and mesmerising.

I put my finger to my lips. She watched me silently as I took the lids off the bowls for her. Inside was rice and more of the vegetable stew. She looked starving – literally starving, not just hungry like me – but she didn't fall on the food. Instead, she took some in her fingers and offered it to the young man, who seemed too weak to move. His forehead was glistening with sweat and his breath came in small, shallow gasps. There was no 'special soup' for him, though. Karim had lied about it to the guards, to give me my chance.

He needed more than special soup anyway. I suddenly remembered the packet of pills hidden in my sleeve, and as I took it out the girl's blue eyes fixed themselves on it. I handed the whole packet over and it disappeared into the folds of her clothes in an instant. Her friend needed hospital treatment, but a few painkillers might bring his temperature down at least. Those eyes flashed me a look of gratitude, then turned back to him.

Outside, Karim raised his voice. 'Have you seen this one before? I will pick the seventh card from the pack. I promise I can do it.' Under his calm exterior he sounded agitated. It was a signal to me to get a move on. Oh my God – Dad. This was the moment.

I gave the girl the biggest sympathetic look I could manage (yeah, right, like that was so going to help), and scuttled out, clutching the last bowl to my chest.

The door to the other cell was still open. Everything I had done since the moment I got on the coach had brought me to this place. The guards were distracted. I hurried silently across the corridor, and I was in.

TWENTY-EIGHT

The cell seemed empty.

'Three?'

My voice hardly made it into a whisper. Nobody answered.

'Hello?'

Had the guard opened the door to the right place? Had I misunderstood?

The bulb outside lit a narrow patch of ground through the open door, but beyond it was a jumbled mass of flickering shadows. This place wasn't so much a cell as a storeroom. I walked a few paces into the gloom and waited. Silence.

'Mr Allud?' Hel-*lo*?'

Nothing happened.

As my eyes adjusted to the darkness, old pieces of furniture revealed themselves among the shadows: tables, chairs and even something that looked like a grand piano. It was a bit like being back in the furniture van, except this time the air smelled of filth, and worse. I spotted the outline of a dark figure hunched over in the corner, behind a leaning stack of broken chairs. He didn't look up – in fact, he made no indication of knowing I was there at all.

I moved in closer. All I could see was hair and bones. He sat huddled in the corner with his knees up near his head and his face resting against them.

'Mr Allud? I bring food.' Nothing. Getting desperate now, I hummed the tune of 'Walk Away' very quietly, but loudly enough, I thought, for him to hear. Roxanne Wills's biggest hit. My ringtone. Maybe Dad would remember it from the last day we'd spent together. He'd know it was me. And then . . .

There was no response.

He couldn't be asleep. He just couldn't! I'd pictured this moment for so long, and now I didn't know what to do. Outside, in the corridor, Karim was laughing and joking, putting on his gleeful voice for all to hear.

'It was the five of diamonds! You see? I know it every time. It is an excellent trick, yes? Shall I try it again? Would you like to bet on it, Mister Gino?'

I didn't dare say the prisoner's real name. 'It's me,' I muttered under my breath, trying to fight my growing sense of desperation. 'I'm here. It's me.'

At this, he grunted. So he wasn't asleep! I rushed over, waiting for the recognition in his eyes. But he wouldn't look up. If anything, this was an angry grunt. A 'go away', practically inhuman noise.

'I've come to help,' I whispered.

The figure shook its head and shrank further into the shadows. There was no recognition, only fear. Whoever he was, I was starting to wonder if he was mad.

Outside, the guards were laughing. Slowly, I held out the bowl in my shaking hand. Bony fingers grabbed it from me. I saw a quick flash of a thin, white wrist as he jammed the bowl between his knees and started to eat, head down, scoffing up rice and stew through his beard like a wild animal. It was disgusting.

'Mr Allud?'

I tried to keep the tears from my voice. This wasn't Dad. This was hardly a person at all. Whatever they'd done to this man, it must have broken him.

Crouching as close as I dared, I couldn't help reaching out a hand to touch his arm. Instantly, a leg came flailing out to stop me. His ankle was chained to the wall and his body came to an abrupt halt, jerking the bowl he was holding and scattering the remains of the food over me and the floor. Even so, he managed to kick at me again, sending me flying.

'*Che succede qui?* What is happening, eh?' A guard put his head round the door. I nearly said something, before remembering at the last moment to keep silent. Instead, I jumped to my feet, bowed low and indicated the bowl.

'Doesn't like the food, eh? Clean it up, girl.'

I was shaking, hard. Without even trying, I was giving the perfect impression of someone who'd just been beaten. The guard watched as I picked up all the rice and bits of vegetable I could find from the filthy floor, putting them back in the bowl with my hennaed hands. I wondered how the prisoner was going to cope without his meal tonight, whoever he was.

Whoever he was.

Maybe he was someone who'd known Dad once. Maybe I had simply made the worst mistake of my life. He wasn't my father, that's the only thing I knew.

'Goodnight,' Karim was saying, through the door. 'Good*night*.'

Oh hell, the signal. I clutched the half-empty bowl to me and hobbled for the door. The guard smacked me, hard, on the side of the head. The flash of pain was blinding.

'Stupid girl. That beating made you slow tonight, eh? And your brother made me lose my money.'

The other guard laughed and patted his pocket.

'Never make a bet, Gino. You know you always lose.'

I nodded and bowed, a pair of eyes peeping out from a scarf. A nobody. A girl. A slave.

Karim loaded the tray with the guards' empty plates and gave it to me. 'We leave you now. Tomorrow I will show you a new trick.'

Down the corridor. Up the long and winding staircase. Away from the dank smell and the flickering light. My head ached. We didn't speak until we were back beside the sleeping body of Amina. Only then did Karim groan and roll his shoulders with the pain of his own beating.

'And so?' he asked. 'Mr Allud? It is your father, yes?'

I stared at him with hollow eyes and shook my head. My journey was over.

TWENTY-NINE

I sat with Amina through the night. Nothing changed. She slept, moaning occasionally as she shifted to a new position. I stayed wide awake, not moving at all.

Who had that been, in the flicking shadows? Not long ago, he had given Karim my telephone number and my special message. How did he know me?

I remembered Dad reading me a story once, about one soldier who told another all his secrets. *The Return of Martin Guerre*, it was called. Maybe Dad had told this man about his goodbye message, before a battle perhaps, and when the man thought he was going to die – down here you would think that sort of thing – he passed it on anyway, even though he

168

didn't know me, and didn't care.

Maybe he was angry that Dad's child had come, and not his own. Maybe . . . whatever. It didn't matter any more. I couldn't help him. He didn't want me to.

The thoughts came at me like knives.

I'd pinned everything on six words: *Never forget, you have the power.*

I had assumed so much. I'd taken so many risks, and I was really bad at taking risks – that much was obvious. I didn't think about what I was doing, and other people got hurt because of my mistakes. I'd got myself into danger, and Karim and Amina too.

Mum would probably never see me again.

Nor would Luke.

Nor would Lacy, or Granny and Grandad. All there would be was that note for Mum on my computer: 'This is not about you.' *Well, yeah – thanks for that, Peta. Thanks a lot.*

The man in the cellar wasn't some great friend of Dad's, who wanted to save me on his behalf.

The man in the cellar wasn't Dad.

Dad wasn't here, he was dead. He'd been dead since the bomb, and I was the only one who was too stupid to admit it. Just because I couldn't *feel* that he was dead, just because I didn't want to believe he'd given up on us, got some dodgy job in a dangerous city and got himself blown up in a stupid car . . . Just because I didn't *want* him to be dead, it didn't mean he wasn't.

People die. They leave you. They don't always say good-bye. Other people come in the night and they tell you that it's happened and when they do, you'd better believe them. You'd better do it soon, because the thought will hit you eventually, and when it does it's like being walloped by a giant hammer and left for dead yourself. That's why Mum's legs collapsed under her the night we got the news, while I just went around in denial, making cups of sugary tea and feeling pleased with myself for coping so well.

A stupid, pointless, crazy girl, being happy for no reason.

With a stupid cat.

I listened to Amina's shallow breathing beside me. She was so sweet and shy and strong, and every day people shouted at her and hit her or ignored her. She was treated worse than an animal. There must be thousands of children like her. Millions, maybe, and there was nothing I could do about it. Just like there was nothing I could do about those two starving 'enemies of the state' down in the dungeons. A packet of pills was hardly going to save that young man's life. He probably wouldn't last very long if nobody came to rescue him. He would die and they would take him away in a bag and throw him in the sea. The girl would be all alone.

Just like me. I was a crazy, stupid teenager, who'd got herself stranded in a big, evil place where 'bad things' happened, and soon they would find me too and nobody who cared about me would ever even know that I had been here.

And Dad was dead.

THIRTY

Amina stirred soon after five a.m., just as the pink dawn lit up the small square of window above our heads. Karim arrived a few minutes later.

'How are you feeling this morning, Peta Jones?'

'Great. Wonderful,' I muttered.

'I do not think so. I am sorry about your father.'

'Yeah, well . . . anyway.'

'And soon you must leave,' he added. 'It is dangerous for you here.'

'*You think?*' I wasn't in the best of moods. He frowned at me, like something was wrong with me. Well, after the horrors of last night, everything was wrong. 'Got any furniture I can sneak away in?'

'No,' he said, still frowning. 'But there is a path I can show you, where the guards cannot follow. It will lead you to the shoreline. There you can hide on a boat or swim far away. Can you swim? It is not a perfect plan, but you are a brave girl, Peta Jones. Nobody is looking for you yet. I think you will escape.'

I stared at him. Was this his sick idea of a joke?

'You know a *path*? Yeah, of course you do.'

He nodded. 'I would have shown you before, but you wanted to see Mr Allud first . . .'

'Seriously, a path?'

'Not a good one. It is just some covered-over steps, built into the rock, going down to the sea. It was built for smugglers, like I told you before. The entrance is small and blocked with bushes. The guards think it is a ruin because I told them so. It is broken and weedy, but it is not a ruin.'

'Just tell me now that you're joking.'

'I am not joking, Peta Jones. It is what I use when I . . . when I need to imagine I am far from this place. I will guide you to it.'

'What, now?'

'No. In two days.'

I didn't ask him why 'in two days'. There would be a reason, and knowing Karim, it would be a good one. But I couldn't really picture having the energy to leave the island, now or ever. Dad was gone and I couldn't really imagine two *hours* ahead, never mind two days.

I'd never felt like this before. Presumably this is how they wanted me to feel in Winchelsea churchyard, during the ashes ceremony. Why would anyone *want* you to feel like this?

Also . . . an *escape path*? Really?

'So they trusted their slave boy to tell them if there was a working escape route, and you told them there wasn't, and that was it?'

Karim looked scornful. 'They are too big to fit inside and check, with their muscles and jackets and boots. They think I am afraid of them, so they assume I will tell the truth.'

'But you're not afraid?'

He shrugged. 'I am very afraid. But I am not as stupid as they think I am.' He allowed the faintest shadow of a smile to steal across his face.

No, 'stupid' was not a word I would use to describe this boy. 'Extraordinary', possibly. Also, 'odd': if Karim knew a way out of here, why wasn't he somewhere far away, like he said, and safe, instead of being trapped in this dingy cellar?

'So why haven't *you* used it?'

He put his finger to his lips and indicated Amina, whose eyelids were fluttering, and motioned me outside. We sheltered in the room with the dripping tap, while he talked in a low voice.

'I have thought about it, but my sister is too afraid. We have no papers, nowhere to go.'

'You don't need papers,' I said. 'Keeping you here is illegal. Nobody would force you back.'

He still looked troubled.

'Also, Amina is afraid of the dark. In the castle tunnels she can use a torch, but to escape it must be totally black. It must be done on a night when there is no moon, so the guards cannot see the tunnel exit by the shore. Which is why you must leave in two days, Peta Jones, when there is no moon. We are lucky it comes so soon.'

Yeah, really lucky. I was feeling so *lucky* right now.

173

I sensed that Karim was making lots of excuses for his sister staying here, but he was just as scared himself. There was one thing he *was* frightened of, it seemed: freedom.

'Well, I'm not going without you,' I said.

He looked into my eyes and he seemed about to argue, but he could tell that I meant it. Knowing that Dad was gone, my lust for escape had dwindled anyway. Without Karim, I wouldn't make it. He was my only hope, this ragged, extraordinary boy. And if he needed help to get out of here, perhaps I could be his.

Our conversation was cut off by the sound of Amina groaning. We both rushed to be beside her. She opened her eyes and saw me, and even though it was my fault that she was in this state, she smiled when she saw me.

'Mr Allud? You see him? Yes?'

'Yes.'

Her eyelids flickered and she looked at me again, sadly.

'Go now?'

Her voice was cracked and raspy. Karim gave her a plastic cup of water, lifting it carefully to her lips. She gulped it down.

'Not yet,' I said. 'When you are better.'

Outside, there was the sound of sandals slapping on the corridor floor. Karim nodded to the space behind the door and I sprang into it. A man shouted harshly at him for a minute or two.

'We must go,' Karim said, glancing anxiously at his sister. 'The young masters brought back some more friends last night. Things were broken. Everything must be made pristine again. Pristine – it is a word, yes?'

'Yes,' I agreed. 'I think so.'

His eyes lingered on Amina. 'She is still not well,' he sighed.

I looked at her, huddled up under a thin piece of sacking. Her back was still hurting.

'Karim, if no one's really watching, maybe I could help you,' I suggested. 'I've got the hands now, look.'

Of course, a lot of things could go wrong, but then – everything had already gone wrong.

Karim smiled at me. 'Perhaps. Then she could rest . . . Yes, yes. If you look down at the ground. Crouch, so you are smaller. Come with me, Peta Jones.'

He whispered tenderly into Amina's ear. I promised her we'd be back soon.

'Are you ready?' he asked.

I wrapped my scarf around my face and hobbled to Karim's side. Slave girl. Head down. Look at no one. Done it before. Besides, what did I have to lose?

Watch me walk right under your noses, kidnapper dudes.

THIRTY-ONE

One thing about the Wahools – they knew how to party. In the dawn light, the castle terrace looked like the aftermath of a hurricane. Broken plant pots and statues littered the area. Colourful silk cushions floated on the surface of the pool. Two wooden sun loungers lay in the shallow end, like shipwrecks. Half a dozen servants in uniform were moving quietly through the gloom with brushes and rubbish sacks, careful not to wake the family in their bedrooms above.

There were four grown-up slaves too, thin and ragged in other people's mismatched clothes, scouring the lawns looking for litter on the perfect grass. They were all bent over, concentrating, but I still turned my face away and made sure to keep my 'brother' between me and them. If they looked up, they would notice instantly that I wasn't the little girl they knew so well.

A butler explained to a lesser servant, who explained to us, that Karim and I were to work in the spa complex, which was the building still covered in scaffolding. Inside, it was bizarre, with its golden floor, central golden hot tub and ancient-looking arched roof. There were two stained glass windows at either end, which reminded me a little of the windows in Winchelsea Church, except those had pictures of knights and saints, and these had mermaids in shell bikinis.

Apparently Omar Wahool had made the servants fill the hot tub last night so he could impress his friends. It had been drained overnight, but the drainage system wasn't working properly yet and the bottom was still covered with wet shards of broken champagne glasses. The servant told Karim that we were expected to clear the glass up with brushes, then go over the gold mosaic floor with our bare fingers, which were more sensitive to finding the almost-invisible shards.

'Can you do this?' Karim asked me, once we were alone.

'Of course.'

He got to work, moving carefully and efficiently across the damp golden floor. I copied him.

'This reminds me of another party, in England,' he said. 'There was a competition to drop champagne bottles from the windows. It took many days to clean up the green glass.'

'Wait – you were in *England*? But England doesn't have . . .' I struggled to get the word out. '. . . slaves.'

Karim looked sideways at me. 'Do you think so?'

I gulped. Frankly, up to a week ago I didn't think anywhere had slaves any more. But then, if they were kept in hidden-away places, how would I know?

'You were in London? In the house on Eaton Square?'

He shrugged. 'A big white house. I do not know the address. We were there for a few months, while the castle was made ready.'

'How did you get there?'

'By boat, like you.'

'And before that? I mean, how did you even get to be a . . .?' I gave up. I couldn't say the word again.

'I was born this way. It is not a good story. You don't want to know.'

'I do. Really.'

For a while he didn't speak, concentrating instead on sweeping around him with a dustpan and brush, then going over each area of gold mosaic with his fingers, feeling for slivers of glass. Like mine, his fingertips were already bloody from tiny cuts, but he didn't let it bother him. He seemed more bothered by his stiff and aching back.

'My family came from an island in the ocean,' he said eventually, stretching painfully. 'It is beautiful, but the fishing was very bad. My mother was with child. Some men came to offer jobs and my parents went with one of them to Marvalia, far away. He promised them riches, but they were taken to a market and . . . the master found them there.'

He wouldn't catch my eye at this point. I sensed that his parents had been sold at market, like cattle.

'What happened?'

He paused to remove a sliver of glass from his finger. 'I was born at the master's house. My father angered him, so he sent him to the copper mines. My mother . . . died while Amina was still small. There was an old servant who was blind and sick. He made the others teach me to read, so I could read to

178

him from the Qur'an. He taught me the path. But he died on our journey to London. We were hidden on a boat – not the super-boat, a different one. It was very dark. That is why Amina is afraid of the dark.'

'Oh . . .' I thought of the children, and the darkness, and the body, lying there . . . 'Karim.'

I didn't know where to look, or what to do or say.

'How do you do it?' I asked. 'How do you keep smiling?'

He shrugged. 'I smile? Do I?' He was smiling as he said it. He couldn't help himself.

We worked on in silence. After a while, he said, 'I live in my mind. Perhaps that is why I smile. My mind is free. Do you understand this?'

'No,' I told him truthfully.

'I can read. The master cannot take that away. Mr Johnson teaches me chess. I watch Mr Omar . . . and learn computers. Sometimes I imagine what I would do if I was the master, with all the money he has. The ruins here were once a chapel. Mr Wahool saw them and made . . . this.' He scornfully indicated the golden spa. 'I would have made a paradise garden. I would have channels of running water, and fragrant plants, and high walls to shade the man of contemplation from the sun. Also, I would learn to play Beethoven. He is the greatest composer, do you not agree?'

I didn't have much of an opinion on classical composers. Karim was kind of ahead of me on slavery and Beethoven. I loved the idea of the paradise garden, though.

'And I would defend my sister,' he added fiercely. 'From everything.'

I was flooded with guilt again, but we were interrupted. The same man who'd brought us here came back to check our progress.

'Be quick,' he said. 'I'll bring you some bleach for the . . . stains.' He meant our blood stains on the gold mosaic. 'We need to get this thing filled up again by lunchtime.'

As soon as he'd gone, I turned to back Karim.

'How come so many of the staff here are English?'

He gave the ghost of a smile. 'Mrs Wahool is from England. Also, the French make the best chefs, the master says, and the English make the best servants.'

I glared at him, affronted. This brought out a grin.

'I didn't think you would like to hear that, Peta Jones.'

Then he put a hand over his lips. He hadn't meant to say my name out loud in this public space. But nobody was around to hear him, and it was good to see his smile.

The tub was slowly refilled while I was sent to sweep up earth from the broken lavender pots by the pool, and Karim went to wait by the family's bedrooms in case one of them woke up and needed anything.

By now the sun was up, and the adult slaves had gone. Beyond the terrace, the sea sparkled in the morning light. The air was buzzy with the sound of motor boats, and thickly scented with lavender. I worked steadily, collecting the pieces of broken earthenware, sweeping up the scattered soil and placing the bare lavender plants along the side of a path, ready to be replanted.

I thought about Karim and his family. Was his father still alive? Yeah. I knew what *that* feeling was like. Or at least, I used to know. Without trying, I was back where I started, with the knife-sharp grief of missing Dad.

A man walked unhurriedly down the path. His beaky nose and square, handsome face looked familiar: it was Mr Johnson, Mr Wahool's security adviser and Karim's chess partner. He took a moment to stand by a stone balustrade near the pool, looking out to sea. I kept my head down and carried on sweeping. Another man wandered across to him from the guardhouse. I caught the scent of lemon aftershave cutting through the air: Muscle Man.

He passed so close I that could have touched him. *Use the fear, Peta. Use the fear.* Somehow, I carried on with my task mechanically, making myself as small and uninteresting as I could.

Anyway, they ignored me. They stood at the balustrade together, looking out at the *Princess Nazia*, admiring her smooth, clean lines and the crew in their smart white uniforms, getting her ready for the family to use.

'Eighty million, she cost, plus the refurb,' Muscle Man said. He sounded just as proud of the boat as when he'd described her to the Wicked Queen. 'She looks good, doesn't she? Biggest boat on the water.'

'Until the Grandfather comes,' Mr Johnson replied, sounding less than super-impressed.

'Oh?'

'Yes. He is bringing his yacht for the party. The *Juno*'s forty metres longer.'

'Really?' Muscle Man sounded disappointed.

'*And* she has a helipad,' Mr Johnson added, like it was a competition. I thoughts servants were supposed to be loyal to their masters, but Mr Johnson seemed more interested in the bigger boat.

'I'm sure you *could* land a helicopter on the *Princess*, if you had to,' Muscle Man said doubtfully, peering out to sea.

'Where? On the jacuzzi? Also, the *Juno*'s got state-of-the-art anti-piracy defences and a submarine.'

'A *sub*?'

'Yup, a sub.' Mr Johnson smirked.

Muscle Man sighed. 'The boss won't be happy.'

I remembered what it was like to be on the biggest boat in the harbour. Even for a stowaway, it had felt a bit special. Being on the *second* biggest boat wouldn't be the same at all. 'Eighty million plus refurb' obviously wasn't enough these days. Maybe even billionaires envied other, bigger billionaires.

The men turned away from the sea, while I quickly crouched down and fiddled with a broken pot.

'Oh, and by the way,' Mr Johnson went on, 'the Grandfather's bringing the Jongleur. He'll be taking over the . . . guest accommodation.'

'Oh God.'

Muscle Man had stopped in his tracks. His 'Oh, God' had sounded very serious, like he'd just been told that somebody had died.

'It has to be done,' Mr Johnson said. 'Gerry Alard has kept us waiting long enough.'

'I suppose so.' Muscle Man shivered slightly and they carried on together down the path.

Alard. Not 'Allud'. *That* was how Mr Johnson pronounced the name. Why did it sound familiar to me now? And why did it make me think of stone, and cold, and death?

Beyond the balustrade, a guard patrolled the castle wall with a large German Shepherd on a leash. I shivered too, despite the heat. Karim was right: it was time to get out of here.

THIRTY-TWO

After breakfast, the Wahool children left to spend the day on the yacht. They wouldn't be needing the hot tub after all, but that was normal: everything still had to be perfect, just in case. Meanwhile, Amina was told to freshen all Mrs Wahool's summer clothes with a lavender-infused steam machine, so they would be ready for when she got in from Paris tomorrow. We did it together, in the laundry room off the corridor that led to the dungeons. In fact, I did most of it for her, squeezing into a mop cupboard whenever we thought anyone might be coming by.

When we were certain we were alone, I talked to her about leaving the castle. I hadn't changed my mind: I wasn't going without her, or her brother. I promised that the family had lied about needing papers, and that there were places where she and Karim could go. I wasn't sure what those places were, but I felt certain there were people who would help her. And even if there weren't, *I* would help her. Anywhere I could take her was better than here.

Karim popped in to check on us. He and Amina talked quietly but animatedly together for a long time in their language. Both of them were scared. Both of them were excited. Each seemed to be trying to persuade the other to go with me. Eventually they turned to face me.

'We do not need papers?' Karim asked.

'No.'

'There is safety?'

'I will find it for you.'

'You can do this, Peta Jones?'

'I promise you I can.' If that was what it took to get them out of this place, I would promise.

He swallowed. 'Then there is much to do.'

I grinned at him. I may not have found my dad, but at least my coming here had been useful for something.

Karim had had an escape plan ready for months, but had just been too scared of the outside world to use it. I convinced him it was less frightening than anything he'd dealt with here. At that he seemed to grow several inches, and the twinkle in his eyes grew brighter.

After the massive laundry session, Amina took me back upstairs, through the tunnels, to find clothes for us to wear after the escape. Karim really had thought this through, but as he'd burnt most of the things I'd brought with me from Rye, we decided we'd just have to borrow something from Yasmin, who had several cupboards of clothes she no longer used.

It was strange to find myself back in the rose-scented bedroom, so peaceful and quiet. Amina showed me Yasmin's walk-in wardrobe of clothes, which was like the one on the *Princess Nazia*, but mirrored, and five times the size. Inside, there were several drawers of shorts and T-shirts that she no longer used, and that were small enough to fit us – even Karim, who was so thin he could easily fit into a girl's clothes.

I took only the simplest things (Amina couldn't bring herself to take anything at all), but instinct told me to remove as little as possible. The longer Yasmin didn't realise that anything was missing, the better.

While we were there, I sneaked a look at myself in the wall of mirrors. Even though I knew roughly what to expect, it was still a shock. The henna was starting to fade, but my face was still patchy under my black scarf. My arms were worse: orange in some places, brown in others. When I lifted the scarf up, my hair was tangled and filthy. I looked thin and dirty and not so very different from how Karim had seemed to me when I first saw him: a beggar child, a slave girl.

Excellent.

My own mother would struggle to recognise me now.

After lunch, as torpor descended on the castle and everyone tried to shelter from the baking heat of the summer sun, I suddenly thought to tell Karim about the conversation I'd overheard by the pool. I thought the news about the bigger boat would amuse him, and it did.

'Mr Johnson said the Grandfather's boat has a helipad. And a submarine.'

Karim's eyes glittered. 'A helipad? For helicopters, yes?'

'Uh-huh.'

185

'And Mr Wahool's boat – she does not have these things?'

'No.'

His face lit up.

'He will be *so upset*! He will be *furious*! He will want a new boat immediately!'

'It almost makes you feel sorry for him.'

A look of cold steel came into Karim's eyes. 'No. It does not.'

'Of course. You're right, I'm sorry, Karim. Anyway, I'm glad we're going to be out of here by then. The Grandfather's bringing this person called the Jongleur, and I didn't like the sound of him.'

I wasn't expecting Karim's extreme reaction. His face went grey. 'The Jongleur?' He had the same note of horror in his voice as Muscle Man.

'Yes. I think that was it. Is he famous? Why does everyone sound like that when they say his name?'

'He was the most famous man in Marvalia,' Karim said bleakly. I could make out his heart pumping in his skinny chest. 'The chief of interrogations. He is . . . a monster.'

'Oh my God. He's coming for Mr Alard.'

Karim stared dully ahead. 'If the Jongleur asks you a question, you will tell him anything.' He still looked sick. 'Nobody survives. Nobody wants to.'

He shut his eyes and I followed his thoughts down, down into the dungeons. The wild man would be cowering in his shackles. They would drag him off to 'the room where they do these things'. There the Jongleur would be waiting . . . He was already broken. What would they do next?

Karim opened his eyes; we stared at each other.

'It cannot be,' he said.

'I know.'

THIRTY-THREE

If something seems too good to be true, it's because it is. The idea of three of us leaving the castle at night and travelling through a *ready-made escape tunnel*? Of course it was never going to be that simple. Now, we would somehow have to take the wild man with us. Who was tall, starving, constantly guarded and chained to the wall.

'And Prisoners One and Two,' I said to Karim. 'What are their names again?'

'Sammy and Parissa.' He nodded and looked, for a moment, desperate. They were 'enemies of the state' and we could hardly leave them behind. But how could we bring them too?

Karim meditated for ages, working through all the options, trying to hit on the least suicidal scheme.

'It is good,' he said eventually. 'Marco is the most stupid guard and will be on duty again tomorrow. After midnight, one guard works alone. I will go up behind him and hit him with something. Then—'

'No! You can't!'

'I can,' he said grimly.

'I mean, what if it goes wrong? Dad says . . . my dad used to say that you shouldn't try fighting people who've had better training. Marco could kill you.'

'We do not have a choice.'

'I'm sure we do. Let me think of something.'

'We do not. I will hit Marco, then we will release the prisoners.'

Much as I would have loved Karim to hit the guard, it was too dangerous. We needed to knock him out some other way.

Knock out . . . Why had I been worried about that recently? Then I remembered: Mum's pills.

'I think I have a better idea,' I said.

When night came I couldn't sleep. Back in the tunnels, curled up under my threadbare blanket, I could almost feel the Jongleur travelling towards us, over the waves. At some point I must have drifted off, though, because I dreamt of Winchelsea churchyard again. Dad's ashes were there, lying in a puddle. They made the shape of a skull. Inside the church, I wandered around looking at the stained-glass windows: death and resurrection, a knight going up to heaven.

Suddenly I woke up in a sweat.

There was a tomb of a medieval knight inside the church, near where Mum and Rupert had signed the register. Dad and I often used to admire it. The name ALARD was carved into the stone beside it. The name was real, I was sure of it.

I felt haunted. Dad was visiting me from beyond the grave.

In the morning, my first job was to crush Mum's strongest pills into a fine powder. I crushed four and hoped it would be enough, then another one for luck. I found an old leather satchel in one of the storerooms and packed it with the clothes from Yasmin's room, and everything Karim had saved from my backpack. Watching me, Amina was equal parts scared and excited about what we were planning to do.

Over hot breakfast rolls, Karim made me memorise the plan. We had to time things carefully to avoid the guard who patrolled the perimeter every hour with his dog: it was vital to be nowhere near the entrance to the tunnel when he passed. Once we were through, Karim would guide us to the jetty, where we would hide on a boat the staff used to get supplies.

'Will six of us really be able to hide?' I asked. *Especially,* although I didn't say this, *as one is very sick, and one is mad?*

'Yes.'

His eyes said *trust me* but the jut of his chin said he was more hopeful than certain. Nor did we discuss how six of us were going to sneak off the boat on the mainland without being spotted. Some things you couldn't plan for. We would just have to take our chances and find a way.

The rest of the day dragged badly. I finished packing my satchel with some bread scrounged from the kitchens, a large empty water bottle for peeing in, and a funnel. My brain didn't really want to go there, but I knew what it was like to need the loo desperately while you were hiding, and even

189

peeing through a funnel wasn't worse.

Karim disabled the cable that linked the CCTV cameras round the castle to the guardroom. The man who could fix it wouldn't be here until morning. The guards checked for suspicious activity, of course, but all they could find was a slave boy, innocently sweeping.

Late in the evening, he took Marco a 'special hot chocolate from the kitchens', laced with Mum's powdered pills. Amina and I sat huddled in the cellar room, hugging each other for warmth, while Karim checked on the guard. The pills took a while to work, but by two-thirty he was out cold.

We left Amina in the cellar. Karim and I didn't want her risking her life during the next, tricky part. She would join us in twenty minutes, just inside the perimeter wall, when the patrol guard and his dog would be as far away as possible.

'It will be OK,' I said, hugging her. 'There's nothing to be scared of. We'll look after you, I promise.'

Her eyes looked deep into mine and she nodded slowly. She was doing to me what I'd done to Karim: believing me because she had to. I tried to make myself believe it too.

In the corridors and the kitchens, everything was dark. Karim made his way light-footed, by feel, and I followed, holding his hand. He looked like a ninja – or at least, the almost-invisible outline of one, which is how a ninja ought to look. I looked like a ninja carrying a satchel. A really nervous ninja, who kept bumping into things.

The stairs down to the dungeons felt familiar by now. With no moonlight outside, they were pitch-black, but the smell was still the same. The stench of rot and sewage grew stronger the lower we descended.

When we reached the lower corridor, Karim went first,

padding silently along, motioning for me to wait. Above his head, the dim bulb flickered. Even so, I could see from the stairs that Marco was out of it. He lay slumped with his head on the table. Karim was already reaching for the bunch of keys and signalling for me to join him.

The near-silence down here was eerie. The only noise came from the buzzing light and the tinny earphones in Marco's ears, still playing Europop from the phone beside him. His head was resting on the football results from today's paper. I put my hand on his neck to check for a pulse and felt him breathing, just.

Karim caught my eye: if the guard woke up, we were dead. If someone came, we were dead. If we made a mistake, we were dead. The only thing to do was to get moving, focus on the plan and try not to think about the other stuff. Using the keys from the wall, he opened the door to the end cell and nodded to me. He handed me a smaller bunch of keys as I went inside. Parissa, the girl, woke instantly from sleep. She saw me and went rigid.

'I've come to get you out of here,' I whispered, indicating the sleeping guard behind me.

Her eyes widened with shock and she nodded slowly. I looked at her shackles and she pointed to the keys I was holding. One of them was small and silver, with a pentagon-shaped head and a couple of small teeth at the bottom. She picked it out with her fingertips and stared at me intently. This must be the one.

Meanwhile, I could hear Karim going into Prisoner Three's cell. In the corridor, the light buzzed and flickered. And all the time, the sound of the guard's tinny music leaked through his headphones.

The small key fitted tightly into the slot on Parissa's

shackles where her wrists were joined. I turned it, and soon her hands were free. She squeezed my fingers, thanking me wordlessly. I freed her ankles too. Then we turned to the young man, Sammy, who was still sleeping fitfully beside her. I fiddled the key into the lock on his wrists. It wouldn't budge.

'Is this the right one?' I whispered.

'Yes,' she whispered back. 'The same key for him as for me.'

I tried again. Sammy woke up, but his breathing was shallow and he hardly seemed to see me as I worked. We had to get him out of here quickly. I fiddled some more, but the lock wouldn't move. Time was ticking by.

'Karim!' I called under my breath.

He appeared at the doorway. 'Is there a problem?'

'Yes. This lock is stuck.'

'Let me try,' he said. He worked on the bracelet, but had no more luck than me.

'This happens sometimes,' Parissa said. 'The guards use oil from a can.'

Suddenly, there was a shadow in the doorway. Prisoner Three loomed over us, wild and threatening. I smelled his stench as he pushed me roughly aside and crouched over the trapped young man. To my surprise, his bruised, hard hands seemed steady as he worked with the key. By now the girl was shaking with fear and I tried to calm her, but I was almost as scared as she was. We'd been here too long already. The guard with the dog would be leaving the guardhouse soon to start his next patrol. Amina would be waiting for us near the tunnel. We couldn't let her stay there: it was dangerous. Everything was dangerous.

The prisoner shook his head in frustration and the key

clattered to the ground.

'Where's the oil?' I asked. 'The can the guards use?'

Nobody knew. Feverishly, we searched high and low, but there wasn't much high or low to search – just the guards' table and the bag Marco used to carry his paper, his bottle and his big, heavy torch. No can. Everybody tried the key again. The lock wouldn't budge.

From his jacket pocket, Marco's two-way radio crackled into life.

'*Ci sei? Castello due? Marco? Dove sei? Mannaggia.*'

We all froze.

'Go!' the prisoner grunted. His voice was harsh and low. It was strange to hear him talk, but what he said was true: if the other guards were worried about Marco, they would come and check on him. Fast.

With glassy eyes, Sammy stared up at Parissa and croaked something. I think he was telling her to go too. She shook her head. The wild man grabbed her arm to pull her away, but she ignored him. She was soaked in sweat from the fear, but she would not leave her friend. The wild man turned to Karim and me, hovering in the doorway.

'Run!' he rasped.

We had no choice. I glanced back at them as I headed down the corridor, just in time to see the wild man grab Marco's large torch from his bag and hit the sleeping guard hard over the head with it. The movement came out of nowhere and shocked me so much I shrieked. Then he came after us, leaving the others where they were and looming down the corridor like a zombie.

I ran as fast as I could, as much to get away from the prisoner as anything. It was all going so wrong. Karim led the way as we panted up the stairs, through the kitchens and out on to a gravel path, with the wild man hard on our heels. We raced around the side of the castle, past the cameras that didn't work, across well-kept terraces that descended towards the outer wall, where Amina would be waiting.

Two of them, trapped in that cell. My brain repeated the thought with every breath, but I kept running.

THIRTY-FOUR

By the time we got to the bottom terrace, I was gasping for air. The wild man dragged me along, running faster than I was. How he had the strength to do this, I didn't know. I'd assumed he was near dead in that cell, but I was wrong. In fact, his strength was frightening.

Far above us came the sudden sound of shouting.

Karim ducked down and we all stayed low as we headed for the meeting point. The leather satchel bounced on my back, bashing me with every step. It didn't matter. I listened for the sound of the guard dog – my biggest fear – and on we ran.

The thick perimeter wall rose up ahead of us. Already the

neat castle terraces were giving way to wild gorse that pricked our clothes. Karim paused for a moment in the darkness, checking the way ahead. Beside me, the wild man waited, breathing hard. I half expected him to attack me, but he was watching Karim, who suddenly moved off again at a run. I followed, pushing through the undergrowth until, just before we reached the wall, the hillside fell away and a hole appeared in the ground, surrounded by thickset thorny bushes.

It was the first of a series of stone steps. They led down steeply under the wall, and I could just about make out the edges of the hidden roof under a canopy of plants. Amina's terrified face was dimly visible in the entrance to the smugglers' tunnel.

In the distance, the guard dog started barking.

'We are here,' Karim said. 'Go fast.'

I moved forward, but sensed him hesitate beside me. 'What about you?'

Just one look at his face told me everything. He wasn't coming after all.

'What's happened? Why?' I cried, stopping and reaching out to take his hand.

'The Jongleur,' he said. 'Parissa and her friend . . .' He pulled away.

'There's nothing you can do!'

'I must try. You have my sister. Look after her, Peta Jones.'

'We can't go without you!' There were tears in my voice, and desperation. 'You *have* to come. Think what they'll do if they find you.'

'I will say I heard prisoners escaping. I tried to capture them. Go.'

'No! *Please!*'

The barking grew louder.

'They will not suspect me,' Karim insisted. 'They think I am nothing. A boy like me could never plan something so ingenious.'

There was a brief flicker of pride in his eyes, but Amina had realised what was happening and now she threw herself up the steps and into his arms, begging him to come. He hugged her hard and pulled away. 'Take her!' he said to me.

All the time, the dog was getting closer, and now I heard shouts and running feet.

'Move!' the prisoner shouted, grabbing the sobbing girl from her brother and pulling her down into the tunnel. Karim nodded. His eyes blazed at me with their maharaja intensity.

'Go with them!'

I had no choice. I couldn't trust that wild man with Amina, and I'd only make things worse if I stayed behind. This was the worst mess in the world. After one last look into those blazing eyes, I turned and flung myself down the steps as fast as I could.

Somehow, the bony prisoner had squeezed himself through the narrow entrance. Ahead of me, I sensed him moving quickly down the steps. They were wider than the ones in the castle, but broken and uneven, and in the darkness I tripped on every one. The roof was low and I had to bend double to keep moving. How the tall, lanky figure of the wild man could exist in this space, never mind move in it, I couldn't understand – especially with Amina clinging to him, keening with distress. And yet he travelled so fast that I could hardly catch up with him.

All the time, I listened for the sound of the dog. I had seen it on patrol and dreaded being the thing it was hunting for.

On we hurtled, down and down, with the occasional gap in the old tunnel roof revealing stars in the night sky. Then a new noise hit us: something more terrifying than anything we'd heard before. Paws pounding on stone. Claws scrabbling, slipping and sliding. The dog was breathing hard, like us. Not barking now, but panting: coming in for the kill.

The prisoner turned round to face me. 'Take her,' he hissed. 'Run.'

He came back and we passed awkwardly in the cramped space. As we did so, his hand seemed to catch on my cheek.

'Move!'

I did. Fast. Amina was almost paralysed with fear, but with my arm around her and my momentum pushing us on, we continued rushing down. Behind us, the dog's hard panting came closer, closer. There was a yelp and a struggle. And the noise stopped.

Amina stopped too, but I forced her on. 'It's OK,' I whispered. 'Close your eyes and hold on to me.'

We moved along together, slipping and stumbling against the rough concrete walls, catching our feet on the broken steps. The tunnels in the castle were paradise compared with this. We slid and fell and crouched and ran. There was the dim sound of shouting far above us, panicked and confused. The men seemed to have found the tunnel entrance, but in their uniforms they would be too bulky to fit inside.

The steep hill began to get shallower and a dim light appeared ahead of us. Then suddenly, the roof was gone. We were out in the open, at the bottom of the hill. The sea breeze hit our faces.

I looked behind me and the castle was way above us. We were near the shore, halfway between the sheer cliff-face under the castle dungeons and the gentle side of the island where the wild flowers grew. To our left, rough waves pounded the rocks. To our right, the jetty stuck out into calm sea, beyond a little bay. The lights of several boats bobbed and sparkled on the water.

Amina collapsed beside me in a heap. Her face was a mask of horror. She didn't even move when we heard footsteps in the mouth of the tunnel. I turned around slowly. If it was the wild man, we were safe, and if it wasn't, there was nothing we could do. We'd used up all our adrenaline in the final run from the dog, and there was nothing left to run with.

It *was* the wild man. He emerged from the tunnel, scratched and bleeding. The dog must have gone for him and there had been a fight, but the dog had lost. The wild man came straight towards me, looked into my eyes and ran his long, bony fingers through my tangled hair. I shrank away instinctively and a shadow of sadness passed across his face.

'Peta, I'm so sorry.'

Dad's voice.

'*Dad?*'

THIRTY-FIVE

No. No. NO. This couldn't be happening to me. The man stared down at me, and his sunken eyes were sad but smiling.

I stared back. I had to be hallucinating.

The wild man reached out his hand again.

'Peta. My love.'

Just *no*.

'Come on. I have to get you out of here,' he insisted.

I couldn't have made such a mistake about him. My dad wouldn't *let* me.

The voice was Dad's, but rougher. The broad forehead could be his, and maybe the eyebrows. The nose was broken and it was hard to see the rest of the face through the bushy beard, but now that he was standing upright, he was the right kind of height. He was several stones lighter than I'd ever seen Dad before, and I felt sick imagining that this bag of bones could be the person who used to carry me on his shoulders.

But this bag of bones had just killed an attack dog. It had bashed the guard to spare Karim and make it look like an outside job, not a drugging – I realised that now. It had folded its large frame into an impossibly small space and kept us moving. It was highly trained, and supremely tough, and it called me 'my love'. Also, I noticed, it had a scar on its right cheek, from a training accident long ago.

Damn.

It was Dad.

'We have to move,' he said. 'Come on.'

Amina and I just sat there, exhausted from our flight. My brain was still struggling to un-know what it had finally accepted, and to believe that the pale figure in front of me wasn't a ghost, or a mirage, or a dream. I'd got so much wrong up to now; my heart couldn't afford to get this wrong again.

First my head got there, then, sluggishly, my heart followed. *Allud, Alard.* The knight in the church. The voice. Dad. My dad.

I rose to my feet and lunged for him, pounding my fists into his chest, howling. 'Why didn't you tell me it was you? Why didn't you *tell* me?'

He held me against him, pressing his face against my hair. 'Oh, love. My lovely girl.'

Oh, Dad. And me howling with grief and my heart still aching. This was how they'd wanted me to feel in front of the urn of ashes, and now I did, and he was standing right in front of me.

'We have to go.'

I clung to him. He spoke gently, but there was an edge to his voice that translated as *move now or those men will find us and we die*. I wanted to run, but I couldn't bear to let go of him.

In the end he leant down and put an arm under each of our shoulders. He was surprisingly strong for someone who'd been locked up in a dark room for the last few months. Of course, my hero dad would have kept himself fit when they weren't looking. He'd have done secret exercises. He'd have never given up, keeping ready for this moment, just in case it ever came.

He half dragged, half carried us round the bay, through the shallow water, out of sight of the castle. Out to sea, the bright lights of the *Princess Nazia* danced on the water. Behind us, beams of torchlight criss-crossed over the hillside, moving fast.

The cold water shocked my body to life again. We took shelter among the puddles and rock pools, using a couple of big boulders for cover and listening to the sound of shouting as guards moved steadily down towards the shore.

Amina was moaning, 'Karim! Karim!'

'It'll be all right,' I whispered through chattering teeth. 'He'll be OK.'

She shook uncontrollably. The horror in her eyes was scary.

'Your brother is clever and strong,' the wild man said to her, gently, echoing my thoughts. *Dad's voice. Dad.* I still had to remind myself.

He turned to me. 'We must keep moving.'

The torch beams were getting closer, and now there was

the sound of a second dog barking. He was right, and he wasn't the wild man any more: he was a trained soldier, trying to stay ahead of the enemy. However, he was a mess. His left arm was bleeding heavily where he'd cut himself on a stone or been bitten by the dog in the tunnel. His feet were grazed from the rocks. And bare. He'd done the whole thing without shoes. Two of his toes were in weird positions and looked broken. My stomach lurched.

'Help me?' he said.

Together we put our arms round Amina and moved her quickly past the rocks and closer to the jetty. Beside the water there was a shelter for the vehicles and a low wooden boat-house with a slipway. People clustered near them, shouting instructions. Men ran. Engines started. Several people seemed to be heading up the hill.

'Good,' Dad whispered. 'I need to find us a way out of here. Stay nearby. Keep talking to Amina, love. Try and keep her warm. Don't let her shut down. I'll be back soon.'

He left us, wading towards the jetty, a dark figure moving through the shadows. I crouched behind the nearest boulder, holding Amina up as much as I could. We were knee-deep in cold water by now, and though I was alert again, she was shivering like she'd been electrocuted.

'Don't worry,' I murmured to her. 'You're safe now.'

'He did not come,' she muttered through chattering teeth, staring dully ahead. Her mind was still trapped at the top of the tunnel, watching her brother fade into the distance.

'He'll find a way out,' I said unconvincingly. 'You heard . . . the man: Karim's clever and strong.'

He wouldn't be able to use the tunnel now it had been discovered. Amina's frightened eyes told me she was worried about this too. I had to think of something else to tell her.

'He'll be so glad to know you're getting away.' This was true. 'He only cares about you. You've got to get free, Amina, for him.'

For the first time she looked at me properly. The horror turned to something else: the need to please her brother, however she could.

'Let me help you,' I said. 'He wanted me to.'

The jetty was empty. Dad had disappeared, and all the men and vehicles had gone up to the castle. Up the hill, the distant shouting was interrupted by the sudden rapid sound of gunfire. It made us both jump. They obviously thought they'd found something, but it wasn't us. Was it Karim? I couldn't bear to think about that now.

To our left, the water just beyond the bay was criss-crossed with torchlight as the searching guards made their way through the dense bushes to the shore. The second dog barked loudly.

By now, Amina was so cold she'd stopped shaking. This couldn't be a good thing. Dad had told us to stay where we were, but he'd also told me to keep her warm. I could only do one of those things. 'Come with me,' I said.

I helped her wade the short distance to the sloping slipway that led up to the boathouse. We hauled ourselves up the slippery concrete and I shifted the door open with my shoulder and felt around the walls for something, anything, to wrap Amina in. A folded sail seemed like the best thing I was going to find, but as I leant against the wall, my body fell into something smooth and padded. A miracle: four thick, warm sailing jackets, hanging near the door.

I grabbed the nearest one, which was enormous. Amina was too cold and weak to get her arms through the sleeves, so

I wrapped it round her like a cloak.

'Better?' I asked.

Even in the jacket, her teeth were chattering. She was swaying with cold and fear. Before she could answer, a new sound pierced the night air: the roar of a motor boat. I peered through the window and saw the large white speedboat belonging to the *Princess Nazia* powering through the water towards us. Great. So now the waters were patrolled too. It wasn't the only boat out there, in fact. Another, smaller motor boat was rumbling around the jetty, taking it more slowly, checking out the rocks for signs of life.

The smaller boat drove out to near where Amina and I had been hiding behind the boulder, almost as if it knew exactly where to go. My heart pounded. Had they caught Dad? How else could they know where to look for us? I peered closer. It was hard to tell in the darkness, but the figure in the boat was about Dad's height. And then a gust of wind from the water caught his hair. Wild and unkempt, it blew around his face. He was scanning the shoreline for us.

I grabbed another jacket from the wall.

'He's back,' I told Amina. 'Come on. Let's go.'

She didn't move. 'Come *on*!' I whispered urgently, forcing my face into a smile. 'For Karim. You can do this, Amina.'

She'd reached her limit. It wasn't that she was weak or fainthearted, but she'd had to face the terror of the dark, and now the horror of leaving Karim behind. The thing was, though, we *had* to get off this island. Now.

I'm not sure how we got to the motor boat. Dad said later that I carried Amina through the water, but I couldn't have done because it was impossible. She must have found the strength from somewhere to wade back through the shallows with me. All I really remember is the sound of the barking

205

dog, and a jeep racing down the hill, and the loud, whiny engine of the superyacht tender getting closer and closer, and Dad yelling, '*Now*, Peta! Yes!'

THIRTY-SIX

D ad hauled me aboard after Amina and set off in a slow, lazy circle away from the shore. My chest ached from the pounding of my heart. A muscle pumped in Dad's cheek too, as the speedboat changed its course and came charging towards us. Dad held his own course, keeping a tight grip on the steering wheel.

Why weren't we racing away? Of course, we couldn't escape the faster boat, but at least we could try . . .

Chess. This must be like chess. Karim always had a plan, and I was sure Dad did too. Maybe we looked less suspicious if we didn't speed off. But as I looked at Dad in his ragged, bloodstained shirt, he stood out a mile.

'Here. Take this.' I shrugged off my jacket and handed it to him. In the past, if I'd offered him something I needed too, he'd refuse it without even thinking, but this time he simply grabbed the jacket and put it on. His brief nod of thanks, like from one team-member to another, made me feel warmer than the jacket had.

The speedboat drew nearer.

'Hide,' Dad shouted over the noise of the engine. 'Her too.'

OK – so hide. In an open boat. Sure. Now is not the time to panic, Peta Jones.

I did the only thing I could think of, which was to curl myself over Amina and huddle in the bottom of the boat with her jacket draped over both of us. I had no idea if it was good enough, or if any bits of us or my satchel were showing. I could feel Amina's pulse beating rapidly, almost in time with mine.

On the water, the engine's note changed down as the bigger boat slowed beside us.

'*Salve*,' the driver shouted down to Dad. Then some sort of question in Italian. He sounded tense, but not suspicious. Dad called something back, also in Italian. I didn't know he spoke it.

Anyway, it seemed to satisfy the other driver, who pulled slowly away. Meanwhile, Dad revved his engine slightly, gradually gathering speed until we were skimming across the water. I risked looking up, to find that we were level with the superyacht itself now, heading round the back of the island, past the cliffs and out of sight of the search party.

There was nothing ahead of us, nothing behind us. For a moment, it felt like freedom.

'Stay down,' Dad said. 'I told them I'd search the cliffs. Any moment now they'll realise what we're really doing.'

He headed straight for the mainland at full speed, his eyes fixed on the shore.

'Check the box,' he ordered, without looking at me. 'Stay low. See what's inside.'

Box? What box? Crouching in my place, I scanned the little boat. There was a built-in store-chest behind the driver's seat. I went over and opened it up to find a couple of oars, some life jackets, some short rubber boots and various ropes. I put on one of the life jackets and did the same for Amina. Our dark, wet clothes looked somehow less unusual with a fat yellow jacket over the top. I passed the wellies to Dad, but they were much too small and he threw them aside. Two minutes later, the speedboat appeared again around the side of the island behind us, travelling fast.

'Just a bit longer . . .' Dad muttered. He seemed to will the little boat to speed faster over the waves.

With every minute that passed, the mainland grew more distinct ahead of us, and the boat behind us grew closer. I tried to calculate the distances in my head. It was a classic maths problem: *Peta, her not-so-dead father and an ex-slave girl called Amina are heading towards safety at* x *knots, being chased by a much faster boat travelling at* y *knots, which is* z *distance away. How long will it take before they are overrun? And will they have reached the shore by then?*

I looked, and the answer was *no. No, they won't. Not even close.* It didn't take a maths genius to see we had too far to go.

There was a dull popping sound from behind us. Looking round, like Dad, I saw a flash and a puff of smoke from the speedboat. Then another.

'They're not *shooting* at us?' I asked.

Dad's lips set in a grim line. 'They're idiots. And desperate. But don't worry – you can't hit a moving target at this range, with this wind.'

They were. They were shooting at us. Out at sea. Dad seemed remarkably calm about this. I, however, was not. True, the bullets weren't reaching us yet, but the speedboat was getting closer all the time

'Stay down. Don't look at them,' Dad said.

I couldn't help it. But a few seconds later, the popping stopped and Dad started slowing down.

'What's happening?' I asked.

Dad nodded ahead of us. 'Company,' he said.

A large fast boat was heading straight for us, with a bright searchlight that suddenly caught us in its beam.

'Polizia!' a voice boomed through the night air.

Rescue, finally!

Dad put a hand on my shoulder.

'Get ready to lie.'

THIRTY-SEVEN

At first I thought he said 'die'. And I did prepare myself, sort of. That is, I stopped feeling so terrified and thought of Mum. I also thought of all those times I'd spent in Winchelsea churchyard, thinking about Dad. Even being here, like this, was better than visiting those stupid ashes.

But he didn't say 'die', he said 'lie'. When the police boat came close, he put on a posh accent, like one of his old officers from the regiment. In fact, he sounded exactly like Rupert – the new stepdad he didn't even know I had.

'Thank goodness you're here. We're off to hospital. This girl's got appendicitis, I think.' He indicated Amina, lying in the bottom of the boat. 'She's my daughter's friend. We're trying to get her to shore as fast as we can. Can you help us?'

Wait – *appendicitis*? What about the castle, and the dungeons, and the people who were chasing us down with guns two seconds ago?

A policeman stepped forward. 'British, yes?' Dad nodded. The man smiled and spoke in careful English. 'Some people have reported guns . . . shooting . . . from the Isola Sirena. That island over there. Do you know about this?'

Dad shook his head. 'Guns? No. I might have seen fireworks. I can't be sure. I'm so worried about this girl. She needs to get to hospital.'

The policeman held up his hand. 'What is that boat behind you, please?'

Dad looked round and gave a start, as if he'd only just noticed it. Nothing to do with him, he said. Nice, though. Pretty tender.

The police agreed. They seemed pleased to have the opportunity of stopping it and getting closer. Would we please wait, while they talked to the people on board?

'Of course,' Dad agreed. But the girl . . . you know . . . appendicitis? Hospital?'

They nodded gravely. They wouldn't be long.

'Da-ad,' I hissed as soon as they'd moved away. 'What are you *doing?*'

He crouched down low so Amina and I could hear him.

'You have a choice,' he said urgently. 'You can go with the police and tell them everything. If you do, they may investigate the island. I don't know what they'd find, but it wouldn't be much by then. Or you can follow me. I got you into this. I promise I'll get you out of it.'

Amina nodded earnestly.

212

'Peta?'

I nodded too. 'But why can't we at least . . .?'

'There isn't time to argue. First, Wahool would rather kill those prisoners than have them discovered. And second, two of his guards have brothers in this police force. I don't know who to trust round here. OK?'

It was a *shut up* kind of OK. I shut up. Meanwhile, the police boat was heading back to us. Dad looked at Amina.

'Can you walk?'

'I think so.'

'Pretend you can't. Hold your stomach . . . *here*.' He pointed to the exact place. 'It's hurting, OK?' He turned to me. 'We'll only have one chance to disappear. Wait till we get ashore, then watch me for the signal. When you see it, say nothing and walk away, fast, both of you. If it doesn't work out and you end up at the police station, make them call the embassy. Say I was just a stranger who helped you escape.'

'What signal?' I asked.

But by now the police boat was back alongside us.

'Watch me,' Dad muttered, then turned away. 'So glad you're back!' he shouted. 'I think she's taken a turn for the worse. Can you possibly give us an escort?'

They did more than that. They took us on board their much faster boat, while one of the policemen drove our motor boat to shore. As soon as we were on deck, the policeman who had spoken to us before gave us a bright smile.

'You forgot this!' he said, holding up a blue holdall.

'I'm sorry?' Dad looked confused.

'The men from the *Princess Nazia*. They were trying to give it to you, for your daughter's friend. They had nearly reached you, but not quite. So, you were staying on the

Princess?' He looked impressed, as if to say that if you were going to go down with appendicitis, a superyacht was *the* place to do it.

They'd said we were staying on the yacht?

Dad considered the new development for a moment, then took the holdall from the policeman and looked through it, as if that's exactly what he'd expected to happen.

'Great. Some useful drugs in here. Thank you.'

'Can I administer some pain relief?' the policeman asked. 'I have training.'

'No, that's fine,' Dad replied quickly. 'So do I.' He was rifling through packets of syringes and phials of liquid, holding them up to the light to see what they were. 'Ah. This looks good.'

The police boat was nearing the mainland. I noticed that the tender from the *Princess Nazia* was still behind us.

'What's it doing?' I asked.

'Ah,' the policeman smiled. 'They are most concerned about your little friend. They will follow us to Amalfi and meet us at the hospital. They fear very much for her.'

Oh hell. So that was their plan. They'd said we were with them so they could follow us all the way. It wasn't over yet. It wasn't nearly over.

Dad gave only the slightest flicker of response. He bent over Amina with cool efficiency, clutching a syringe. Anyone would think he was a doctor with his patient. 'Here,' he said, rolling up her sleeve. 'I'm going to give you something for the pain. It will hurt, but don't worry.'

Bending lower, he muttered quietly in her ear. She flinched and moaned as he wielded the syringe. Then the policemen motioned him back across the boat to talk.

'What did he give you?' I asked her, as quietly as I could

over the roar of the engines and the hiss of waves splashing against the speeding hull.

'Nothing,' she said. 'He told me to pretend.' She groaned as if in serious agony, so I really hoped she was acting.

I looked back to where Dad now stood with the policeman, shifting uncomfortably from foot to foot. A thought struck me: what about his bare feet and broken toes? Wouldn't they cause suspicion? But when I checked, I realised he'd somehow shoved his feet and the bottoms of his ragged trousers into the too-small rubber boots.

'Mr Allud is so brave,' Amina murmured.

'Yes, he is.'

'You called him your father . . .?'

'Yeah, he is.'

'But you said before . . .'

'Mmm. I know. I was wrong.'

She frowned in confusion. How could anyone be wrong about something as important as their own father?

Especially me. I always thought Dad and I had a bond that nothing could break. The more I discovered, the less I understood.

By now the coastline was a necklace of sparkling lights. Clusters of pale-coloured houses emerged from the gloom, clinging to steep hillsides. They looked precarious, and beautiful. The police boat swung to the right and headed for the marina of a smart seaside town.

As the boat swerved through the water, Dad lost his footing and fell against the policeman, who clutched his leg in pain. Dad was hugely apologetic, patting him down. The idiot English father, with his bad sea legs. Except that Dad was always brilliant on boats. He was definitely up to something, but I didn't know what.

We drew up alongside rows of tall, shiny yachts bobbing on the water. Two police cars were waiting for us onshore, along with a couple of police motorbikes and a small late-night crowd of curious locals.

On the dock, policemen surrounded us. I didn't see how we could possibly get away. Their faces were kindly, but their hips were bristling with guns. I followed as they gently placed Amina in the back of an open police car, where a police-woman stood nearby to keep an eye on us, while the rest went to the water's edge to watch the graceful speedboat arrive behind us.

All the time I didn't take my eyes off Dad, who hung back, hardly moving as he surreptitiously discarded the too-small boots. He mimed slipping off a life jacket, so I took off mine, and Amina's too. We were all in black again.

And then it happened. Without warning, the policeman who'd been chatting to Dad on the boat collapsed on the dock, moaning and clutching his stomach. The group around him called out anxiously as he knelt over and threw up. Everyone watched the scene, horrified.

Everyone except me. Because that looked like a signal to me.

I glanced back at Dad, who nodded very slightly. He'd said to trust him. Well . . . OK.

First, I gasped and pointed at the sick man, and the police-woman next to me rushed over to help. Then I turned to Amina. 'Now!'

In one fluid movement, she opened her eyes, sat up and slid silently out of the car. I took her hand and we walked quickly towards the crowd of onlookers. Only one or two of them glanced at us as the rest focused on the incident by the dock. Soon our dark clothes helped us disappear among their bright ones.

'Keep going,' I said, as the sound of a siren pierced the air from a distance.

'But Mr Allud . . .'

'He'll find us.'

A minute later Dad was striding alongside us, barefoot, as if we were out for an evening stroll.

'Good job, girls. I'm looking for a Mercedes.'

'Er, how about that one over there?' I said, pointing to a coupé parked further down the road.

He took a key fob out of his pocket, pressed a button on it and shook his head.

'Not that one.' There was a quiet *chirp* sound from behind us and he turned round with a smile. 'That one.'

A large silver saloon sat next to the pavement, a few metres away. Dad opened the back door and motioned us in. Then he got into the driver's seat and drove away.

Just like that.

OK. So my father lied to the police and stole cars now. As we raced out of town, I wished it didn't feel so cool.

THIRTY-EIGHT

We rounded the corner and Dad sped up the road, narrowly avoiding an oncoming ambulance with some expert steering. He drove uphill, through winding streets, slowing only slightly for the switchback turns.

'Did you inject that policeman?' I asked him.

He glanced at me in the mirror. 'How did you guess?'

'That syringe you had on the boat. You did it when you fell into him, didn't you? What was in it?'

'Morphine from that damn medical bag he gave me,' Dad smiled. 'Don't worry, he'll be OK.'

Actually, my first concern hadn't been the policeman's

long-term health, but that was good to know anyway.

Outside, dawn was breaking and the sky was slowly shifting from purple to pink. At the wheel, Dad looked perfectly calm.

'So we're in Amalfi?' I asked, remembering the policeman mentioning it.

'Yes.'

'Where's that?'

'About an hour's drive south of Naples,' Dad said. I thought you'd know that,'

'Why?'

'Because you must have come this way to get to the island.'

'Nope. Came on the *Princess Nazia*.' I yawned.

Dad shook his head. 'Very funny.'

'I know that's what they said on the speedboat, but I really did.'

'What? How on *earth* . . .?'

Our eyes met in the mirror again.

'I could ask the same question.'

'We have a lot to talk about,' he admitted. However, at that moment he was busy punching instructions into the satnav. As we reached the top of the town, the land dropped away to our left, with the sea beyond it almost invisible beneath the pale sunrise. Dark trees cast unfamiliar shapes against the skyline.

Amina stared out to sea. She was looking towards the island, I realised.

'By the way,' Dad said, his eyes back on the road ahead. 'They'll be looking for this car. We'll have to ditch it soon – and find disguises. We'll be travelling for a while. What's in that satchel, Peta? Anything to change into?'

'Yes, actually.'

'Good. Do it now. Is there anything for Amina?'

'Uh-huh.'

He raised an eyebrow at me.

'Good girl. Change now, if you can. I won't look.'

We did as we were told, scrambling out of our filthy, wet rags and into the soft, dry-ish vests and shorts from Yasmin's wardrobe. There were even designer sandals. They were too big for us both, but we weren't fussy. We shoved them on anyway.

'Where are we going?' I asked.

'West,' Dad said absently. He was obviously thinking about something else. 'You stowed away on the yacht to find me,' he murmured, 'and even though you thought it wasn't me, you still decided to rescue me. Sammy and Parissa too.'

He broke off and shook his head. He made it all sound a lot more intentional than it felt at the time, but basically he'd worked it out OK. I shrugged. 'Yes, I suppose so. Well, Karim and I did.'

Amina looked round. Her tired eyes were haunted. 'What will happen to my brother?' she asked.

Dad turned to us. 'If anyone can survive in there, Karim can. He did the most amazing thing, Amina, to stay behind for those people . . .'

Please let that gunfire not have been for Karim.

'He'll be OK,' I said, putting an arm around her. It was still hard to believe he wasn't with us, grinning gleefully.

'But they will say what he did,' Amina said blankly. 'Then he will be killed.'

A chill ran through me. Now she'd said it, it was obvious: the prisoners would describe what had happened in the cells, and then the guards would take Karim to 'the room where they do these things' and . . .

'No, they won't,' Dad said firmly. 'She's extraordinary, that girl. So's Sammy, but he's too ill to talk. Parissa will tell them that I did everything. She may say I had outside help. I suppose she might say it was you, Peta. Did you tell her who you were?'

'No. Nobody knew who I was. The guards didn't know I was there.'

'They didn't . . .? That's . . . *Really?*'

I shrugged. 'I laid low. Well, kind of low.'

Dad shook his head for a moment, trying to take it in. 'Well, anyway, Parissa will protect your brother, Amina. You saw what she's like – how brave she is.'

'Why is she even there?' I asked.

Dad scrunched up his face, like this was going to be complicated. 'Do you know anything about a little country called Marvalia?'

'Yes. And the Blue Revolution. And that they were revolutionaries.'

'Oh.' He seemed surprised. 'OK. So, Parissa was particularly famous. She ran a blog, telling the demonstrators where to meet and letting the outside world know what was going on. She did more than that, actually. There was one time, near the Great Palace, when the army moved in on the demonstrators—'

'Oh my God.'

'What?'

'She was the girl on the tank,' I said. 'Wasn't she?'

Those blue eyes. Those haunting blue eyes in the thin, dirty face. I knew I'd seen them before.

Dad smiled. 'Yes, that was Parissa. And Sammy was a lawyer who helped write the new constitution.'

'The Grandfather hated them,' Amina added quietly.

'He did,' Dad agreed. 'When he was exiled, he had them kidnapped. Wahool does most of the Grandfather's dirty work, so he was holding on to them.'

'What for?'

'Revenge. He was storing them up for later things.'

'What things?' I asked. It sounded very ominous: *later things*.

'You don't want to know,' Dad said.

'I do.'

'No, you don't.'

Dad's mouth set into an unrelenting line. This was annoying. It was a part of my father that I'd forgotten in all those months of missing him. The part where he told me I was 'too young to understand', or it was 'none of my business', just when things got interesting.

'And you worked for this man, who kidnapped teenagers and lawyers?' I asked pointedly.

'I did.' The muscle in Dad's cheek started pumping again.

'And you did nothing?'

He flushed with anger. 'No, Peta, I did not do nothing. I wanted to get them out. But Wahool got a new security adviser, and that was bad luck for me. Johnson had served with me once, in Kosovo, years ago and he recognised me. It was always a risk – Wahool liked to hire British staff. Anyway, Johnson got suspicious about why Mike Jones was at the castle, pretending to be Gerry Alard, and before I could arrange anything, I ended up in a cell next to them.'

'And why *were* you there? Are you still working for the army, then?' I asked.

'No.'

'MI6? The CIA?'

'No.'

'Then . . . what, Dad? Why?'

'I can't talk about it,' he sighed. 'You know what it's like.'

But those were the only legitimate excuses I could think of. I'd lived without him for so long. I thought I deserved more of an explanation than *You know what it's like.*

'No, I don't,' I said coldly. 'Tell me.'

He glanced at me again, frustrated. 'I can't tell you the details. It was about . . . money. More money than you can imagine . . .'

Wait. *Hello?*

'You were doing this for *money?*'

'It's not as simple as that.'

That's all he had to say. I was dumbfounded. I just couldn't believe he was talking like this.

The car was quiet for a long time.

On we drove, and now the sky behind us was streaked with orange. Each bend in the road revealed a new cluster of houses, like limpets on a cliff, or a stunning bay where fast boats carved foaming wakes into the sea. Dad frequently checked the mirror for pursuing cars, but so far he seemed happy there were none.

'It'll be a while before we get to the next town,' he said. 'You might as well get some sleep.'

Amina curled up obediently in her seat. Her tired face had just enough energy left to gaze wonderingly at the back of Dad's neck. Any minute now, she'd be asking for his autograph. It was mildly sickening. I mean, Dad had his awesome moments – I knew that better than anyone. But he clearly had . . . issues.

'I'm not tired,' I said grimly.

He saw the expression on my face and patted the empty

223

passenger seat.

'Join me?' he asked.

Beside me, Amina's eyelids were fluttering closed. I climbed into the front. It felt odd to be here. The passenger seat was Mum's place; I always sat in the back while she and Dad chatted. It was beyond amazing to be so close to him, but at the same time, everything felt out of place. Dad was swiftly piecing me together, but even though I could finally reach out and touch him (I did – he winced with pain, but he was solid and real), I couldn't work him out at all.

I kept having visions of the filthy cell, and reliving the moments in the castle when Dad was dead, then not-dead. Dead, then not-dead. He was like one of those particles Mr Sarfield likes to tell us about in physics, which can exist and not exist at the same time. I didn't understand Mr Sarfield, and I didn't understand this.

'Were you ever going to tell me?' I asked. My voice was low and growly. It made me sound tearful, and that annoyed me.

'About what?'

'About being alive. About not being in the churchyard where we scattered you?'

He winced. I might have said 'scattered you' quite force-fully. It might have sounded a bit angry, even. Possibly.

'Yes I was. One day.' His eyes were focused on the road. They wouldn't meet mine. He felt me go silent. 'Peta! Honestly! Of course I was! Who do you think I am?'

I rolled my eyes. Suddenly all of this was supposed to be obvious to me? After the *urn full of ashes* and the *memorial service*?

'You worked for a slave master. What am I supposed to think?'

'It was part of a job,' Dad said.

'For money.'

'Yes, for money.'

I stared down the road ahead. Cars raced by with their headlights still on. The road was getting busier all the time.

'Were there other jobs?'

'Not yet. There would have been.' He kept his eyes on the road.

'And me?' I asked.

'I'm sorry?'

'What about me?'

Dad hesitated for a very long time.

'You were . . . you were safe, love. You had Mum. I thought that if you knew what I was doing, you'd understand.'

'But I *don't* know what you were doing. I *don't* understand.' Now that he was safe, I felt myself getting angrier with every sentence. I was his only child. How could he *do* this to me? 'And the bomb . . .?'

'Ah, the bomb. We organised it so I could disappear.' He sounded a bit guilty. Not very guilty, though. Not guilty enough.

'"*We* organised it", you said – who's "we"?'

'I can't talk about that.'

'Aargh! Dad! Stop it. Who's "we"?'

His mouth was a grim line. 'I really can't talk about it,' he said. 'Not now. You need to trust me.'

'I have a therapist who kept telling me you were dead for *six months*. How can I trust you? How?'

He looked hurt for a moment. Then he seemed to get it. The bomb, the urn . . . the TWO YEARS OF LYING were making the whole trust thing a little difficult right now.

'You have a therapist?' he asked, changing the subject entirely.

225

He was right: we had a lot to talk about.

'Did you ever give me a cat?' I said.

'Er, what?'

'A cat. A kitten. A tortoiseshell.'

'Oh.' He looked sheepish. 'I thought it might be nice for you. I got an old friend to deliver it. To cheer you up.'

'To *cheer me up?*'

He looked even more sheepish. 'OK, you needed more than cheering up. But I thought you always wanted a kitten.'

'Well, I did. And when it arrived, on my *birthday*, I assumed it was from you, and it proved what I always thought, which was that you didn't die. And Mum thought I was *insane*. So yes, I have a therapist.'

His jaw dropped. 'My God . . . I was trying to fool some of the sharpest brains in Europe and I couldn't even kid my own daughter.' He shook his head. 'So you didn't ever think I was dead?'

Silence.

'Yes,' I said quietly. 'I did. In that cell.'

We were passing through a sleeping village, and all the time the sun was getting higher and the sky was changing from orange and pink to blue. Behind us, we could hear the growing whine of a siren. Dad put on a small burst of speed, but the traffic was getting busier now and he kept having to slow down for passing trucks. Luckily, there was a big tourist coach a few cars behind us, and it would be almost impossible for the police car – if it was a police car – to pass on the narrow, winding road. For a while anyway.

'We'll be stopping soon,' Dad said, checking the satnav again while the muscle worked away in his jaw. 'Get ready to do whatever I tell you.'

Thanks, Dad. So enjoying this new relationship.

THIRTY-NINE

The next town was small and sleepy too. Almost everything was closed, but a few shopkeepers and café owners were starting to put up the shutters on white-walled buildings and pull down the heavy awnings to shield customers from the sun. Dad dumped the Mercedes in a side street and my satchel in an industrial rubbish bin two streets away, after I'd rescued the few things I still needed, stuffing them into the pockets of my shorts.

Dad was limping and Amina's sore back was aching, so she leant against me for support as we headed through the market square. We passed a large group of sleepy tourists waiting to board one of the big coaches, and headed into the back streets, where we found a small tobacconist's shop with a bar serving coffee to busy locals.

Dad bought us all orange juice and croissants at the bar, while Amina and I found an empty table at the back. Dad also bought a couple of things from the tobacconist part, but I couldn't see what. Was he a smoker now, too? I had thought nothing in the world would surprise me any more, but Dad with a fag in his mouth still actually would. And, excuse me, but how did he pay?

Amina and I fell on the food while he disappeared into the toilets for five minutes. When he came back, his hair was wet, quite short and much tidier. His beard was shorter too, cropped close to his face. He must have bought a razor at the bar. And he was wearing a pair of trainers and an old blue cotton jacket I'd never seen before, that smelled strongly of dog. Where had those come from? They made him look less 'wild man of the hills', and more 'rugged hippy lecturer'. Judging from the sideways glances he was getting from the two women behind the bar, it was definitely a look to go for.

He downed his coffee in one gulp. 'Right,' he said, leaning across the table. 'We don't have long. Amina, well done so far. Your brother would be so proud of you. Peta, you're in charge. Listen to me carefully.'

'*I'm* in charge? But—'

'Just listen. You're going to catch a bus to Sorrento. It's the next big town up the coast. You're two tourists, admiring the scenery. Here are your tickets.' He handed over two printed squares of paper and I stuffed them in my pocket. 'When you get there, go to the train station and buy tickets for Naples. Wait for me at Naples station, top level. It's big. Leave a message with the left-luggage people to let me know where to find you.'

'What do I say? Where do we wait?' This was too much. I wasn't ready.

Dad stayed calm. 'It depends what's safe. You'll have to work something out. You can do it, love – I've seen trained soldiers less good at improvising than you. Wait three hours, no more, then catch the next train to Rome. If I'm not there by the time it leaves, go without me. When you get to Rome, go to the British Embassy and tell them everything. You'll definitely be safe there.'

'But what if we don't find you? Where are you going? Why can't we—?'

'I can't travel with you now,' Dad said flatly. 'They'll be looking for the three of us together. Don't worry about me. But don't forget: I don't know who we can trust and who we can't round here – so don't trust *anyone*, OK? Not until you get to Rome. Promise me?'

He waited until we promised. A couple of men in dark uniforms paused at the window of the café, deep in conversation, and Dad turned away, pretending to fiddle with something in his pocket. I could feel panic rising in my chest, but after a few words together, they moved on. Dad made sure they were gone, then carried on.

'If you're followed, it'll be by a team. So don't assume that just because you lose sight of someone, they've gone. OK, what did I just say?'

This was absurd. This whole thing was absurd. But he didn't seem to be joking, so I dutifully replayed all the stuff about the bus and the train and the message and the *other* train to Rome, and the team of watching people. All the time, Amina gazed at Dad, mesmerised.

'Good,' he said. 'Oh, and you'll need this.' He took a wallet out of the pocket of his new jacket and subtly handed me a large wad of euros from it. 'For the train tickets. And food. And get yourself some sunglasses too. Big ones. And . . .'

'Where did you get that wallet, Dad?'

'For God's sake!'

'Was it from someone here? . . . Or one of those people getting on the coach? God, Dad! They were just tourists. That's *loads* of money. What are they going to do? They'll have to cancel all their cards.' This wasn't cool any more. The jacket . . . the wallet . . . the car . . . all he'd done since we escaped was give orders, lie and nick stuff.

He grunted angrily. 'Blimey!' In a whisper he continued, 'Without this money we'll all be caught in about ten minutes. This isn't a game. When did you turn into such a stroppy teenager?'

'When did you turn into a thief? And—' I wanted to go on, but I was too angry to talk. *Stroppy teenager?* After everything I'd just been through? Kidnapped, shot at, scared half to death? Between us, Karim and I had saved his bloody *life*.

Stroppy teenager?

My eyes were hot with tears. I couldn't bear it in the stuffy room, so I ran out into the street to calm down. The café door opened and Dad came running after me. He glanced cautiously up and down the empty street.

'Love, I'm sorry. We'll sort this out, but we can't do it now. You—'

'*Sort this out?* Really? You think so?' My voice was snotty and unsteady and I didn't want to talk, not here in the stupid road, but I was about to lose him again and the words couldn't stay inside any longer.

'Do you know what Mum said to me after her *wedding*, when I was choked up with the pain of missing you?'

Dad looked startled about the wedding, but said nothing.

He shook his head.

'She said you loved me, and that if there was any way you could come back to me, you'd have done it. Which meant you had to be dead. And I wondered – for the first time I really wondered if she was right, because how could you possibly leave me on purpose? How could anyone *do* that? But I kept looking for you. And then I got to the castle and I found this . . . *thing*, like a man . . . but he didn't know me, and . . . it was over. You *must* be dead.' I was shaking by now. 'So I'm sorry if I'm a stroppy teenager, but my dad has died *twice* and I've been through a lot recently and—'

'I'm sorry,' he murmured, moving in and putting his strong, thin arms around me, pressing my face to his chest. 'I'm sorry I'm sorry I'm sorry.'

Under the whiff of dog hairs from the stolen jacket, he smelled of Dad. Sweaty Dad, after an army exercise, or back from tour. He let me go and I looked into his face. He was crying. I'd only ever seen him do that once or twice and it scared me. Behind his tears, he looked genuinely sorry, and that was worse. My hero dad made mistakes. Big ones. My hero dad was an idiot and he knew it. I felt weak.

'Listen, love, I need to tell you something,' he said. 'I can't do it here. Let's go back inside.'

Amina looked up anxiously from our table. Dad went over to her.

'Stay here. But if you see any trouble, come and find us in the back.'

She watched us as we headed towards the door marked *Toilette*.

There was only one cubicle, which was already hot and smelly, even this early in the morning. I sat on the seat while Dad squeezed next to the basin. This had to be the worst place ever for a serious conversation.

He took a breath. 'Leaving you,' he said, 'was the most selfish thing I ever did. I always meant to come back, but they threw me in that . . . place and I thought I'd never see you again. When you came in . . .' He paused and his voice wobbled slightly. 'Karim had said you were in the castle and I didn't believe it, but then I heard your voice. You even hummed that song. I thought I'd explode with joy. You'd found me, and you were incredible. *Incredible.*'

He reached out. I pulled back. I'd imagined that reunion with all my heart, and he'd ruined it. I didn't want him to think I was moved by this little speech.

'All I wanted to do was hug you and never let you go,' he went on. 'But they knew about you and it was my fault. They wanted to kill you. Slowly. In front of me. To make me talk. If they'd ever found us together they would have done things . . .' He trailed off. 'I had to get you away from me as fast as I could. It was the hardest thing I've ever done. I know you don't believe me any more, but you have to believe that.'

I bit my lip. There was a knock at the door.

'Didn't you trust me to keep quiet?' I asked.

'I'd hardly seen you for two years! You were a little girl then. I didn't know what you'd do.'

'I grew up, Dad.'

The knocking grew louder. 'Men are coming,' Amina whispered fiercely.

We let her in.

'Who?' Dad asked.

She shook her head. 'Men in dark glasses . . .' She shrugged helplessly, frightened.

'Right,' Dad said, looking up at the high window above our heads. 'Peta – up you go.'

The window frame was small, but I was half starved and desperate. Dad gave me a leg-up and I squeezed through, landing clumsily in the alley outside. Amina came quickly afterwards, followed by the jacket, then, somehow, Dad.

'I trust you now,' he said to me as we caught our breath. 'We passed a supermarket on the way here. Go there fast. Get food and sunglasses. Then do as I told you.'

He stroked my cheek tenderly, then ran down the street while Amina and I walked quickly in the opposite direction. A minute later, I heard a scooter start up and zoom off. That man could steal *anything*.

FORTY

When the bus to Sorrento arrived at the market square, a large group of people was already waiting to board. There were lots of local Italian ladies with shopping bags, some German backpackers, a large French family, impeccably dressed . . . and two teenagers in sunhats and big, dark glasses, listening to music on their iPods. (We didn't actually *have* iPods, but we had the headphones, bought at the supermarket, which trailed into our pockets.) The taller, patchy-skinned girl was holding a plastic bag containing fruit, salami, bread, and a maxi-pack of wet wipes. We kind of stank, but hopefully the wet wipes would fix that.

A police car was parked up nearby. Two officers scanned the crowd, but they seemed more concerned about checking out fast cars and stopping any bearded men who passed by.

We boarded the bus and showed our tickets to the driver. From behind my sunglasses, I looked for signs of anyone who might be following Amina and me. Several of the men on the bus seemed to be watching us closely, but when three beautiful German girls got on behind us, all eyes turned to them. The men were just 'checking out the laydeez'. Ew, but good.

I found us a couple of empty seats near the back. The driver pulled into the heavy traffic now crawling slowly along the coast road. I cleaned my face and filthy hands with a wet wipe and handed the packet to Amina while I set about getting out the picnic food we'd bought at the supermarket. One croissant had hardly made a dent in my permanent hunger.

I made Amina a sandwich, but when I turned to her, she was already falling asleep again. Her head gently sank on to my shoulder and stayed there throughout the long, hot journey to Sorrento. Eventually, with nothing better to do, and two sandwiches satisfyingly in my stomach, I slept too.

At Sorrento we simply followed the crowd and copied what they did. It wasn't hard to find the train station, or work out how to buy a ticket. Even the machines spoke English.

We caught the first train to Naples: an old commuter line, stopping at every crumbling concrete station along the way, with grey plastic seats that soon stuck to our legs in the heat. Among the mix of tourists and local travellers, I counted at least six people who stared at us oddly, but all of them got off before we did.

Amina finally ate her picnic. A team of not-so-musical beggars worked their way down the train. Most people ignored them, but I saw the way Amina looked at their ragged clothes as she ate her sandwich, and I gave them some notes I'd secretly removed from my stash.

According to the very loud and chatty English family at the other end of the carriage, this railway line skirted around the edge of Mount Vesuvius. The mother was giving her children a quiz about the ancient volcano. I half listened – years ago, that would have been Dad and me – but today I was distracted. After the loneliness of the castle cellars, it was strange to be surrounded by so much life.

Amina felt it too. Now she was awake, she was sensitive to everything: the seats, the crush, the laughter, the noise. She sat very, very still. At first, I thought she was terrified of it all, but she wasn't. This was the girl who'd survived in the pitch-black belly of a boat next to a dead person; who'd lived with psycho-Max all her life; who'd kicked me out of sight without a moment's hesitation when she needed to. She was just drinking it all in.

'Mr Allud – he will meet us soon?' she asked.

'Soon. When we get to Naples,' I said.

But I looked more certain than I felt. What if I never saw Dad again? How would I explain to Mum, or anyone, that the last time we'd talked was outside a smelly toilet in a town near Amalfi? No one would ever believe me, but I suppose I was used to that.

In my head, I replayed every second of our time together, from the moment I recognised him on the shore. All of it – even the sad bits, even the arguments, and especially the smelly toilet part. It hurt, but I couldn't help going over and over the memory. He was gone again already, and it might be all I'd ever have.

*

At Naples station, we took an escalator up to where the fast trains were. After the run-down little stations of the Circumvesuviana, the huge futuristic building stretching ahead of us was a shock. Between the modern platforms and a row of shiny shops and restaurants was a vast, air-conditioned concourse, criss-crossed by armies of busy travellers. It was like we'd leapt forward a century in time.

I spotted the left-luggage place straight away, in the middle of the concourse. Amina gripped my hand. Her eyes were big circles. I pointed to a bright yellow shop-front, not far away.

'I think we need better disguises. Can you look for some clothes to buy? That shop is full of them.'

She nodded. 'I remember.'

'You do?'

'I was in a shop with Yasmin. Long ago.'

I smiled encouragingly. 'It's easy. You'll be fine. Stay there and I'll find you.'

She headed straight for the shop. Meanwhile, I checked the departure boards for trains to Rome and went to buy our tickets, so we'd have them ready. It was what Dad would do.

I was standing at the machine, picking a train time, when I smelled it. Aftershave. Strong. Like lemons. It hung in the air for a moment, then it was gone.

Very slowly, very slightly, I turned my head to look – just in time to see a tall, compact figure moving away from me through the concourse. He was wearing a baseball cap, but I knew him instantly.

Muscle Man. Here. Watching the platforms, scanning the crowd.

With my instincts newly tuned to danger I looked round and spotted another man, in mirrored sunglasses, standing very still and staring in the same direction. He could have been waiting for a passenger, of course, but something bothered me about the way he stood so impassively, how his neck bulged and how, behind the glasses, his eyes seemed to miss nothing. This man wasn't like the random passengers we'd seen at Sorrento. He wasn't waiting, he was working. Once you spotted the difference, it was obvious.

It was only by luck that they hadn't seen me yet. With my head bent low over the machine, I finished buying the tickets. I didn't try to look for any other followers. They were here. It wasn't over.

FORTY-ONE

My first thought was Amina. I had to get to her, fast. The clothes shop was small. I should have been able to see her as soon as I got inside, but there was no sign of her among the colourful racks of summer clothes. And I couldn't go back out looking for her, with Muscle Man so close.

The shop assistant looked up calmly from her magazine and saw me hyperventilating. She said something in Italian. I shrugged helplessly.

'Are you looking for your friend?' she asked, switching to English.

I nodded.

She gestured towards the back of the shop and went back to her magazine. At that moment, Amina came out of a tiny changing room near the back, wearing a long green skirt, a yellow T-shirt, a belt, two large necklaces and a floppy hat. My would-be heart attack subsided. She did a shy little twirl for me.

'So many clothes!' she murmured, her eyes glittering, enchanted. 'So many . . . I was not sure . . .'

She looked happy and strange, like a child let loose in her grandmother's dressing-up box. Bizarre, but very, very different from before, and as her brother would say, different is good.

'Gorgeous!' I said, forcing a smile. 'Let's get them.'

I marched her back towards the changing room. As soon as we were alone I put my hands on her shoulders: 'We have to be brave,' I whispered. 'They're outside, the bad men.'

She met my eyes and nodded gravely, but calmly. In fact, she took the news much better than I had. She was used to being scared, I realised, and I was still learning.

'Will you find me some clothes?' I asked. The longer we stayed here, the better. They wouldn't be looking for us in a changing room.

Amina grinned. Despite everything, she was enjoying her first shopping trip. I sank on to the chair and waited.

She came back a few minutes later, arms piled high with things for me to try. I smiled at her Yasmin-approach to clothes shopping, and her choices. Everything was bright and sparkly. The girl didn't know the meaning of camouflage.

I took my time trying things on. There was a blue tunic: terrible. And a white, tiered maxi dress that made me look like a wedding cake. Then came a multi-coloured, flowery number with flowing silky sleeves. I wouldn't be seen dead in it in England. Which made it perfect for right now.

'And this . . .'

I took a long silver scarf that Amina had brought in earlier and wound it round my matted hair. We kept our sunglasses on. Together, we looked like a fortune-teller recovering from sunburn and a thin green-and-yellow overdressed granny. We would never be more disguised than this.

Outside, the girl at the till coughed pointedly.

'Ready?' I asked.

Amina risked a grin.

'These are fabulous,' I said to the girl. 'We'll just wear them, if that's OK.'

The girl didn't seem particularly surprised at this, or the fact that I paid in cash, with large euro notes peeled off from a big wad that I kept in a plastic supermarket bag.

'Oh, and I'll take this handbag,' I said, picking the nearest one off the rail. Then I remembered about the message for Dad. 'And is that a notebook? That too.'

By now there was a woman waiting behind me at the till, who started to tut loudly and look at her watch in an obvious way. Her son, who looked about ten or eleven, kept yanking on her skirt and saying in English, 'Mum, I'm hungry. When can we get a burger, Mum?'

'Soon, sweetie,' she said in a tight voice. 'As soon as this nice lady has finished paying for *all her things*.'

That made me go slower.

When I was finally done, she flashed me a fake smile. I fake-smiled back. Beyond her, opposite the shop door, the man in mirrored shades was scanning the crowd in our direction. I put my hand on Amina's elbow.

'Wait.'

I nodded back towards fake-smile lady, who was paying

241

for a tote bag. When she headed out with her son, I whispered 'Now!' and linked my arm into Amina's. We slotted into place right behind them, like two extra children. Hopefully, if anyone noticed the lady and the three kids, all they would see was one big happy, hippy family.

Our 'mother' threw us a couple of confused stares as we walked along the concourse. I smiled cheerfully back. As I'd hoped, she was heading for the big McDonald's a few shop-fronts further down. We all went in together. I couldn't see any obvious Wahool men inside, but just in case, I stuck close to 'Mum'. When our burgers came, we followed her to a table near the window and sat with our backs to the glass. She clearly thought we were weird. I didn't care.

The left-luggage place was only a few metres behind me. I risked a glance at it through the window, but – *oh, fabulous* – the Wicked Queen was busy positioning herself right outside it, staring out towards the trains. It looked like the whole team were here.

Amina watched me from under her floppy hat. 'Are they outside?'

'Yes, but don't worry. Like your brother says, they're very stupid.'

She gave me a smile. She knew that wasn't totally true, but she was good at humouring me.

Meanwhile, Annoying Boy beside us had finished his burger and was complaining to his mother that it wasn't big enough and he wanted another one. His mother went off to join the queue again. I had an idea.

Dad had said to tell him where we were waiting. With the Wicked Queen right outside it would be madness for him to join us here, but there was a plan and I needed to follow it. Besides, I couldn't bear the idea of going all the way to the

British Embassy in Rome without him.

I took the notepaper from my new bag and a pen from my pocket – one of the few things to make it through from my original backpack – and thought about what to say. What if the Wicked Queen got hold of the note and realised who it was for? Quickly, I tried to work out a code.

In capital letters, I wrote SORRY I MISSED YOU at the top of the paper. The M had slightly rounded loops, which I hoped Dad would realise were the McDonald's arches. Then PLEASE CALL ME TOMORROW, followed by a number. The first four digits were the time of the train I'd chosen to take us to Rome, but to make them look more like a phone number I added 1015. My power, and kind of like my signature. Nobody but Dad would associate those numbers with me, and Dad wouldn't think it was anybody else.

It probably wasn't the most professional code, but it was the best I could do in the time I had, and I was quite proud of it. I added an illegible squiggle at the bottom, folded the paper over and wrote MR MERCEDES on the front, because I was running out of code ideas and if he got it, Dad would think it was funny. More rounded Ms, to make the point.

Then I called Annoying Boy over, checking his mum was still in the queue for food.

'Wha'?' he asked with a sneer.

'Want to earn some money?'

'How much?'

'Ten euros.'

'No.'

I ignored that. 'I have a message,' I said, holding up my piece of folded paper. 'I want you to deliver it to that booth over there.' I pointed through the window at the left-luggage place. 'Tell them someone will come to pick it up soon. That's

243

it. Ten euros. Easy money.'

He narrowed his eyes and looked at the paper.

'Twenty.'

'Fifteen.'

'Twenty.'

I sighed. I didn't care about the money, but he was very irritating. 'OK. Here you are.' I counted out two ten-euro notes.

He held out his hand. 'What's the message?'

I knew he'd open the paper and check anyway. I sighed. 'I'm an international spy,' I said sarcastically. 'And this is a message for my partner. OK?'

He tried to stare me down, but I'd had enough practice with Jason 'Kaboom' Ridgeway at school. Only one person was going to win this game.

'OK. OK. Whatever,' he grunted. He took the paper and money from me and wandered off to Left Luggage, almost brushing past the Wicked Queen as he went.

Moments later, his mum came back, saw his empty chair and panicked loudly. 'Kevin! Kevin!'

When he came back, she shouted at him solidly for five minutes. He took it well. Those twenty euros in his pocket seemed enough to keep him quiet.

Soon afterwards, they left. Amina and I shifted tables to the back of the restaurant and watched the left-luggage place when we dared, waiting for Dad to show up and wanting him to, and dreading it too, because if he did the Wicked Queen would surely find him first.

But although many people used the booth, there was no sign of him. I saw a station sweeper pause to unfold a piece of paper. For a moment I wondered if that was my note and

Kevin had dropped it after all, but I lost him in the crowd.

An hour ticked by. And then another. Our train was announced on the departure board. Still no Dad.

'Shall we wait longer?' Amina asked.

I shook my head. 'He said three hours. We'll have to go without him.'

She nodded sadly. She would miss 'Mr Allud', but only a fraction as much as I'd miss Dad. However, I couldn't think about that now. We had to catch that train.

A week ago, I'd have suggested we just run for the barriers and hope for the best. But that was before I met her brother. Karim didn't 'hope for the best'; he planned for it. I was playing chess with Muscle Man and his friends – a chess game where we were the pieces. I had to imagine my opponent's moves and make better ones. He would win unless I made it as difficult for him as possible. *So . . . make it difficult for him, Peta.*

One thing was certain: we could never make it from here to the platforms without being spotted. *Fine. Work with that. Remember how you felt just now when you wrote that note. Cheat these people. Come on!*

Cheesy football-coach talk to myself over, I checked the arrival and departure boards through the window and worked out, move by move, exactly what we would do. Like Karim and Dad, I made Amina repeat it to me to be sure she understood it. She did.

Five minutes before our train was due to leave, we ran, hand in hand, helter-skelter across the concourse. I didn't look to see if the Wicked Queen had seen us – of course she had. We simply ran as fast as we could for the barriers, fed our tickets through them and kept on running for platform 20, where the train for Caserta was about to depart. We were both out of breath, but we pulled each other along, fighting through the crowd who were piling into the carriages.

A third of the way down the platform, I tugged Amina's hand and we ducked behind a vending machine. We crouched low and waited. I saw a pale face and wavy hair madly searching for our flamboyant headgear, pushing people roughly aside as she wondered where we'd gone. *Yes!*

By now Amina had whipped off her floppy hat. I stuffed my silver scarf inside it and shoved it under the vending machine. We made ourselves still and small as rocks, while on the train doors banged. Officials shouted. Our trackers leapt aboard before it was too late.

Meanwhile, another train had just arrived on the next platform and started to disgorge its passengers.

'OK. Now,' I said.

Bareheaded, Amina and I casually joined the new set of arriving passengers, blending in with the crowd. As the Caserta train moved off, we retraced our steps to the ticket barriers, then, just before we got there, I yanked Amina over and we hared across to platform 15, where the train to Rome was closing its doors. They shut behind us with a whoosh of compressed air. We were the last passengers aboard.

One other man nearly made it, but missed the train by a single second. He ran like an athlete down the platform, arms pumping, until long after it was too late.

Muscle Man. He didn't look happy.

As the train moved away, I caught sight of my reflection in a glass panel near the door. I was smiling. Karim had taught me chess, and I liked it.

FORTY-TWO

Soon the conductor came round to check our tickets.

'*Ma questo è sbagliato.*'

'Sorry?'

'Your seat reservations, signorina. You reserved a different train.'

He showed me my ticket. I had absolutely made a mistake. When I bought the tickets I was so freaked out by seeing Muscle Man that I must have pressed the wrong button.

I still had so much cash from Dad I could probably have paid for new tickets on the spot, but instead it was more fun to play the confused English schoolgirl.

'But we only have these tickets and we *have* to get to Rome or we'll miss our flight! Please, mister! It goes this evening.' My eyes brimmed with tears. 'I don't know what to *do*. We have to get *home*.'

My lower lip wobbled. He let us off with a smile.

Amina grinned at me. 'You are good. Like your father.'

'And your brother. Thank you. It was easy.'

It had been. After running away from attack dogs and being shot at by armed guards, it was almost too easy. Now I *knew* I was crazy. It felt good crazy, though.

Outside, the weather was changing. Grey clouds slowly blocked out the blue sky, threatening rain. This seemed to change Amina's mood, or maybe it was just that now she felt safer, she had time to think again. Anyway, she stared glumly out of the window. I did too, trying not to think about Dad, but thinking about nothing else, remembering those last moments together and wondering what would happen when we got to the Embassy.

Halfway to Rome, I suddenly sat bolt upright.

'What is it?' Amina asked.

'Nothing.'

I'd realised that Muscle Man would have guessed where we were going, and he could have called ahead. Perhaps new followers were already waiting for us in Rome. I started to wonder if this nightmare would ever end.

As the train pulled up to the platform at Roma Termini, my heart was pumping and that buzzing was back in my ears, louder than ever. Amina and I held hands, ready to run for the first policeman we could find. But almost as soon as we stepped off the train, two powerful hands grabbed our shoulders and pulled us aside. We tried to resist, but we weren't strong enough.

'Stop fighting,' a low voice hissed.

I looked round and saw a grey raincoat and a hat. The head was down, but I recognised the voice. I stopped fighting. So did Amina.

He pulled us behind another of those vending machines.

'Hi, Dad,' I murmured.

This was getting to be a Jones family trick.

'Shh,' he said. 'Duck down. And put these on, fast.'

He pulled two dark blue packets out of his pocket. They turned out to be folded plastic rain ponchos. We scrambled into them, and he grabbed our hands and pulled us back into the flood of passengers heading off the train. By the time we reached the barriers, half the people in the station were in rain gear of some sort. We were just three covered heads, hidden in the crowd.

Dad quickly checked the departure boards.

'How did you know it would be raining?' I asked. 'Did you steal someone's smartphone in Naples?'

'Give us a break, love! They had a TV on in one of the bars.'

He led us to another platform where an express train was shortly leaving for Turin.

'So we weren't going to Rome after all?' I asked, holding tightly on to Amina's hand as we walked alongside the new train.

'Merely a stop on the route,' Dad said.

'Where to after Turin?'

'We're not going that far. Don't worry – you'll like it where we're heading.'

'And then?'

'Then home. For you, anyway, love. I'm not sure about you, little one,' he said to Amina, 'but we'll find you

249

somewhere safe.'

Amina bowed her head. I put my arm around her. 'I'm not going anywhere without you.'

'You are,' Dad insisted.

Ignoring him, I gave Amina a look that told her I wouldn't leave her.

Dad found our carriage. He was constantly scanning the station for followers, but seemed confident we'd finally lost them.

'You did a good job, love,' he said to me.

'Were you watching us all the time?'

'Most of it.'

'You got my note, then.'

He smiled. 'I did.'

'Did the station sweeper give it to—? Oh, wait. You *were* the station sweeper.' I hit my head.

He smiled. 'I liked your code.'

I did the raised-eyebrow thing. 'Oh, I'm an international spy. Didn't you know?'

As the train sped northwards, Dad spent some time in the corridor, on the phone. He *had* stolen one from somewhere – or bought it with stolen money. All decked out in my own criminal finery, I was more forgiving now.

Beside me, Amina did her usual staring out of the window as a summer storm lashed the landscape with rain. I linked my arm through hers.

'I mean it – I really won't leave you,' I said.

But the look in her eyes told me she wasn't worried for herself. She was only thinking about her brother. Trapped. And the Jongleur coming. I didn't try and say anything to comfort her, because I knew there wasn't any point.

Dad came back and settled down opposite us. He, too, was oddly quiet and glum. He didn't speak, but every now and again he winced, as if in pain. Maybe he was thinking about his broken foot. He'd travelled halfway up Italy on it already and it must be hurting like hell. I hoped he wasn't remembering 'the place where they do these things', but the look on his face made me feel that perhaps he was. Eventually he noticed me watching him. He turned to me, careworn and sad.

'So . . . er . . . Mum got married?'

Excuse me?

We were on the run from bad guys with guns, and three people were in mortal danger – and he was thinking about Mum's *love life*?

'Sorry?'

'Was it Rupert Miller?' he asked, looking uncomfortable. 'I lost touch. In the, er . . . the place. You mentioned a wedding. Is she –' *cough* – 'OK?'

Seriously?

'Yes,' I said, sticking my chin out. 'She's fine. You're dead, remember?'

He winced. 'So is he, um, looking after her?'

'Yes. Very well.'

'That's . . . I'm glad,' Dad muttered, not looking very happy. 'He's a good man.'

I stared. *He's not you!* I wanted to shout. Plus . . . *other stuff going on*, plus . . . you know . . . *already married?*

'He always liked you,' Dad went on.

'Oh yeah, right.'

'No, really,' he said. 'When you were little and we were based near Salisbury, there was a mini-assault course for the kids. You won't remember this. It was meant for ten-year-

251

olds, but when you were three you'd throw yourself over it, or under it, whatever it took to get through. You'd do it laughing. He thought you were such a cool kid. His own girls wouldn't go near it. How are they now?'

We're talking about the Darling Ds now? *So* whatever.

'They're beautiful,' I said grimly. 'Very, very beautiful. Rupert wants me to go to boarding school with them.'

'Does he? That's nice.'

What?

'Nice?' I flared up. How could Dad be so relaxed about my rubbish home life? '*Nice?* Those girls are totally perfect. They're terrifying. You don't get my life *at all*.' I glared at him furiously. I didn't want to think about home. In all the recent craziness, I'd actually forgotten how bad it was.

Dad seemed to find it funny. He leant forward, smiling, and ruffled my hair. 'You're right, my love,' he said. 'There is nothing more frightening in this world than a beautiful teenage girl.'

'You're teasing me.' I pulled away.

'I'm not. Honestly.' He laughed. 'I should know. I married one.'

It was true. I thought of his wedding pictures with Mum. The two of them laughing outside Brighton Register Office. Mum, nineteen, in her jeans and a T-shirt saying 'Kiss the Bride', looking so happy she could float.

So why wasn't Dad furious that she'd just married a different man? Why did he just look sad?

Suddenly, it was clear. It took me a while to find my voice.

'You weren't coming back, were you?'

'I was, love! I told you. I'd always come for you.'

'For Mum, I mean.'

He stared at the floor. His shoulders slumped. When he

spoke, his voice was as rough as mine.

'I love your mother more than anything or anyone, except you.'

'Then why . . .?' I tried to stop the tears from coming.

'I'm not very good with . . . families. Sitting back and settling down. I know you thought I was, but you were wrong about me, love. I was always away, on exercise, or fighting. Isabelle said I was married to the army.'

'But she didn't mind! She loved you,' I pointed out. 'You should have seen her. Every time we knew you were coming back she'd spend days getting ready. She'd have her hair done and her nails and . . . everything. And buy new dresses and pick your favourite perfume. She'd be so excited, and so would I.'

My memories of those days were still so vivid: my latest drawings stuck to the fridge for Dad to see, Mum glowing with excitement, the babysitters booked so they could have 'special time' together.

'She bought new dresses?' Dad asked.

He was trying to remember too, but I could tell that for him it was a struggle. How could he not have noticed those dresses? How could he not picture those coming-home days, like I could?

New memories crept in slowly. Different images that I'd buried somewhere. Things I'd tried to forget.

The babysitters cancelled, because Dad had invited his mates home to share stories about their adventures, while Mum sat upstairs in her new dress, unnoticed, crying.

Dad shouting, because Mum had changed our car without consulting him, and Mum saying he was never there to drive it.

Dad announcing that he was heading off early, to help

organise a training mission, or because he'd volunteered for something extra-dangerous that started soon.

Mum finishing *The Count of Monte Cristo* with me, because Dad had gone again, before we were even halfway through.

My father, the absent hero.

Rupert bought Mum new things, and always noticed if she wore them. He even married her in the church she wanted, though he knew it was full of memories of Dad.

Once again, I was back in Winchelsea. Everything seemed to come back to Winchelsea.

'You took the name Alard from the church, didn't you?' I said. 'From our church. The one we went to every Christmas. Why did you do that if you didn't care?' My voice was too cracked to go on.

Dad shook his head. 'Trust you to spot that, Peta.'

'So?' I wiped tears and snot from my nose and waited for him to explain.

He paused for a while, searching for the right words. 'I care,' he said quietly. 'I care very much. I just . . . I was made an offer I couldn't refuse. I wanted to keep you both with me somehow, while I was away, so I chose that name.' He faltered for a moment. When he spoke again, his voice was very low. I had to lean right forward to hear him properly. 'And I did something else, Peta. Something worse. I wrote your name in a notebook I was putting together at the end, in case someone had to take over from me.'

'What notebook?'

'It was a kind of instruction manual. A clue to various codes and passwords. But they found it before I could hide it properly. Of course, I shouldn't have used your name, even encrypted. I was an idiot. That's why they came after you.'

A notebook of codes and passwords . . . Why did my dad have to be so cool and so annoying at the same time? Really. Why?

'What . . . what was it for?'

'I'm sorry, I can't tell you.'

Aargh! He was *infuriating*. But it was hard to ignore the warm feeling I got when I pictured him in the castle, thinking about Winchelsea, while I'd been right there thinking about him. Actually, despite the complete mess we were in, that warm feeling seemed to seep through everything.

'Isabelle must be going mad with worry about you,' he went on, looking guiltier than ever. 'But . . .'

'What?'

'I'd be glad if you could give me just one more day before we call her. The thing is, as soon as we do, she'll want to see you – and I want to talk to you first.'

'Debrief me, you mean.'

He smiled. 'Yeah, exactly. We'll get you clean and give you some rest. Then as soon as we're ready, well call her. Deal?'

'Deal,' I agreed.

Thirty seconds later, he was fast asleep. He had a soldier's ability to grab a nap wherever he could. Another thing that used to drive Mum crazy. He looked as if he didn't have a care in the world.

Amina turned and stared at me. I thought she'd been lost in thought about her brother, but apparently not.

'You are worried about going to school?'

Oh God, the boarding school. 'Yeah. Kind of. School's OK. It's just the girls that worry me.'

'Why?'

'They're pretty scary. It's hard to explain.'

She looked confused. 'You are not scared by guns, but you

are scared by girls?'

I shook my head. 'I'm scared by guns *and* girls,' I corrected her. 'I'm actually a pretty scared person.'

She grinned, a wide smile that came from nowhere and took me straight back to her brother in his cellar room.

'You are very funny, Peta Jones.'

FORTY-THREE

As soon as they announced Florence as the next stop, Dad woke up, like someone switching on a light. We got off the train and were met by two fit ex-soldier types who reminded me of the watchers at Naples station, except they were Dad's friends and greeted him like a brother, and Amina and me like two long-lost princesses. They seemed to create an invisible safety bubble as they shepherded us carefully through the throng.

'Anyone here?' Dad asked the shorter, tougher-looking of the two, whom he introduced as François.

'No sign so far,' François said. 'But let's get you out of here anyway.'

Outside, a driver was waiting for us in a luxury car with the engine running. He moved off as soon as we got inside. By now the storm had passed and the evening sky was a muddy blue. The driver had Italian pop music playing quietly on the radio. We drove slowly through narrow streets, where shops and restaurants flooded the road with light and the pavements were full of people happily strolling. It was another world.

Beside the river, tourists crowded over an old bridge that seemed to be covered in houses. 'The Ponte Vecchio,' Dad explained from the front seat, pronouncing it *Pont-eh Veck-i-oh*, in his new-found Italian accent. 'It's famous. Those buildings on it are mostly jewellery shops. They were used as secret passages across the Arno River during the war.'

I smiled to myself. Dad was always great with his research, but between the Smugglers' Inn and the castle, I was probably the expert on secret passages now.

The city itself was like a living jewellery box, where every building, church and square looked like a work of art. As we drove beside a massive stone palace, François (a short French version of Dad, I was beginning to realise) told us that Michelangelo had worked for the Medici family here. He reeled off a list of famous local artists' names and I nodded sleepily from the back, next to Amina. I was just glad the place didn't seem to be full of people who wanted to kill me.

After a few more minutes, the built-up streets of the city gave way to a tree-lined road, bordered by larger houses and scraps of countryside. We drove on, passing fields and olive groves, until the driver took a sudden left turn up a hill, and stopped a few metres further along, in front of a pair of elegant wrought-iron gates. A gold plaque beside them said *Colombo*

Foundation in subtle black letters, just big enough to read. So this was it: Dad's secret headquarters. Dad explained that *colombo* was the Italian for *dove* — the dove of peace. I'd never experienced a less peaceful time than the last two weeks, but whatever. It had a nice logo of a bird anyway.

The gates opened as if by magic and we continued up a winding drive flanked by rows of tall, thin cypress trees. Amina gripped my arm as we rounded the last bend, and there, lit up against the darkness, was a long white villa. It was two storeys high, with square windows flanked by dark green shutters and a shallow, tiled roof. The front door was already open and a tall man stood framed against the light of the hallway.

As we got out of the car, he came forward to greet us. He was barefoot, I noticed, but wearing a loose silk shirt and a green embroidered jacket. He held his arms out wide.

'Welcome! Welcome, both of you!' His voice was soft and his accent was American. 'And welcome back, Mike. It's been too long.'

'Hi, Henry. This is Henry Phillips,' Dad said. 'Our host.'

He had a young-looking face, softened by a stylish, stubbly beard. His eyes were pale blue, framed with long lashes, and when he looked at you it was hard to look away.

'You must be Peta. It's good to meet you,' he said, holding out his hand to me.

I shook it, stony-faced. He seemed very charming, but this must be the man who'd persuaded Dad to go to Baghdad, fake getting blown up, and then head for the castle, where I very nearly never saw him again. If my eyes said *You stole my father*, I wasn't going to try and stop them.

Amina, of course, was perfectly polite. Dad's glance at me said *Why can't you be more like your friend Amina?* My

glance back said *You wish*. He hadn't been in that churchyard.
I had.

Inside, the villa was stuffed with silk rugs and antique furniture. Whatever else the American was, he was very, very rich. Modern paintings and sculptures provided flashes of colour against pale pastel walls. Every room looked good enough to feature on the cover of a magazine. It was impressive – some of it even looked comfortable – but it didn't make me feel relaxed. Money made me nervous now. I'd seen what people would do for it – including, it seemed, my own father – and people who had a lot of it made my skin crawl these days.

The American showed us to a small room where a round table was set for two, lit by flickering candles in silver candlesticks.

'You must be hungry. Maria will look after you both. Please excuse us for a while.'

A friendly-looking housekeeper arrived and offered us all sorts of food, but after a simple bowl of pasta our shrunken stomachs couldn't handle any more. Disappointed, she went off to the kitchen to see if she could find something sweet to tempt us with.

Meanwhile, Dad had disappeared with his mates from the Foundation. They'd arrived, one by one, at the door of our little dining room, to introduce themselves while we ate, before heading off to join the gang. There seemed to be about a dozen of them: men and women, all different shapes and sizes, from the lean, fit soldier-types to the soft, shy boffins. Some were English, some French and Italian, and the rest I wasn't sure, but all of them – each and every one – reminded me of Dad's best friends from his army days. They had a certain glint in their eyes, and you could just tell they were up for danger. They seemed friendly enough, but kept saying that we must be tired, and they wanted to leave us in peace.

They didn't want to leave Dad in peace, though: they wanted to hear his adventures, and I could just about make out their voices from a distant room. This was how it must have been for Mum, I realised. You think you've got him back, but you haven't: he's sharing his war stories with people he's closer to than you.

Back in the dining room, Maria, the housekeeper, persuaded Amina and me to try some home-made strawberry ice cream, which was, to be honest, the most delicious thing I'd tasted in my life. 'And now, your bedrooms,' she said. 'You're sleepy, I bet. Let me show you where to go.'

She took us upstairs. My room was white, with a carved wooden bedhead and painted furniture. Next door was a white tiled bathroom, which I shared with Amina. Her bedroom was similar to mine, but decorated in blue.

After inspecting the shop fresh summer clothes that had been laid out for me to choose from in the morning, I found Amina sitting in the corner of her bedroom, arms clasped round her knees, rocking. I knew that feeling from the boat, and it wasn't a good one. A part of her was still stuck in that tunnel, screaming for her brother, and no amount of pasta, ice cream and candlelight was going to make it better.

'Go to bed, Amina,' I said gently.

She looked over at the king-size bed and shook her head.

'Then come with me.'

I put her in my bed and curled up next to her to keep her company. Having sworn she couldn't use the pillows and soft white duvet, she was asleep before I'd even turned out the light.

I sat up next to her for a while, flipping through a guide-book that had thoughtfully been placed on my bedside table. I could see why Dad liked it here. Florence was perfect Dad country – full of history and adventure. Through the open window, I could hear the strains of laughter from downstairs. His voice was one of them. He *was* home, I realised: back with his friends, where he belonged.

FORTY-FOUR

In the morning, the house was quiet. The space beside me was already empty. So was the other bedroom. I went to the window and saw Amina down in the garden, staring up at a distant olive grove in the hazy morning light, as if staring far enough could bring her brother back to her. I decided to go and keep her company.

Among the smart summer clothes laid out for me to try, someone had thoughtfully added some soft sweatpants and a comfy T-shirt. I put these on and wandered downstairs. It took a while to find a room with an unlocked door to the garden. As I was about to step outside I heard a gentle cough behind me.

Henry Phillips was standing there, dressed this morning in a floor-length blue robe that brought out the colour of his eyes. They reminded me a little of Parissa's eyes, but hers had been sapphires, whereas his were more pale turquoise.

'Good morning,' he said.

'Hi.'

'Would you like to see the grounds?'

'Don't worry – I'm fine.'

'Perhaps I can show you my sculpture garden.'

The man couldn't take a hint. I sighed, but I didn't seem to have much choice. He led me down a series of paths to an area enclosed by tall hedges, where abstract sculptures sat among rills of running water and low, dense bushes carved into geometric shapes. *Karim would have loved it here*, I thought bitterly.

'I guess I should apologise to you,' the American said.

'For what?'

'For what happened to your father.'

'Oh. OK.' *That* was a surprise.

He sighed. 'I'm sorry. I really am. But I must tell you, Mike Jones is the very best at what he does. I wouldn't have asked for him if he wasn't. He's the only man that could have taken on this job with the Wahools. Did he tell you what he was trying to do?'

'No he didn't. Dad likes to keep his secrets.' I didn't try and hide how I felt about this.

'I think he was just trying to keep you alive,' the American said with half a smile. 'You see, according to what he told me last night, his cover was blown at the castle.'

'I know. There was a man who recognised him from his army days.'

'Correct. Even so, Mike had almost managed to convince

264

them that he was still Wahool's loyal servant. He said he'd faked his death in Iraq so he could work for people like Wahool and earn some decent cash. Wahool's the kind of man who'll believe that people will do anything for money. But this man Johnson – do you know him?'

I nodded. 'I've seen him. Yes.'

'He found out about you. He decided to pull you in and use you to get the truth out of Mike, once and for all. If they'd caught you yesterday and thought you knew anything about his real mission, they'd have killed you. No question.'

I listened to the sound of water trickling through the rills by our feet, and doves cooing in the distance somewhere. Perhaps Dad didn't keep his secrets purely to be annoying, although it felt that way sometimes.

'You said Dad's "real mission",' I said eventually. 'So he *was* a spy, then?'

'I prefer to think of him as a campaigner for justice,' the American said. 'But they would have called it spying. You see, he's uniquely talented, your father. An elite soldier and also a great IT man. That's exactly what I needed. I heard about him, found him in Afghanistan and told him I was trying to help six million people. I asked him to join me, and he agreed.'

'Six million people. That's not the population of Afghanistan?'

'No.'

'Marvalia, then?'

'Clever girl.'

'You didn't organise the Blue Revolution, did you?'

'Oh no!' he laughed. 'They did that by themselves. I don't do revolutions – I mostly do money.'

Money. That word again. No amount of money was worth what Dad had suffered in those dungeons, or what I'd gone through, missing him.

The American waited for me to ask him what he meant. When I didn't, he carried on anyway. 'Yeah, well . . . money. You've probably noticed that some people have far too much of it, and millions don't have enough. When Wahool and the ex-president went into exile, they smuggled billions of stolen dollars out of the country, some of it in gold, some of it in secret bank accounts. They were living the billionaire lifestyle, while back in Marvalia the people had no money for food, or farms, or even machinery to work the copper mines. That made me angry. I was working with the new government to try and get some of the money back. Then I discovered we had a bigger problem.'

He waited for me again. This time I couldn't help myself.

'Which was?'

'Wahool was using a chunk of the stolen money to plot a coup, so the Grandfather could go back to Marvalia and take over again. If he did that, it was game over.'

'Oh! So *that's* what Mr Wahool wanted the guns and missiles for.'

'You know about the arms deal?'

'Uh-huh. I heard him talk about it.'

Henry Phillips looked astonished. I had his full attention. 'Is it happening soon?'

'I think so. It sounded that way. The dealer was at the castle.'

'You're a fascinating person, Peta. We need to talk some more.'

'And . . . Dad?'

He considered for a moment, obviously wondering exactly how much to tell me. Then he seemed to decide that I knew a lot already. Besides, we were safe now.

'We could have just alerted the authorities about the coup, of course, but we had a better idea,' he said. 'Mike was posing as an IT security expert so he could monitor the bank accounts Wahool was setting up to fund it. He was supposed to intercept the money online, before the arms deal took place. That way, we could stop the coup *and* give the Marvalians some of their money back. It was always a danger-ous mission, working at the heart of Wahool's household. That's why I needed someone with Mike's survival skills too, in case there was a problem. And, of course, there was.'

His sigh was brisk, but heartfelt. He obviously felt very bad about what had happened to Dad. As he should.

'How much?' I asked.

'Excuse me?'

'How much money was Dad trying to intercept?'

'Oh, I see. Two hundred million dollars. That's what Wahool had set aside for the coup. But the Grandfather and his cronies had stolen at least ten times that. The Marvalians could have used the coup money to find the rest. '

Two hundred million times ten was . . . twenty billion dollars. *More money than you can imagine.*

So Dad hadn't changed. He still saved the world every day. Or at least he tried.

'Peta?'

'Sorry, Mr Phillips. I was distracted.'

'Anyway, that's what I wanted to tell you. You've earned the truth, Peta. I don't believe in secrets between friends. But I've kept you too long. Come and let me feed you up. And call me Henry.'

He led me back inside, through a suite of rooms hung with wall-sized paintings. The all-out luxury everywhere still bothered me.

'How did you get all this?' I asked, indicating the art and antique furniture.

He smiled. 'You're very direct.'

'I s'pose.'

'I inherited some of it,' he shrugged, 'and I made some money on the markets. I created a little company that made computer games . . .' He named it – it was a super-famous internet giant. Luke was addicted to their games. 'And that did OK, so I created another one.' Same story, except the second company was bigger. 'Money's a burden, Peta. If you're not careful, it owns you. In Florence, it owned the Medicis. Half of them ended up murdered, or mad. I want to make my money work. Some people give theirs to charity but I'm . . . I get bored easily. This is what I do.'

At first I thought he meant the villa, then I realised he meant the Foundation.

'It sounds interesting, but not exactly . . .' I searched for the right word '. . . legal.'

He nodded thoughtfully. I noticed he didn't disagree.

'Legal usually takes time,' he said carefully. 'If we only did what's strictly legal, Marvalia would stay poor for decades. I shouldn't be telling you this. All I can say is, I try to be ethical, and I know that's a different thing. I'm not asking you to join us – I just want you to understand.'

I thought about it. He'd persuaded Dad to balance my happiness against the lives of six million people. For six people, I'd have been pretty hacked off at losing him, but for six *million* . . . In a weird kind of way, I was proud to have been a part of it. And anyway, I had Dad back.

He'd said that if I knew what he was doing, I'd understand. Perhaps I did.

FORTY-FIVE

We'd reached a large, airy kitchen with a wall of windows overlooking the gardens. There was a big but homely cooking area at one end and a long trestle table at the other, where some of the people from the Foundation were starting to gather. Not a chef was in sight: in this house, people made their own breakfast.

There was lots of banter, teasing and good-natured swearing as the early birds grabbed food and chose somewhere to sit. But all of that stopped when Henry and I walked inside.

'How are you doing, Peta?' a woman with tattoos from shoulder to wrist asked me politely. 'Can I get you something?'

'No, I can do it,' I said.

There was no sign of Dad yet. I hoped he was still catching up on sleep. Meanwhile, I set about choosing the biggest, fattest yellowy-golden croissant from a pile on a nearby counter, and pouring myself a big tumbler of orange juice. As I sat down, I waited for the conversation to return to its original energy level, but that didn't happen; they chatted in muted voices now. My presence seemed to put them off, and that hurt.

'I've been telling Peta about Mike's mission,' Henry said, making himself an espresso from a high-tech coffee machine. 'I thought she should know.'

Again, I expected them to relax, knowing I was in on the secret. But again, I was disappointed. Instead, there were lots of surprised faces around the table, and a couple of furrowed brows. This was so annoying! I'd personally been shot at on that mission, which is more than any of them had. I at least deserved to know what it was.

'Not exactly our biggest success,' Henry went on. 'But at least we learnt lessons.'

'You got him out alive, boss,' François said.

Er, *hello*?

Henry came to sit next to me.

'We need to talk,' the bald-headed man on my other side muttered to him, leaning across me to get his attention. 'About the intel Mike gave us last night. Those other prisoners . . . Shall we go outside?'

Henry turned to me. 'You don't mind if we talk here, do you, Peta? I need this coffee.' I shook my head, scattering croissant crumbs. 'Go on, Steve.'

The bald-headed man looked uncomfortable. 'Er, right. OK. So if Wahool's really planning to kill them the day of the coup—'

'*WHAT?*'

Steve glared at me. I shut up.

'—we need to get them out fast. He'll want to use them as battle trophies. It'll be messy.'

Henry nodded, considering the problem. I was thinking, *What are battle trophies?* It sounded nasty, but I didn't say anything. Steve disliked me enough already.

'I've been wondering about a rescue,' Henry said. 'I'd love to do it, but we don't have the manpower. We're set up for covert ops, not snatches.'

'We could do it,' François insisted from the other end of the table. 'Just. There's a blind spot on the island, up the cliffs. We know exactly where to locate the prisoners. Only two guards outside the cells. In and out. Fast and clean.'

The others agreed. They were all obviously up for the job, glad to do something to save the mission from being a failure. Quickly, the idea became a plan. This was fantastic!

'There's another boy there,' I said excitedly. 'Karim. Amina's brother. He got us out, but he stayed behind to try and protect Sammy and Parissa. You've got to get him too.'

'Mike told us about him last night,' Steve said. He turned to me with an unexpectedly kind, pitying expression that made me nervous. 'Look, I'm really sorry, sweets, but this has to be a lightning-fast operation. Otherwise we'll get into a firefight, and that won't be pretty for anyone.' He put a hand on my shoulder. 'We can only rescue people we know how to find, and according to Mike, that boy could be anywhere. I know he was kind of your friend, and Mike's too, but—'

'He was more than our friend! He saved our lives!'

Steve sighed. 'We'll do what we can, OK? But I have to be realistic. And we need to get planning.' He patted me on the shoulder. 'You've been through a lot, kid. I know Mike wants to talk to you about what happened at the castle and on the yacht and everything. Why don't you go upstairs and have a bit of a rest till he comes down? And don't worry – everything's under control.'

I looked down at my shoulder, where he'd *patted me*. It was like Sergeant McCrae telling me to rustle up sandwiches all over again.

They were going to the castle, but they weren't going to find Karim. They weren't even going to try.

Everything so absolutely wasn't under control.

I went to find Dad. I didn't even know where his room was, until I found Maria, the housekeeper, to ask her. She explained that Dad was with the nurse in the medical suite. Because naturally, this villa had a medical suite. I mean, don't they all?

She showed me to a little pavilion next to the main house, where Dad was sitting on what looked like a massage table, having his foot strapped up by a smart-looking woman in a shirt and suit skirt.

'Hello, love,' he said, beaming at me. 'Having a good day?'

His hair was now beautifully cut and his skin was shaved. He looked rested and slightly more like himself, but he sat stiffly on the table and winced when he moved. I could just make out a swathe of tight bandages under his T-shirt, and more around his arm and foot.

'No.'

I didn't want to make things worse for him, given how much pain he was obviously in, but the business with the rescue was too important. I told him about the job the team were planning, and what they'd said about Karim. He nodded and winced. Even nodding hurt.

'I'm sorry, love. Steve's right. You know I like Karim as

much as you do. The boy's fantastic. But he's not in danger like the others are, and the team can't get him out if they can't find him, and I can't tell them where to look.'

'I could tell them where to try.'

'Sure,' he said absently. 'You do that, love.'

I knew my dad so well, and the way he said 'You do that, love,' meant *You do the thing that we know won't work, and we'll listen politely and then get on with the real stuff.* I thought he'd be the answer, but he was just as bad as Steve.

'Va bene così?' The nurse straightened up and got Dad to see if he could walk on his strapped foot. Every step was obviously painful, but Dad pretended it wasn't. He nodded vigorously.

'Fantastico, Allegra! Grazie.' He looked at me. 'Are the others still in the kitchen?'

'Yes. Shall we—?'

'Great. I'll join them. See you later, OK?'

I let it get to me. Maybe I shouldn't have, but I did. I sulked around in the gardens for half an hour, furious and frustrated, with Dad as much as anyone. Eventually, though, I went back to the kitchen too, because it was the only room with any life, and this time the noise level didn't drop when I walked in, because they ignored me completely. Dad gave me his polite *Hi, but not now, love* face. I'd forgotten he even had that face.

I listened while they discussed explosives, crampons and the castle layout. Maria arrived and started making soup for lunch. Amina came in too and offered to help her, glad of something to do. Maria got her stirring a pan of sizzling onions. Assuming I felt the same about helping out, she gave me two bowls of water, one scalding hot and one cold, and showed me how to peel tomatoes at the counter: scoring them

273

with a sharp knife and plunging them into hot water, then cold. It was about as much fun as it sounds. All the time, the Colombo team sat around drinking coffee and making plans.

'So how close did you get?' one of the guys asked Dad, during a quieter moment.

'To the money?'

'Yeah.'

'Close,' Dad sighed. 'I got into the accounts, but most of the cash won't be there until just before the deal. It was a waiting game.'

'Ha. You wouldn't have had to wait long,' Steve chipped in. 'The boss heard the deal was close to happening.'

Oh yeah, I thought. *That would be because I told him.*

Dad groaned. 'If I'd managed to hand over to you, François, and if we just knew where the Grandfather was, we could've . . . Damn!' He thumped the table in frustration.

'What about the Grandfather?' I asked, looking up from my half-peeled tomatoes.

Dad glanced round, surprised. I think he'd forgotten I was there.

'It's just that they won't do the deal without him. When he gets together with Wahool, that's when it'll happen. But he dropped off the radar weeks ago. About ten agencies are searching for him.'

'Oh, right.' I went back to peeling my tomatoes. 'That's tricky.' They went back to their conversation. 'By the way,' I added, 'I know when they're meeting. And where. It's happening in five days. If that helps.'

Major swear word.

Steve had tipped hot coffee all over himself. Everyone was staring at me.

I forced myself not to smile.

FORTY-SIX

What happened next was very satisfying. Everyone clustered round. They took the tomatoes away from me, sat me down at the table and took turns to ask me questions while I explained about being on the yacht, and hearing about Yasmin's birthday party, and how the Grandfather was on his way.

'We'd heard rumours,' François admitted.

'But he's supposed to be in the Caribbean,' said Elena, the girl with the tattoos.

'Or doing a deal in Moscow,' added a boffin-type called Syed from across the table.

'Wahool's security people confirmed it,' I insisted. 'He's

bringing his big yacht. And besides, Mr Wahool told Yasmin about this visit when he thought no one else was listening. I don't think he'd lie to her for no reason.'

Across the table, François spoke up. 'Yes, it makes sense. The Grandfather was always fond of Yasmin. They say she was like the daughter he never had. And imagine: a big party, a castle full of important guests. Wahool could invite all his cronies and nobody would notice. It's the perfect cover to finalise the coup.'

They thought about it. The more they thought about it, the more they agreed. The more they agreed, the more impressed they were with my eavesdropping skills. They were even more impressed when I went upstairs and got the torn and dirty invitation from the last of my belongings, to prove the date of the party. Steve didn't look remotely tempted to call me 'sweets', or pat me, or tell me to 'go and have a rest'.

Then a bad thing happened.

Dad said, 'It's not too late. We can combine operations and I can finish this. It's my set-up. I know the systems. I'm going back in.'

No. No! NO. This was *not* what I had in mind.

For months, Dad had been a prisoner. They were bringing someone in specifically to torture him and I'd only just got him out of there. (*Karim* and I had only just got him out of there.) He was finally safe and he was NOT going back. No way. No way ever. Not Dad.

'But you said . . . Couldn't François do it?'

I looked across to the Frenchman. I didn't want *anyone* going inside the castle unless they absolutely had to, but surely François was better than Dad?

'I never did hand over,' Dad said dismissively. 'François

hasn't seen the layout, doesn't know the systems. If this gets done, it has to be done fast. By me.'

Henry Phillips walked in two minutes later, looking exasperated, with Steve hot on his tail. Steve must have told him about the whole stupid idea.

'Mike – we need to talk,' Henry said.

Dad stared at him levelly. 'You're right. We do.'

'I know you want to finish the job, but come on. You're Wahool's Most Wanted. Everyone in the place will be looking for you.'

Keep it up, Henry. Liking your angle so far.

'They won't,' Dad said, sticking his chin out. 'They'll think exactly what you think – that I'd never go back. All I need is thirty minutes with Wahool's laptop. I know exactly where to find it . . .'

'Thirty minutes? That's a lifetime. Who's going to give you thirty minutes?'

'At a party? Everyone. They'll all be busy saying happy birthday to Yasmin and watching the fireworks. You know it makes sense, Henry. I worked on that banking program for months. I installed the virus, I know how to activate it. If anything goes wrong, I'm the only one who can fix it.'

The trouble was, when Dad looked at you a certain way, it was hard to resist. He was super-confident and totally convincing. Around the table, I sensed the others starting to waver.

But not the boss, thank goodness. 'Can we step outside, please?' he asked.

'Sure,' Dad said.

They went out into the garden and everyone left them to it. Everyone except me. I took my bowls of tomatoes to a spot near the open window and listened as hard as I could.

'You can't do it, Mike,' Henry insisted in a lowered voice.

'The virus is installed. All I need is—'

'I don't mean the IT. I mean, look at you. You're a wreck. We're talking swimming in, scaling a cliff-face, taking on the guards. Even at peak fitness it's hardly a walk in the park, but you're held together with tape right now.'

'I'm fine,' Dad insisted. 'I got out of there, didn't I? I got the girls out.'

With help, I shouted in my head. *With a little bit of help, Dad.*

'You need time to heal . . .'

'I don't have it. Trust me, Henry, this is our only chance.'

'And even if you go, I don't have the people to support you. We'll be at our limit as it is, getting the prisoners out. You'd be on your own in there.'

They wandered off towards the olive grove, too far for me to hear any more. But by the time they came back, Dad had worked his magic. Even Henry was on board. Dad was part of the operation again.

Now the kitchen was full of *Way to go, Mike*s and high-fiving. What had happened to being held together with tape, or 'Wahool's Most Wanted'? Only I still thought of his bandages and broken toes. Only I had seen Karim's face when he talked about 'the room where they do these things'. The whole idea was insane.

'You can't do this!' I shouted.

'Look, Peta,' Dad snapped at me, losing it completely. He was as angry as I'd ever seen him. 'If I don't stop the deal, the coup goes ahead. Maybe we save Sammy and Parissa, but six million Marvalians get the Grandfather back, and – think about it – he'll take his revenge. He'll put the Jongleur in charge. Do you really want that to happen? *Do* you? And even if we somehow stop the coup, the people will still starve. Everything they had has been taken from them. In thirty minutes, I could change that.'

So basically, I was back where I'd started. To save my dad, I'd have to sacrifice the lives of six million people. Or to try and save them, I'd have to sacrifice my dad. Whatever happened, it was my fault.

I stood there shaking for a moment, too overwhelmed to think straight. In the silence that followed, François coughed uncomfortably. He knew who would win this fight, and so did I. As usual, I had tried to do something good, and ended up making everything worse.

FORTY-SEVEN

I'd noticed Amina running out of the room, looking almost as upset as I was. Twenty minutes of searching later, I found her in a coat cupboard, with the door half open, sitting among the boots and sandals that littered the floor. She seemed to need its familiar smallness and semi-darkness. I joined her there.

'Mr Allud, your father . . . he will be all right?' she asked.

'Of course he will,' I lied.

'And when they go, they will rescue my brother?'

She must have missed the earlier discussion, where they'd categorically said they wouldn't do that. 'I think so,' I said, putting my arm around her. Lie after lie.

She pressed into me, fighting tears. 'They must get Karim too. Promise me they will find him.'

I paused for a guilty beat. 'I promise,' I said.

I felt too bad to stay with her much longer, with the air so stuffy with hopeless lies. So I left her in her cubby-hole and went back to my room, where I stood at the window, staring out blindly.

Dad was crazy, but at least he was trained. At least he'd *chosen* his suicidal mission. Karim was trapped. Only I could ever find him in that maze of tunnels, and he needed me, and if I didn't help him nobody would.

Outside the window, a dove cooed. Then another, and another. That sound was so *not* peaceful when you listened to it long enough. Stupid doves. Stupid cooing.

That broke my mood. God, I was so uptight that even doves annoyed me! It made me laugh out loud and somehow, a weight was lifted from my chest.

The problem was suddenly crystal clear: Karim needed me. Not Dad, or Steve, but *me*. So I must go back and help him. If Dad could do it, then so could I. At least Wahool's people didn't really know what I looked like. And if I went back, then maybe I could help Dad too.

How? I had no idea. I wasn't Tom Cruise in *Mission Impossible*. I couldn't scale cliffs at night – not with less than a week's training, anyway – or take on guards, or blast through solid walls. But I'd survived on the *Princess Nazia* and escaped from Naples station. I'd got into the castle, and out of it again. And, unlike Dad, I hadn't got caught.

I needed a plan: a good plan – better than the one Dad and his mates were making downstairs. Plans were the only thing these people listened to. I calmed my breathing and started to think properly. Once more, I pictured the chess game. I was learning that you didn't win by getting angry and rushing into things: you won by thinking them through.

So do it, Peta. Make a plan.

On the table next to me were the remains of my possessions from the backpack. They included the spare pills, the torch and my old phone – fully charged now, because that's the way they did things round here.

I remembered the first time I heard Karim's voice on the line. And gradually, like solving an equation, the answers came one after the other.

One: how to get into the castle.

Two: how to smuggle Dad past the guards.

Three: how to find Karim and get him out of there.

I paced around for ages, thinking through all the possibilities, examining them from every angle. The more I examined them, the better they looked.

I practised my lines in front of the mirror, doing my best Darling D impression. Then I went over to the bedside table and searched the guidebook for Florence's most glamorous hotels. When I was ready, I picked up the phone, turned it on and unlocked it.

Do not call me on this number, Karim had said, as if his life depended on it.

I dialled the number.

It took a few rings. Then a sultry drawl came on the line.

'Omar. Uh-huh?'

'Is that Omar Wahool?' I tried to sound sophisticated and posh.

'Yeah, Omar. Uh-huh?

'Oh, cool. This is Ella. From Cannes. You probably don't remember me.'

'Er, no.'

'There was a party in June? You gave me your number, but I took it down wrong. I've been trying to call you for ages.'

'Oh! The chick from Cannes! Nice to hear from you, er . . . Ella. Is that what you said? How are you, sweet thing?'

'I'm great. How's Yasmin?'

'She's fine. You know my sister?'

'Yeah. We go way back. She's having her party soon, right?'

'Uh-huh.'

I made happy-sounding, non-committal noises. I let the silence play. I let Omar's flirtatious mind work out things for itself. *Chick, party; chick, party; chick, party . . .*

'Hey, you coming to that?' he asked at last.

'Well, no. I'm in Florence, but I'm supposed to go to New York that day. And I never got my invite . . .'

We chatted. Omar was in a good mood, as usual. There was the sound of squeals and splashing in the background. He was either by the castle pool or, more likely, showing off the *Princess Nazia* to some new friends. This was a bit like fishing, I decided. Grandad had taken me down to the river a few times, but we'd never had much luck. This was like reeling in a big, juicy, flirty fish.

After a few minutes, I rang off. I let the conversation play over in my head for a moment before heading back down to the kitchen, where Steve, Dad and a few others were huddled in a group, over a large-scale map of the island.

Dad glanced up.

'Not now, love. We're a bit busy.'

'Sure,' I said. 'I just wanted to see if you were OK. Oh, and to let you know that I've been invited to Yasmin's party. We'll be ferried out from Positano. My invitation's on its way.

You can be my bag carrier, if you like.'
  I turned on my heel and walked out.
  TAKE THAT, COLOMBO DUDES!

FORTY-EIGHT

That wasn't the end of the story They spent hours trying to talk me out of it. Literally, hours.

All through supper, they came up with reasons why I couldn't go. Dad was the worst. He kept going on about the danger, and the risk, and my lack of training, and the risk, and the danger . . . He really was incredibly pig-headed. And hypocritical too. I had to keep pointing out that *his* plan was more dangerous, more risky. This way, he could just walk into the castle two steps behind a party guest. It wouldn't matter quite so much that he was held together with tape, or that he was a wanted man. As my bag carrier, nobody would be paying him much attention. I'd learnt that much about servants recently. And as for my lack of training . . . I'd had a crash course in survival over the last couple of weeks. Plus, I was a *teenage girl*. Like, who was going to suspect me of anything?

'You're being ridiculous,' Dad said.

'*You're* being ridiculous,' I snapped back. 'Two years I lived without you, after you went to Iraq. TWO YEARS. And for half of that I had to visit your *grave*. You owe me.'

Steve laughed at the end of the table. 'She has a point, Mike. You do owe her.'

Guilt and anger fought on Dad's face. 'I'm sorry,' he said. 'But this is too much.'

'No it's not. If I don't go, Karim will die. I have to go.'

Dad looked at me, and for the first time since we emerged from that tunnel, he really saw me. He saw *me*, not just a taller version of the girl he thought he knew.

'I know what I'm taking on,' I said quietly. 'I've been there, remember?'

Dad looked craggier and guiltier than ever. Beside him, it was Henry's turn to laugh. 'Who does she remind me of?'

'Shut up, Henry,' Dad grumbled. 'You're not helping.'

'It won't be climbing up a cliff-face,' I pressed. 'I'll be a guest at a party. They don't know my face – I'm just a girl. I'll find Karim and we can hide in the tunnels till you're ready to get us out.'

The look in Dad's eye said that as an operative, he thought this could work. But as my father, *no way*.

'Look, love – it's not just me. There's your mother. It's bad enough that I haven't let you call her yet. But at least I can keep you safe.'

'I don't *want* to be safe!'

'Think of her, Peta. If you could see her now . . . She's in

286

pieces.'

'I don't care! She's got Rupert to look after her.'

Dad looked grim. 'There's something you need to see.'

So they showed me.

Dad took me to a small, plush sitting room, where a large TV was set into the wall. Henry came too, and sat on a chair next to me. Dad turned the TV on and inserted a disc into a slot below it, before joining us. The screen went blue. Eventually, an image came up of a news conference. Two people sitting either side of a policeman, behind a bank of microphones. Grandad and Mum. The camera zoomed in on Mum's face. She was super-pale, holding back the tears. She looked as though she hadn't slept for days.

'I have a short statement,' she said. 'If you are watching this, Peta darling, I want you to know that you are not in any trouble. Please come home. Everyone is missing you very much.' She could hardly say those last two words because her voice was breaking, but she composed herself and carried on. 'And if someone knows where she is, please call the police, in confidence. I need my daughter back.'

She didn't break down exactly, but she couldn't carry on either. The police officer gave a phone number that people could call. All the time, Mum stared, red-eyed, straight into the camera.

'Do you see now, my love?' Dad said. 'You can't do this to her.'

How *could* I do this to her?

I'd seen her reaction when she got the news about Dad and the bomb, and that was bad enough. I was her only child. When she wasn't busy marrying her new husband, we were close.

Mum . . . I missed her so much. I missed her smell, her hair, the way her face lit up when we hugged . . . I missed her telling me off for leaving my blazer on the floor *every day*, and lying on my bed with her shoes off, talking about growing up and how to survive super-embarrassing social situations. I wanted her back easily as much as she wanted me.

But if Mr Wahool ever found out that Karim had helped Dad, or if Karim ever did some other brave and risky thing – which, being Karim, he would – then the Jongleur would take him 'the room where they do these things'. That was the baddest 'bad thing' I could imagine.

Mum had Rupert, and Granny and Grandpa. Karim only had me.

My voice, when it came, was a whisper.

'If she knew what I was doing, she'd understand.'

Dad recognised the quotation. He snorted with frustration. Henry leant back in his chair and made a face.

'I can't imagine *where* she gets this from.'

'Shut up,' Dad told him irritably. 'It's different for me.'

'No, it isn't,' I argued. 'Except that you were doing your mission for total strangers. At least I'm helping someone I know.'

Henry got up. 'You're quite a girl, Peta. I've seen many a teenager do extraordinary things – just look at Parissa. But this is between you and your dad. You know where to find me.'

'We'll talk in the morning,' Dad said stiffly, getting up too.

'You can't tell me what to do any more,' I snapped. 'You're officially dead, remember?'

He didn't reply.

*

I went up to my room and sat on the bed.

288

I'm sorry, Mum. I have to do this.

And when it was over, if I wasn't back to explain everything, Henry Phillips would tell her what I'd done and why. It wasn't perfect, but it would have to be good enough.

It might sound all brave and noble and everything, but that wasn't true. The truth – the secret I'd been discovering since that first step I took on the coach – was that I was starting to like this stuff. Every time I thought about stealing food on the yacht, or getting Amina through the smugglers' tunnel or watching Muscle Man miss the train, I wanted to hug myself.

There were many things I wasn't good at: believing what people told me, tidying my room, hanging out with scary, beautiful girls . . . but this – this was something I could do.

All my scariest moments were the ones I was most proud of, looking back. Henry was right: I was just as bad as Dad.

FORTY-NINE

Dad sat opposite me at breakfast, looking miserable.
Actually, I wasn't *totally* like him, I realised. I trusted
my family a bit more than he did.

'I have an add-on to the plan,' I said. 'It'll let Mum know
we're OK. Do we know anyone in the Caribbean?'

Dad looked at me like I was totally mad.

'Yes,' François interjected, leaning over. 'Why?'

'Because we need to make up a postcard of a woman called
Ada Lovelace – I'll explain who she is – and get someone to
send it to Mum at the inn. No message. She'll know it's from
me, because I named my cat after Ada Lovelace. And she'll
guess I found you, Dad. I made all that fuss about Lacy being

290

really from you.'

Dad just grunted, looking miserable as ever, and sceptical about the plan, and guilty about the kitten.

'I don't think we can do that,' François said to me gently. 'Wahool's men are probably watching your mother. It would alert them too.'

'I know they're watching her,' I said. 'And whoever's doing it will think we're in the Caribbean, where the Grandfather's supposed to be right now. It might put them off the scent for a while.'

Dad took a long sip of coffee and said nothing.

'That's not bad,' François smiled, nudging him.

'So?' I asked.

'I'm thinking,' Dad said. But something in his eyes had already changed. If Mum knew we'd found each other, then she'd know I was OK and his last excuse for leaving me behind was gone.

'Way to go, Dad!' I ran over and gave him a big kiss.

'It's only because I could hardly get out of bed this morning. Those bloody cliffs . . . And I know you'd just follow me if I tried to stop you. But you're not taking a step on that island without me. The second I'm done, we're leaving. I can't believe I'm doing this.'

'It's too late,' I grinned. 'It was too late from the moment you gave Karim my number.'

A few hours later, Ugo the chauffeur picked up my invitation from Omar at the Four Seasons Hotel, where 'Ella' had said she was staying (thank you, guidebook). The theme was handwritten in neat, flowing ink: *Roman Holiday*.

Maria, the housekeeper, was dispatched to get me a party outfit. She came back with two streaky-blonde wigs, a long, sleeveless black dress in a variety of sizes for me to try, some VERY expensive underwear, a fake pearl necklace, mini-tiara, gloves and a few pairs of high-heeled shoes. It turned out she was an expert on Audrey Hepburn.

'This is not the outfit from *Roman Holiday*,' she said. 'But in that film Audrey only wears a heavy evening gown or simple summer clothes. This is Audrey's look from *Breakfast at Tiffany's*. It's very famous and elegant. The shoes will make you look taller.'

'Won't it seem odd that it's not the right film?' I asked.

Maria laughed. 'They won't notice. You'll look glamorous – that's all that matters. I'm sorry about the necklace: it isn't perfect, but it's the best I could find this morning.'

She and her niece, Flavia, worked on me for a couple of hours, getting the make-up right, choosing shoes I could actually walk in (well, almost) and the dress that fitted me best. Then came the wig, which they worked into a chignon high on my head, held in place with the tiara, and finally the gloves and necklace.

Amina watched, fascinated. They all had great fun telling me I couldn't look at myself, which really, *really* annoyed me, and finally – just as the delicious smell of home-cooked pizza wafted in through the window – they covered my eyes and took me to the full-length mirror. At last, I was allowed to see what they'd done. Yeah, yeah, the whole 'magical transform-ation' thing.

And I stared. Because that stuff actually *works*.

For a start, I was taller. When you are balancing precari-ously on four-inch platforms, carefully hidden under your extra-long dress, you tend to look taller. I could easily pass for sixteen. Apart from no longer being midget-like, I also had big eyes with huge, cat-like sweeps of eyeliner and not one

292

but two sets of false eyelashes. My face was plastered in foundation to hide the last patches of henna. They'd done clever things with blusher and lipstick too, and the other million and one products they'd used on me. The wig shone like liquid crystal and the underwear had given me the hint of a shape. I definitely wasn't Marilyn Monroe, but I was no longer a broomstick, either.

'So?' Maria insisted. 'So? So? What do you think?'

'It's great,' I said.

She sighed. Flavia groaned theatrically. 'It is not just "great". Look again, Signorina Jones. Act the part. You will see.'

Now it was my turn to sigh. I had to be Ella, 'the chick from Cannes'. The closest I could think of was Davina, the middle of the Darling Ds. She was the right age. She was the right sort of drop-dead sophisticated girl who would go to a party on an island at the drop of a hat. Davina could do this, no problem.

I closed my eyes and thought of her. I breathed in.

I opened my eyes. I possibly batted my double eyelashes. And there she was. Davina-Ella. Ella-Davina. Scary-hot sixteen-year-old beauty, dripping with money and boys.

'Madonna! Straordinaria.'

'Che bella! Ma guarda!'

Even Amina grinned.

I smiled. 'Oh, Omar, how *fabulous* to see you.' My voice came out deeper, more assured: Davina's voice.

Everybody laughed. But it was kind of good.

Late in the afternoon, Henry Phillips took me into Florence itself. We parked near the Ponte Vecchio and he took me into one of the jewellery shops on the bridge. Inside, the owner was waiting for us. As soon as we arrived, he brought out a slim black leather box, stamped with a gold pattern around the edge.

'I know Maria did her best today,' Henry said, 'but the people at the party will know good jewellery. It's like another badge that you belong.'

Inside the box, a five-strand pearl necklace sat on a cushion of oyster silk. It was fastened at the front by a massive clasp, the size of my fist, set with hundreds of tiny diamonds.

I didn't know what to say.

'Just think of it as a tool for the job,' he told me when we got outside. 'It looks right, and it's the kind of thing Ella might need a bodyguard to look after for her. But once you've got it on, don't worry about it, OK? Just focus on what you need to do.'

Right, fine, sure. I'll just forget about the THOUSANDS AND THOUSANDS OF POUNDS' worth of pearls and diamonds I'm wearing and run around trying to find Karim.

Actually, when it came to practising, the necklace was easy. I was more worried about breaking my ankle in those shoes.

FIFTY

By now we had three days left. As well as learning how to walk in the platforms without falling over, I had a crash course in self-defence from Steve and Elena, in which I learnt how to break a man's nose and his arm in two places if required – but mostly, as usual, to stay out of trouble if at all possible.

I scrubbed my skin to get rid of the last traces of henna. With the help of Dad and Interface, I made up a story for 'Ella', about how she met Yasmin on holiday in Paris, and knew lots of her friends from the school in Switzerland, and how her dad had a villa near Cannes, which was how she'd met Omar Wahool.

My plan was to avoid him at the party. If he saw me, he wouldn't recognise me, of course, but the Crystal Ball was ages ago, so he probably wouldn't remember *who* he'd met there exactly. Hopefully he'd be so busy having fun on the million-dollar dance floor that he wouldn't care.

I memorised all the names. I practised the posh voice. I learnt how to do my own make-up (which took most of one evening) and use the earpiece I would have to communicate with Steve, who would be on a nearby, borrowed yacht, directing the operation.

I wrote a letter to Mum, just in case. It was the hardest thing I've ever done. I imagined the letter I would have wanted Dad to write to me before the bomb thing. It included lots of *sorry*s, and *I love you*s, and *goodbye*s. It wasn't long, but at least it was better than *'This is not about you'*. I gave it to Henry to look after for me.

I wrote a letter to Luke too. That was easier. It was mostly pointing out what an idiot I'd been at various stages, and leaving him all my Forza points, my stash of Toxic Waste and my computer, to use for parts when he wanted to upgrade his.

On the last evening, we danced around the kitchen to Syed's playlist of pop and rock classics. Dad and I did our diva moves, Steve taught us some Gangnam Style, and Amina – after a few minutes watching the video – did a scarily accurate impression of Freddie Mercury singing 'One Vision'. François and Elena proved they could jive to anything with a beat, and Syed and I proved that I couldn't. Then Maria fed us all strawberry ice cream, before dragging Amina and me off to bed.

The next day, saying goodbye to Amina was tricky. We'd been through so much. In the end I was pathetic: my face was wet with tears as we hugged.

'I'll find your brother, I promise,' I told her. 'I'll bring him back to you.'

'I know you will,' she whispered. '*In bocca al lupo.*'

'What's that?'

'It is "good luck" in Italian. I've been learning it from Maria. It means "in the mouth of the wolf".'

'In the mouth of the wolf? Great. Thanks.'

She grinned at me. 'I have seen you in the mouth of the wolf. I worry for the wolf.'

It was a kind thing to say, but I worried for *me*. I'd been in that castle. I'd seen the guns, and knew that they wanted to kill me. I'd seen how they beat a little girl. I was excited, I was ready, but I was scared to my bones. You'd be crazy not to be.

'Focus on the training,' Dad said. So as we drove out of the villa gates, I focused on everything they'd taught me, as hard as I could.

With Steve and the snatch team travelling separately, Dad and I set off for Positano, where the guests would be picked up for the party. Having done the journey one way, I wasn't particularly looking forward to going back, but I hadn't factored in that this time we would be flying from Pisa to Naples in Henry Phillips's private jet. All I can say is that on the whole, being a billionaire sucks, but when it comes to air travel . . . it kind of doesn't. They had even stocked the galley with Toxic Waste and Haribos.

Dad sat opposite me in a comfy leather armchair. We were quiet for most of the flight.

'You know you still don't have to do this, love,' he said, leaning forward and looking anxiously at me as we came in to land.

'Way to encourage me, Dad.'

'I mean it. We might . . . Look, things can go wrong. I can't guarantee to get you out safely.' He frowned, angry with himself for getting me into it, but I met his eye.

'I know that. I can't guarantee to get *you* out safely. But we can try.'

'Ha! Your mother will never forgive me. Ever.'

'True. I was expecting a bit more of a pep talk, though,' I complained. 'Is that what you say to all your teams?'

'No,' he admitted. 'We say something about being the best and it's time to show the bad guys what they're up against.'

'So . . .?'

He reached out and put his hands to my cheeks.

'Go and get the bad guys, Peta, my precious girl. It's entirely my fault that you're as messed-up as you are. We're the best. It's time to show them what they're up against.'

FIFTY-ONE

In the late afternoon, a group of party guests gathered on the quay at Positano, where a fleet of boats was waiting to ferry them to the Isola Sirena. I was wearing a long, streaky-blonde wig (the chignon one was in my bag) and a cotton dress that looked like 'any old thing' and had cost three hundred euros in Florence (I saw the price tag).

Dad stood nearby, with my matching designer luggage, in wraparound sunglasses and a blond wig of his own. Despite the heat, he was dressed in the standard jewellery-guard uniform of white shirt, dark jacket and tie. He had a completely different way of standing and walking from normal, which meant even I had to remind myself he was him. The security guard checking our tickets threw him a casual glance, but seemed more interested in checking out the party girls.

All the other guests in my group were young, tanned, happy, and slightly drunk already. Many of them knew each other, and lots of air-kissing went on. Being Ella Van Cleepels made things easier. I practised listening in on people's names and going over to them and air-kissing them too, shouting, 'Kitty!' or 'Alexei!' or 'Masha!' or whatever it was. 'It's Ella! *Darling!*' And without fail, they kissed me back and pretended to know me. It was freaky at first, but I quickly discovered that Ella *loved* seeing all her old friends.

We were picked up by the tender of the *Princess Nazia*. As soon as it came into view, my heart started beating faster. I was fairly sure that the guy at the wheel had recently been shooting at me. He gave all the girls – Ella included – the same respectful smile as we climbed aboard. Even so, I joined 'Robbins', my jewellery guard, at the back of the boat, as far from him as possible. We watched as the mainland rapidly shrank into the distance. I tried to think about the training, and Karim, and not what I was leaving behind.

Soon one of the girls squealed and everyone turned to see where she was pointing. The island loomed ahead of us: craggy cliffs at one end and a gentle sloping hill at the other, bathed in sunlight and studded with wild flowers. Nearby, too heavy to bob about on the waves, were two absolutely enormous boats: the *Princess Nazia* and the *Juno*. At the top of the cliffs, the castle stood magnificently against the sky. Flags fluttered on the ramparts. Its stone glowed gold in the afternoon light.

Only 'Robbins' and I knew what lay underneath. He put

his hand briefly over mine. I was shivering, but this time, I recognised the exhilaration as well as the fear.

We landed at the jetty, and several of the girls squealed happily at the sight of the flower-festooned buggies lined up to take us up the hill. The last time I'd landed here, I'd been stuck inside a trunk. Today, I stepped lightly on to the dock as a crew member took my hand to steady me. I muttered to 'Robbins' to find me later and went off to join the others. Did Ella squeal? I decided she did.

Yasmin was waiting for us in the castle hallway, next to a very beautiful, glacial woman in big jewellery. This had to be her mother, the 'fifty-first most stylish woman in the world'. Yasmin was wearing a bikini and mini-kaftan, glowing from an afternoon by the pool. Everyone from the buggies queued up to hug her.

'So good to see you again!' I squealed, going in for the hug like a pro. 'Happy birthday! I love your place!' Squeal, air-kiss. Air-kiss, squeal.

'We're all getting changed upstairs,' she said giving me a slightly odd stare as she tried to work out who I was. 'The servants will show you where to go. If you're down early, they're showing *Roman Holiday* in the cinema.'

'Oh how lovely! Everything's so . . . lovely.' Ella didn't have a massive vocabulary, I decided. She giggled, though.

Just beyond the staircase was a vast collection of rocks and statues that hadn't been there before, down which bubbles cascaded into a pool of pale gold.

'What's that?' I muttered to Robbins, who was waiting for me beside it, bags in hand.

'A scale model of the Trevi Fountain,' he said. 'In champagne.'

'Oh, nice.'

Robbins said nothing, but his face suggested he didn't approve.

Next to it, a trio of musicians played old-fashioned tunes. Servants were everywhere, carrying trays and escorting guests. Outside there was the regular *whoop whoop* of helicopter blades, signalling the arrival of guests who couldn't be bothered to come by boat.

Robbins carried my bags upstairs for me as I was escorted to my top-floor room, where he politely left me at the doorway. We were allocated four to a room, but nobody seemed to mind sharing. In fact, the girls in my room seemed very happy to parade around in their underwear while they examined all the furniture, the gifts on each pillow, and the contents of each other's cases.

'They've got the same sound system as our place in Ibiza. Shall I put something on?'

'Oh, Mitzi, this bed is just like the one in your summer palace.'

'Gabby, I just *love* your dress. Is it Valentino? It's too cute. You must wear it to my party in Salzburg.'

'Oh, but I couldn't wear it *twice*. By the way, will Alexei be there?'

This time, with the party approaching, Ella didn't join in. I'd been worried that they'd notice that I wasn't unpacking or dancing around in my knickers, but they were so pleased to see each other they didn't seem to notice me at all.

I slipped my make-up case out of my bag and spent the time doing my eyes and lips while they danced around getting ready. Then they all went downstairs together without saying goodbye.

If this had been my first day at boarding school, it would

have been the utter humiliation I expected. But as it was, it was perfect. Nobody looked in my case, and I was left alone to continue the tricky process of transformation by myself. Undies, including push-up bra; dress; wig and tiara; dangly earrings; little earpiece to talk to Steve; full-length gloves; heels. Then I got out the phone from my evening bag and called Robbins, who brought in the black leather case.

'Good evening, miss.'

'Good evening, Robbins.'

'May I say you look absolutely delightful this evening, miss?'

'You may.'

'And may I suggest that you are very careful and don't drink any champagne or anything else alcoh—'

'Shut up, Robbins. Ahem. I know perfectly well what to drink.'

'Yes, miss. Well, good luck. Enjoy the party.'

He put the pearl necklace round my neck and fiddled with the clasp until it was secure. Then he put his hands briefly on my shoulders and said a proper *good luck* to me with his eyes.

'See you later, Robbins.'

'And Miss . . .'

'Yes?'

'You really do look beautiful.'

'You said that, Robbins.'

'Good. Well, you do.'

I grabbed my little bag and smiled at him. A small, nervous smile, which wouldn't do, so I switched on Ella.

'Blimey! Er, be careful, miss.'

'I will, Robbins. You too.'

After he'd gone, I checked myself in the mirror. Dad was overreacting, I thought. I would have said I was eighty per cent incredible pearl necklace, eighteen per cent glamourpuss Ella, and two per cent me in a wig.

Ella winked at the mirror. I'd left it very late and I could already hear the sound of hundreds of happy voices down below. It was time to join the party.

FIFTY-TWO

There was a huge commotion in the hall, but as I got halfway down the staircase suddenly everything went quiet. All eyes gazed upwards. Wow. This was a bigger reaction than I'd been expecting. In fact, it was just like Audrey arriving at a ball. Well, only one thing for it. Ella put on her biggest smile and carried on walking down as graciously as she could.

It was only as I neared the bottom step that I noticed a minor detail: nobody was looking at me. They were all staring up at someone behind me. I glanced around to see two enormous bodyguards and, several steps up from them, a small, stumpy man dressed as a Roman emperor, in a white and purple toga, with a huge wreath of golden laurel leaves on his head.

He stared straight at me. He didn't have much hair under the laurel wreath, but what little he had was dyed black and slicked straight back over his scalp. His face seemed to be stretched over his skull, too: it was unnaturally smooth and shiny.

For a moment, he fixed me with a cold, dead gaze. Then he noticed everyone watching him, and the bottom half of his face broke into a smile. His teeth glowed ultra-white and he gave a regal wave.

'Welcome, Grandfather! Welcome!' came a voice from below me.

Mr Wahool strode forward through the crowd, arms outstretched, also dressed as an ancient Roman of some sort. As I'd learnt on the yacht, this was a confusing party theme.

'Grandfather! We are honoured to have you in our presence. Or, may I say, we are honoured to have you *back*!'

He bowed low and there was a smattering of applause, which continued until everyone in the hall was clapping.

I scuttled down the last few stairs and stood with the others as the ex-dictator made his way slowly down, flashing his teeth at everyone, seeming to take in every face and assess it for how enthusiastic it was, then acknowledging their applause. The bodyguards made sure that nobody got close as he headed on towards the terrace outside.

As he drew level with me, the Grandfather seemed to give me an extra-penetrating stare. For spoiling his entrance, I supposed. Or perhaps he was sizing up my pearls and diamonds. I bowed my head. When I raised it again, the small, be-togaed figure had moved on, but for the first time I noticed the man walking a few paces behind him. It was odd

I hadn't spotted him before, but then, the Grandfather was pretty mesmerising.

The man behind him must have been nearly seven feet tall. Despite this, he had the knack of seeming almost invisible in his simple grey suit, and yet, when I looked up, I felt myself wobbling on my platforms for the first time. There was something about his face. It seemed to be an endless series of bags: under the eyes, under the bags under the eyes, under the cheeks, under the chin. The skin was a strange greyish-purple colour, and the eyes themselves looked empty and hollow. They seemed to look into you, and through you. He passed close by me and I felt I couldn't breathe until he'd gone.

In a few moments the procession had moved on and the hall returned to normal. I found a white-gloved servant with a tray and asked him in a whisper: 'Was that the Jongleur?'

He stared straight ahead, face blank. 'We do not talk about such things, signorina. Champagne?'

'No. Thank you.'

I paused by the mini Trevi Fountain to regain my composure. Nobody should ever be left alone with that man.

My first job was to create a distraction at precisely six minutes past nine. I looked at my watch (a vintage silver one that had belonged to Henry's mother). It was eight forty-five, which gave me a little while to check out the party, so I did.

Everyone, it seemed, was moving out on to the terrace and the lawns, soaking up the music and enjoying the view. I stood on the edge of the terrace, where the breakfast table had once been, and looked out. The place looked even better than before. The scaffolding had gone, and coloured fairy lights nestled among the climbing roses. Hundreds of candles flickered in little glass vases along the pathways. The terrace was set with white-clothed tables, while below it the dance floor took up most of the area by the pool. What I'd thought was DJ music turned out to be a South American superstar, dressed in nothing but spangles, singing last year's biggest number one.

The guests were a mixture of old and young. The older ones sat at the little tables near where I was standing, while the younger ones played about on the lawns, laughing loudly and taking pictures of themselves on jewelled phones. Some were dressed as Audrey Hepburn or ancient Romans – there were two other *Breakfast at Tiffany's* and several togas – but most had just gone for straight-up high-fashion evening wear. Maria was right that I needn't have worried about theme accuracy. Meanwhile, waiters in white jackets circulated round them on little scooters like the one Dad had stolen, serving trays of mini ice-cream cones and champagne.

For my last birthday we ate chocolate cake and deloused a kitten. Just saying. But Ella had been to *lots* of parties like this. She just *adored* them.

A few boys smiled at me and waved me over, but I ignored them. I glanced at my watch: 9 p.m. exactly. I had work to do. I went over to one of the tables and picked up one of the starched white napkins.

At 9.01, I wandered back inside, taking the napkin with me, as well as a little candle in a vase. *Doop de doop de doo.* Ditzy Ella. The poor girl somehow ended up in the sitting room, where she put down her vase and accidentally left the napkin folded on top of it. Oops.

I went back into the hall and started to go back up the staircase. *Three. Two. One.*

I think I was the first to smell smoke. Seconds later, somebody shouted 'Fire!' just as an alarm bell went off. Sprinklers started sprinkling, servants and security came running. I couldn't see the corridor outside Mr Wahool's study from here, but I assumed that 'Mr Robbins' could now walk along it undisturbed.

Job over. Pausing only to look vaguely surprised by the commotion, I carried on up the stairs.

Part two of the plan was harder. Now I had to find Karim and explain why I was back. Preferably without giving him a heart attack at the sight of me dressed as Audrey Hepburn. I'd considered going through the kitchens to look for him in the cellars, but too many servants would pass me on the way and wonder what a guest was doing down there. The tunnels were my best option. I just had to pray he'd be there, on the way to one of his tasks.

I slipped into Yasmin's bedroom, which was closest, and let myself through the invisible door, leaving my shoes just inside it. I hoiked up my dress and made sure I bent as low as possible, so as not to rub my wig on the rough ceiling. My outfit really wasn't designed for this part.

'Karim!' I hissed. 'Where are you?'

No answer. Not so surprising. The music outside was very loud, and he could be anywhere. I moved forward, calling louder: 'Karim!'

Still no answer. On I went, and down, crouching all the time and calling as loud as I dared. Then round and up again, via a different staircase, on the other side of the castle. This *had* to work.

'Karim!'

Stillness and darkness and nothing, apart from the

pounding of a heavy beat from the dance floor, which seemed to vibrate through the stones.

'*Karim!*'

There was no sign of him on the basement floor or the ground floor, but I carried on searching, calling as I went. No answer. I retraced my steps down the passage towards Yasmin's room.

'Peta Jones?'

I whipped round. He was standing in the stairwell behind me, silhouetted in a stairwell in the moonlight.

'Karim!'

I moved towards him as fast as my dress allowed and threw my arms around his neck. He was too shocked to hug me back.

'I've come to get you,' I told him.

He stood back and clasped my hands. His skin was cool but his grip was tight. For a moment, we just stood there. His face was just as I'd remembered it: elegant, curious, brave. His bright eyes glittered in the gloom.

'You are a mad girl, Peta Jones.'

'No, I'm not.' It was hard to pull away, but there was a lot to do. 'Come on – follow me.'

I led him back to Yasmin's room, where I collected my shoes and repositioned the wig, which was half over one eye by now. Then I remembered Yasmin's walk-in wardrobe. It seemed an excellent place to talk.

'My sister,' Karim said, still staring at me in wonder as we stood among the endless closets, 'she is safe?'

'Very safe,' I smiled. 'You've no idea how safe.'

He relaxed a little. 'You should not have come. This castle is a bad place.'

'That's why I'm here,' I told him. 'I'm getting you out.'

'But Sammy and Parissa—'

'Don't worry, they're coming too.'

Quickly, I outlined the plan. Something was bound to go wrong – I'd learnt that by now – but we had plenty of back-up plans in case it did. Karim listened carefully as I told him about the spare waiter's outfit in my bag upstairs – his disguise for the escape – and where to meet after Dad had finished in the study. I thought I'd have to explain the details a few times, but he understood everything instantly. He looked worried, though.

'Does Mr Allud . . . your father . . . know about the new pressure pads Mr Wahool installed in his special room? They are the latest security devices.'

'No! There are pressure pads?'

'After the incident with my sister . . .'

Karim looked uncomfortable, because of course it wasn't his sister who'd got caught in the 'special room'. Pressure pads weren't in the plan. What if Dad had tripped an alarm?

'Aargh!' My two-second encounter with the wide man seemed to have led to endless trouble.

'Perhaps they are not working yet,' Karim said hopefully, seeing my face. 'They are very—'

He stopped at the sound of rustling outside. The door opened. Yasmin Wahool stood there, one shoe in her hand, staring at us both.

Oh seriously no. Bad thing.

Karim bowed almost to the ground and muttered, 'I am so sorry, Miss Yasmin. I was just . . . I am so sorry.'

She stared at me. She was now dressed in a vintage 1950s sundress, like the ones Audrey Hepburn wore in *Roman Holiday*, which clashed somewhat with the two hundred and eighty-nine diamonds around her neck.

'Who are you?' she said accusingly. 'What are you doing here?'

I took a breath. Ella batted her eyelashes and looked ditzier than ever.

'Oh, hi, Yasmin. I'm *so* lost. I don't think this is the bedroom they gave me. I—'

'You're lying. What are you, some kind of thief? I'm calling security.' She made to leave the room.

'No! Listen!' I pleaded. 'We're not stealing. I was hiding. It's just a party game.'

'Hah. Nobody plays party games with the servants.'

Yasmin bent to rub her aching foot. She must have come in to change her shoes, which were even higher than mine. As she bent down, her big diamond necklace slipped round and banged against her collarbone. Underneath it, I spotted a glint of gold – a charm on a slim chain. I remembered the last night on the *Princess Nazia*, and it gave me an idea. I turned off my begging face.

'Some of us *like* to play games with servants,' I said in a different voice, more threatening and mysterious.

'What do you mean?' She looked up, startled.

'I like your necklace. The gold one, I mean. Who gave it to you?' I gave her my best mock-innocent stare.

She gulped and looked frightened. Her hand went to her neck. 'But . . . but . . . but . . . How did you . . .?'

I let her sweat. So Dad stole stuff, and I blackmailed people with their guilty secrets.

Yasmin's eyes were pleading now. 'You mustn't . . .'

'Don't worry. I won't say anything, if you don't. I just wanted this boy here to help me with . . . a trick I'm playing on someone.' This was actually true, up to a point.

She frowned. It was clear she didn't exactly believe me, but she didn't know what to think. 'You swear you're not stealing.'

'I swear. Of course not.'

Two hundred million dollars, baby. But it wasn't hers anyway.

'OK,' she said reluctantly. 'But get out. Now.'

Without a word, Karim disappeared through the door in the bedroom wall. Yasmin watched me suspiciously from the landing as I headed down the main stairs, just in time to see several of the older male party guests file into the dining room. Two bodyguards stood impassively either side of the door. Something not very party-like was going on in there.

FIFTY-THREE

I paused for a moment, watching. Was François right? Was the coup being finalised in that room tonight? But that was the Foundation's problem, not mine. Right now, I had quite enough problems of my own.

I had to find somewhere quiet, fast, to talk to Steve, so he could warn Dad about the pressure pads in the study. But before I could think of anywhere safe to do it, two girls called after me.

'Hey! You! Tiffany girl!'

I spun round. They were sparkly and smiling.

'Are you Ella?' they asked. 'They said you were the one in the pearls. Ooh, are those real?'

'Yes,' I said, in answer to both questions.

'Cool. Omar wants you. We've been looking for you for *ages.*'

'Oh . . . lovely,' I said, smiling brightly.

Oh hell. Oh big time hell.

The girls took me by the hand and led me back to the terrace, where the air was throbbing with music so loud they could probably hear it on the mainland, and two boys were having a competition to see how much champagne they could spray over each other from the bottle.

'Here she is!' the girls called out, skirting round the champagne fight and heading towards a group of people watching Max Wahool, down to his shirtsleeves, do balancing tricks on a waiter's scooter.

One of them was Omar. His bowtie was draped round his neck, and three long-legged girls were draped over him, like furs. He turned round and slowly looked me up and down.

'Who are you?'

'Ella,' I said in my deepest, most husky voice, glancing nervously over at Max. 'Ella Van Cleepels. Hi! We met in Cannes. Don't you remember? We got very drunk that night.' I giggled. At least, I tried to giggle. It came out as more of a gurgle.

'So you're the chick from Cannes.'

'Uh-huh.'

'That's weird. You're a honey, you know that? I've been wanting to talk to you all night. But I just met this girl here . . .' Omar indicated the six-foot blonde next to him, also watching me curiously. 'And *she's* the girl I met in Cannes. And her name's Sophie. So, like I said, who are you?'

'I met you there too,' I said, thinking fast. My smile was slipping, and so was my voice. 'And I just, like, really really wanted to see you again.'

Silence. Omar didn't believe me. And Max didn't believe me. And even the drapey girls didn't believe me. 'Gold-digger,' someone muttered.

I had underestimated the Wahools, and how suspicious they were of anyone outside the family. Big mistake. Huge, much-too-late, can't-go-back-now mistake.

Omar's eyes hardened. 'Come on. We're going to meet my dad.'

He grabbed my arm. Behind him, Max stopped his balancing act to stare at us. Now everyone was staring.

Omar steered me back through the party, past the champagne fight and more waiters on wheels and a boy being sick in the bushes, through several doorways, past the Trevi Fountain and into the hall. His grip was like steel.

'Ow! You're hurting me.'

'Shut up.'

We reached the closed doors to the dining room. Omar nodded to one of the bodyguards, who let us in.

Ten men were standing round an enormous marble table, covered in maps and plans. It reminded me of the kitchen table at the Colombo Foundation when we were planning our operation, but bigger, and surrounded by men in togas. It would have been funny, if it wasn't the scariest place I'd ever been. Yes, they were definitely planning the coup. No, I wish I hadn't found out this way.

The wide man was there, in the smartest toga of all. I glanced at him nervously, but he didn't seem to recognise me. Like the others, he was watching the Grandfather, who stood at the end of the room in his purple finery. I checked for the Jongleur, but there was no sign of him.

'Why are you here?' the Grandfather said to Omar coldly.

'Where's my father?'

'Elsewhere. There's been a disturbance.'

Oh no. The pressure pads . . . *Oh no oh no.*

Omar didn't seem to notice me shudder. 'It's just, I've got this girl. She faked her way in to get to me. Papa hates it when they do that.'

'Not now, boy. Tell security. Go back outside.'

'OK, fine,' Omar sighed.

'Wait! She was not invited, did you say? Bring her to me.'

Omar marched me up the room, past the table and the men in expensive Roman party gear, to the place where the Grandfather was waiting. In my platforms, I was about the same height as the ex-President of Marvalia. His black eyes looked directly into mine. They were sharp and intelligent, and pitiless.

'Can it be a coincidence that this girl should appear at the same time as our intruder?'

'I . . . I'm a party guest. I just wanted to see the castle . . .'

'Take her to your father's study.'

Whatever makes your knees work gave up on mine. Omar had to hold me up as he pulled me back out of the room. Dragging a girl wearing platforms isn't easy, but he was strong and he managed it.

Oh, Dad, I'm so so sorry. Please don't be where I think you are.

FIFTY-FOUR

The plan had gone so wrong so fast I felt giddy. There wasn't a back-up for this.

We reached the study door and it was locked. Omar bashed against it.

'Papa! It's me!'

The key turned in the lock. Mr Wahool opened the door and breathed cigar smoke in our faces.

'Go away, my son.' His body blocked most of the doorway.

'I found this,' Omar said, pushing me forward, like a cat with a dead bird.

Mr Wahool looked unimpressed. 'Get rid of her.'

'But, Papa, the Grandfather said—'

'You went to the Grandfather?'

I craned my neck. Behind Mr Wahool's toga-clad shoulder I could just make out Dad near the desk, kneeling in front of the Jongleur. The tall grey man was holding a pistol to Dad's head.

Oh no oh no oh no.

Mr Wahool saw that I had noticed the scene behind him and motioned us in angrily, locking the door behind us. Omar's casual glance at Dad on his knees suggested he'd seen this kind of thing before.

'What did he say?' Mr Wahool asked.

'The girl faked her way in, Papa.' Omar nodded across to where Dad was kneeling. 'The Grandfather said she might be to do with him.'

Meanwhile, I looked around the room desperately. The window was shut. It was miles to the secret door. The walls looked soundproof. And if I tried anything, the Jongleur would surely do something to Dad . . .

Right now, the giant's baggy face was studying mine. I looked away.

'Bring her here,' he said. His voice was hollow, like his eyes. There was no emotion in it at all.

Omar dragged me across the room, just as the door shuddered under more thumping.

'Hey! Omar! It's Max! What's up with that girl?'

Mr Wahool swore under his breath and opened the door again.

'Be quiet, my son. Leave us.'

Like I'd done, Max peered beyond his father to see what was happening in the room. He took in Omar and me, Dad, the Jongleur and the pistol. His eyes lit up. 'Hey, party! Can I join?'

'No you may not,' Mr Wahool said crossly. 'Get out, both of you. Leave the girl.'

Omar sighed and turned to go, but Max stood his ground.

'Let me stay, Papa. You look like you could use some help.'

His father eyed him coldly through a haze of cigar smoke, then softened. 'I don't need help. But you may as well learn how we contain our enemies.'

A look of pure enjoyment stole across Max's face, which only increased when Omar's turned to thunder.

'But, Papa, I found her. I'm the oldest. *I* should stay.'

'Get out!' Mr Wahool commanded. 'We don't need the whole family here. For God's sake, boy.'

Omar backed out, furious, while Max, the favourite, strutted across to me.

'Have you been a naughty girl?' he whispered, smirking. His face was almost touching mine and his breath was hot and sour. His eyes gleamed dangerously in the lamplight.

'We're about to establish that,' Mr Wahool said. 'We found *Mr Alard* here working on my computer. Or should I say "Mr Jones"? He has been blocking access to my money. He was just about to explain how to fix the mess he made. Weren't you, Mr Jones?'

In a lightning-fast move, the Jongleur hit Dad, casually but hard, across the face. Dad's head snapped back and I gasped – I couldn't help it. Mr Wahool watched me closely.

'Interesting.' He smiled at the Jongleur and turned back to Max. 'I do believe this young lady may be able to assist us. You see,' he went on, walking over to the desk, 'there is a book –' he stubbed out his cigar in a crystal ashtray and picked up a small black notebook – 'which was among the possessions of the charming Mr Jones. It was hidden, but we found it.'

He paused. *Thump.* Dad groaned.

'It was written in code, but I had it decoded. And at the end of this *fascinating* book it mentions "the power of Peta". Mr Jones has a daughter called Peta. Would that by any chance be you, my dear?'

I said nothing. Max jabbed me in the ribs with his elbow, causing my bag to drop to the floor and the contents to spill on the carpet. 'Answer my father!'

'I – I don't know what you're talking about. My name's Ella. I just wanted a free invitation to a party.'

They all looked down at my scattered lipstick, phone and hairbrush. I think they'd been expecting something more high-tech and incriminating. But I was Ella Van Cleepels, ditzy party girl.

I risked a quick look at Dad. He was still on his knees, head slumped forward, so close I could nearly touch him. The Jongleur had thumped him in the chest, where he already had at least two broken ribs from his time in the cells. It was hard to tell how he was coping. I looked away.

Mr Wahool stretched out his arm and yanked at my necklace so hard that the strands broke and pearls scattered over the carpet. I gasped again. Still not satisfied, he grabbed my tiara and pulled the wig off my head. My earpiece fell to the floor. With slow deliberation, he stepped forward and crushed it under his smart leather heel. Suddenly, my excuse that I was just a normal party guest was starting to look a bit thin. I found it difficult to breathe.

'Yes, yes,' Wahool muttered, looking at me. 'Put them side by side.'

'I don't know what you mean. I—'

'SHUT UP!' Wahool ordered.

Max and the Jongleur pushed Dad and me together and

made us kneel in the middle of the room, facing them. The scattered pearls hurt my knees. My limbs felt like ice. I focused on a pool of golden lamplight to make myself feel warmer, until the Jongleur tipped our chins back with the gun. It had a big fat silencer on it, I noticed. Not that you really needed a silencer with the massive disco going on outside. By now I was rigid with fear.

Mr Wahool walked across the thick carpet to join his monster and his son. I could just hear Dad's ragged breathing beside me. The others stood over us and examined our faces, like we were exhibits at a freak show.

'The same eyes,' Mr Wahool said. 'Don't you agree?'

'And the same chin,' Max said. 'The daughter, definitely.'

'I've never seen this girl,' Dad muttered through a thick lip.

The Jongleur kicked him hard in the abdomen and he doubled over.

'I think you have,' Wahool said coldly. 'I think she's your daughter. You see, Peta,' he continued, taking care to say my name this time, 'we have a problem. Your father has infected my computer banking system with a virus that has blocked my bank accounts so the money can go in, but I can't get it out again. A very, very –' *thump, groan* – 'irritating virus. I need him to fix it *now* so I can pay some people. If he doesn't help me I will kill him. You understand that, don't you?'

That wasn't quite how I thought Dad's mission was supposed to work, but I didn't want the Jongleur to kick him again. I nodded. 'I understand.'

'The notebook says you have a power. What *is* that power?'

'It's nothing! It's just my name! It's—'

THUMP.

The Jongleur kicked Dad even harder than usual, and all the time he watched me with those hollow eyes. I stifled a scream. I was panicking and desperate, and that seemed to please him.

'It's just my name,' I cried out, my face wet with tears. 'He just wanted to use my name.'

The Jongleur nodded to Mr Wahool. Torturing Dad was some sort of honesty test for me, it seemed, and I had passed.

Wahool sighed at me. 'In that case, I would like you use your "power" to ask your father, very nicely, to fix the virus for me. Will you do that?'

Well, no. I would do many things, but not spoil the mission. Dad wouldn't want me to. I knelt up as tall as I could and said nothing.

'I COMMAND IT!' Mr Wahool went bright red with the sudden force of shouting at me, and spittle came out of his mouth. 'JUST TELL YOUR FATHER WHAT HE MUST DO! Please.' In that last word, he went from fire to ice. The ice was scarier.

'Fix the virus, Dad,' I said obediently. I sounded about as animated as when Yasmin talked about diamonds.

Thump. The Jongleur kicked Dad. *Slap.* Now Max joined in, hitting my cheek with his free hand. Something hard – a ring? – caught the bone. My vision went blurry for a moment.

'Try a little harder,' Wahool said.

'Fix the virus, Dad.'

Thump, thump. Slap.

Mr Wahool sighed. 'I can see this isn't going to work. Let's try it differently. Sit over there.'

He pointed to a big armchair in front of the window. It was the chair that the wide man had sat in when he had

323

talked about helicopters and art. I was so scared I couldn't move, so the Jongleur stepped over, picked me up by the hair and dragged me to it. I couldn't tell what he was going to do, and the uncertainty made it worse. At least Dad was still kneeling upright, just. At least he was still breathing.

'One bone at a time,' Mr Wahool crooned to the Jongleur.

The giant handed his gun to his boss, who in turn passed it to his favourite son. 'Can you use this?' he asked.

'Of course,' Max smiled, feeling the weight of it in his palm. 'I have my own collection, remember?'

'Good. Keep an eye on Mr Jones.'

Dad was kneeling in front of the chair, with his head down. Max pulled his chin up again with the pistol, forcing him to face me. For the first time, our eyes met. Dad's were calm and sad and sorry and full of love. I forced a smile. Whatever happened, we were in this together. We would not let them beat us.

The Jongleur moved into position beside me and stretched his arms out, clicking his fingers. I wasn't sure what he intended to do, and I didn't want to know. *Lalalalalalalala . . .*

'No! Wait! No!' Dad shouted.

The room went quiet.

'I'm sorry?' Mr Wahool asked silkily.

'Enough!' Dad shook his head. 'I'll fix your bloody virus.' His voice was rough from having been thumped so much, and his words were slurred from a cut on his swelling lip.

What? 'Dad?'

'I'm not sure I believe you, Mr Jones.'

I wasn't sure I did, either.

Dad stared Mr Wahool down, ignoring the trickle of blood from his lip. 'It's the only way. You've got my daughter. The virus for her life.'

Mr Wahool looked at his son. 'What do you think, Max? Is he lying?'

Max laughed. 'He loves his little girl. He knows what we'd do to her.'

All the time, my brain was racing. Some people were stupid – Max Wahool certainly was – but not my dad, not *ever* my dad. Why would he offer to go along with them, to save me, when it was obvious they would kill us both anyway? I mean, what else were they going to do?

Dad must have a plan. Maybe he was just buying time for the others to escape. Whatever it was, I had to make Wahool trust him. I looked Dad straight in the eye and sobbed desperately. 'No! Daddy! Don't!'

I never called him 'Daddy'. He gave me a flicker of an odd look, but everyone was looking at my face, not his.

'It's too late, child,' Mr Wahool said smugly. 'I must have my money.' He seemed more confident about the deal, now that I'd begged Dad not to do it. Dad's odd look turned into the faintest flicker of a smile.

'We must help them, honey.'

Dad never called me 'honey'. OK, so he'd got my code. And there was a plan. And we weren't helping. That's all I needed to know.

'Do it,' Mr Wahool instructed, after a moment's deliberation. 'Max, take Mr Jones to where he can see the computer. You –' he turned me – 'come over here and type.'

The Jongleur started to drag me from the chair, but I pulled away. The secret pact with Dad had given me strength. I walked unsteadily to the desk and stood in front of it. This was where I'd tried to call Mum. I pushed her out of my head.

Max forced Dad to kneel to my left, at the end of the desk, and stood over him with the pistol, while on my right, Mr

Wahool turned the laptop to face us and pressed a key. The screen came to life. It was already open on a page of a banking website, full of names and numbers. I stared at them and forced myself to concentrate. They looked as though they might be different bank accounts.

'And now,' Wahool said blandly, 'give me my money.'

'Peta, click on the third line down,' Dad instructed. His voice was perfectly calm – the epic calm that I really needed right now.

On the web page, the third line down had the most digits in the numbers column. I blinked and checked them out. $114,617,933. The lines above it had over $50,000,000 each. And there were others too. I clicked on line three, as Dad instructed. The website asked for a password.

'I need that,' Dad said grimly to Wahool. 'I can't disable anything until I get into that account.'

'You're lying,' Wahool sneered.

'Of course I'm not lying. You've got my bloody daughter.'

Wahool thought for a while, then nodded to himself. He leant over me, opened a file on the computer, found the password and entered it. Now the screen flickered and a new page showed details of transactions – or rather, one transaction: $114,617,933 paid in two days ago. The words 'ACCOUNT FROZEN' appeared in red at the top.

'Click on that message, love,' Dad said to me. I did, and a new page came up, with the Colombo Foundation's bird image showing faintly in one corner, asking for another password.

'And now?' Mr Wahool said with icy fake politeness. 'This is your work, I believe. Can I have my money? Please?'

Dad sighed. 'Do I have your word you'll let Peta go?'

Mr Wahool nodded. 'You have my word.'

Of course you don't, Dad.

'Thank you. I gave Peta the password. That's why she was in the notebook.' Dad looked across at me. 'I'm so, so sorry, love,' he said. 'It's over. But if you help them, they'll spare you.'

No, they wouldn't. I heard the Jongleur crack his fingers behind me. Beyond Dad, Max's hand was tightening on the gun.

I'd never felt this close to death before. It was like a void opening up in front of me. In front of both of us. Did Dad really want me to help these people?

'Daddy?'

'Just do what they say, love. Never forget, you have the power, and the Grandfather and his cronies are just worthless little piles of—'

THWACK.

It was Max who did it, cracking the pistol against Dad's head. He didn't seem to know his own strength. Dad crumpled like a rag doll. *Oh, my dad.*

The Jongleur took two steps and pushed him over with the toe of his shoe. Dad toppled to the floor in the darkness beyond the lamplight. His eyes were closed. His mouth was slack. I wanted to scream but I couldn't, because I couldn't even breathe.

'Is he faking?' Wahool asked, unmoved.

Another kick in the ribs. No reaction.

'Is he dead? No matter. Max, be more careful next time. Girl, the password, please.'

I gulped some air. 'But I don't *know* it!'

Mr Wahool picked up the black notebook and waved it in my face.

'I SAY YOU DO! Tell me the password or I will have you

killed. Slowly.'

OK, OK, so I got the bit about 'slowly'. I suppose my alternative was to be killed quickly and, yes, at this moment that seemed a better option. Even so, I wanted to resist. But when he asked me to obey them, Dad had said 'love', not 'honey'. He meant what he said. *He wants you to do this, Peta.*

Slap. Slap again. My cheek burnt.

'You are thinking too much. The password. Please.'

Focus, and don't fall apart.

Then I realised what Dad was trying to do. It was brilliant. It was beautiful. But there was a problem: he said he'd given me the password, and he hadn't.

The Jongleur loomed ever closer. Mr Wahool waved the notebook madly.

A notebook of codes and passwords, Dad had said. I took a breath and concentrated.

Never forget, you have the power.

Finally I understood. Those six words explained everything.

'I think I've got it,' I whispered, trembling.

The Jongleur grabbed me by the throat and yanked me up so my face was level with his. Behind him, I could just see Dad crumpled on the floor, with Max standing triumphantly over him. The purple monster forced me to look into his cold, hollow eyes, then dropped me. I landed with a thud.

'Let her try it,' he told Wahool.

My fingers shook so much I could hardly use them. Very carefully, one key at a time, I typed in '1015'.

Dad *had* given me the code. I'd used it myself. I *was* the code.

I held my breath, not sure what to expect. Wahool peered at the screen over my shoulder. The page didn't change. 'It's not long enough. Try again.'

328

Oh hell. The Jongleur got me back by the throat.

'You're not trying hard enough. Think! Think!'

Like being shouted at by a seven-foot psycho was going to help me think.

'OK, I'm thinking.'

He dumped me down, walked a few steps across the carpet and picked up my phone from the floor.

'Your mother's number will be in here. Maybe she would like to listen to your final moments. That would be good, yes? Your mother listening?'

I just stared at him. Did he honestly think that these mind games were making it any easier? Well, he'd have trouble with *that* little threat because, first, that wasn't my original phone with Mum's number in it, and second, the phone had a PIN and there was no way I would ever tell him what it was just so he could let my mum listen to . . . whatever.

The Jongleur was hissing at me now, talking in a low voice about Mum and stuff. I tuned him out and thought about home. Dad always made me have a PIN for my phone. He was fussy about that kind of thing. The password on my laptop was quite complicated. Dad had made me think of a phrase I knew well and take the first letters from each word. So that password was *atbab* – the first letters of Mum's favourite hymn, 'All Things Bright and Beautiful'. Funny – I could remember it easily, but Dad said it was surprisingly hard for even computers to crack.

Oh, OK. So . . .

I closed my eyes. My power. If I was Dad and I wanted an unbreakable password using my daughter's power, what would I have done?

I let the Jongleur rumble on at me for a while. He seemed to be enjoying himself. I caught the occasional word –

'muscle' . . . 'ligament' . . . 'agony' – but his voice was surprisingly easy to tune out now. I sang 'All Things Bright and Beautiful' to myself in my head and thought about the knights in Winchelsea Church while I waited for him to finish.

'I've got it now,' I said when he shut up at last. These might be the last words I ever said, I realised. Oh well. At least they connected me to Dad. And to Mum too, through the day I was born.

Carefully I typed *tttpof*.

Ten to the power of fifteen. Easy to remember, hard to guess.

Dad had done what he said, I thought with a smile. He'd put me at the heart of everything, even the most dangerous bit of his most deadly mission. OK, so it had got us both killed, but it was a nice gesture. He loved me dangerously well.

Nothing happened.

Really?

'We have all night,' Mr Wahool said, his voice dripping with sarcasm, 'but the next time you make a mistake, it will annoy me. This will not be good for you.'

Max smiled. The Jongleur cracked his fingers, while outside, muffled explosions announced the start of the fireworks. They were the signal for our rendezvous. At least that noise meant that Sammy and Parissa would soon be safe.

Computer passwords generally had a mix of numbers and letters, didn't they, to be really hard to crack? The code adjusted itself in my head slightly. This was my last shot.

Bye, Dad. Bye, Mum, and Luke. I'm sorry, Karim, but at least you know I tried. Dad, I hope I understood you right, because those six million people really need that money.

Forcing my fingers to press each key without a mistake, I slowly typed '10ttpo15'.

It looked like nothing on the screen. Just a jumble of numbers and letters. My code. My power.

The room went silent, apart from the whizzes and pops of the distant fireworks. A few seconds later, the password page disappeared and the columns of numbers were back. The red message was gone.

'It's working!' Max said, looking excitedly over my left shoulder. 'Is the money all there, Papa?'

Mr Wahool snorted with relief. 'It is, my son.'

Max smirked. 'He gave it to us so easily!' he crowed.

'A father would do anything for his daughter,' Mr Wahool declared, with a pitiless glance at me. 'He – wait. What's happening? What . . .? Where's it all going to? I didn't authorise this . . . Stop this! Stop this!'

He shoved me out of the way and furiously pressed the keys, but there was nothing they could do. A message had come up saying *Transferring*, and we watched as the amount in the account changed from $114,617,933 to $0. The screen returned to the main list of accounts, and while Wahool fussed and panicked, the money disappeared from each of them, until it was all gone.

Dad's mission had always been to divert the coup money to the Marvalian people. This wasn't the password that undid his virus: it was the one that finished the job.

Way to go, Dad!

I turned and grinned up at the Jongleur. He hit me so hard that I flew across the floor.

'Kill her!' Wahool screamed. 'Kill her now!'

With a hideous grunt of fury, the Jongleur lunged towards me, but he was distracted by a movement in the shadows. I looked behind me. Max Wahool was falling to the floor. His startled face said he didn't understand how, or why. He hit the ground with a thud, smashing his head against the desk on the way.

There was a loud *PHUT PHUT* and I felt the air hiss and sizzle near my head. Something hot and wet hit my face. Now the Jongleur was crumpling to the ground in front of me. Blood oozed on to the expensive carpet.

Beyond him, on the other side of the room, the secret door was open and Karim was standing in front of it, dressed as a waiter, with a shiny silver revolver in his shaking hand. I stared at him. He seemed as astonished as I was.

'Peta!' he said. 'Mr Allud! You are safe?'

Mr Allud?

I looked back. Dad was sitting up, with his legs wrapped around Max's, breathing hard. At the desk, Mr Wahool looked around, utterly confused. His money was gone, his son was unconscious, his pet torturer was shot. And now Dad was pointing the Jongleur's gun at his head. Dad must have swiped Max's legs from under him when no one was looking, and grabbed the gun as Max fell. So *that's* why he'd played dead. *Seriously, way to go, Dad.*

He smiled at me briefly, then turned to Karim.

'Perfect timing,' he said. 'You can keep an eye on the boy while Peta helps with these.' With his free hand, he took some plastic ties out of his trouser pocket and threw them to me. His voice was still muffled by his thick lip. 'Move quickly.'

I did. The ties worked as handcuffs. Dad told me how to put them over Wahool's wrists, then pull them tight. I thought the old man might try and fight, but it's amazing how helpful people are when there's a gun pointing at them.

There was a knock on the door: *rat tat tat tat*.

'The boss is busy,' Dad called out in a muffled imitation of the Jongleur, while keeping his gun trained on Mr Wahool. Whoever it was seemed happy enough. They went away.

I moved across to Max, sprawled on the floor where he'd fallen. As I pulled his hands behind his back, he groaned and opened his eyes. The first thing he saw was Karim standing over him with the silver revolver.

'But that's . . . *mine*,' he said.

'I found it in your room. You used to point it at my sister,' Karim told him coldly.

Max grunted and resisted, thrashing his body around, but it was too late. I had his hands tied by then.

We gagged them with pieces of torn-up toga and dragged them to the secret tunnel. Dad shoved them roughly inside, one by one, removed the door's rope handle and together we blocked the door with the desk.

'That will keep them for a little while,' he said. 'Long enough, I hope. Karim, will you check the corridor is free?'

In the centre of the room, the Jongleur moaned. He was badly injured, but not dead. Dad seemed disappointed by this.

'I fired twice. Where'd the other bullet go?'

'*You* fired?' I said. 'But I thought Karim . . .'

'I have not yet learnt to shoot,' Karim said, grinning. 'Mr Allud shot the Jongleur. Ah, there it is, Mr Allud. Your other bullet.' He indicated the picture beside the secret door.

Dad had got the Picasso, right between the eyes.

We left the Jongleur where he was and locked the door behind us. Dad found a bathroom to wash the blood off his face. Then we walked out of the castle, through the main hall, where none of the servants or guests who saw us bothered to ask why the girl, the waiter and the jewellery guard looked so rough. It really is amazing what people get up to at these parties and nobody turns a hair.

The last of the fireworks were exploding in the night sky.

A flower-festooned buggy drove us down the hill. Dad used my phone to tell Steve to come and get us, and heard the news that Sammy and Parissa were free. As we arrived at the jetty, a speedboat was already racing in to carry us away. 'Robbins' explained to the island guards that Ella Van Cleepels was feeling sick and needed to go home. I'm sure I looked the part. I was tempted to do a few Amina-like groans, but decided that would be going too far.

François and Elena drew up with the boat. I took Karim's hand and led him aboard. As we headed out to sea, we heard the first faint *whoop whoop* of helicopter blades. Now we were safe, the American had called someone *very* high up in Italian security to say that this would be a good time to catch an international gang of criminals planning a coup.

The moon and stars were bright above us. The sound of helicopters grew louder. We watched the island disappear into the darkness until it was just a dot.

FIFTY-FIVE

We had two precious days together in Florence before I had to go home. Sammy and Parissa were recovering in hospital, but the rest of us spent most of our time round the kitchen table at the Foundation, regaling the rest of the team with our stories.

That first morning, Karim had walked into the villa like he owned it. This not-so-ragged, extraordinary boy. He wore super-skinny jeans, and a T-shirt with an image of six chess pieces that said 'Weapons of Choice'. Maria, who'd met him off the jet with the outfit all ready, had been listening carefully when I'd told her all about him. He glanced around the rooms, approving the American's taste in art and furnishings, nodding like a connoisseur. Which, in a way, he was.

When we joined the Foundation guys for our debrief that evening, Karim sat at the table with Dad and me, noticing everything, saying little. Amina quickly crawled into his lap and stayed there. His thin, strong arms wrapped themselves around her and held her fiercely close.

He had hugged me fiercely too, when we'd reached the safety of the mainland. It was the only time he showed just how much his freedom meant to him. Now he was learning to wear it nonchalantly, like the T-shirt and his cool new haircut. Sitting in the kitchen, he looked perfectly at home.

I felt it too. Here, round this table, with these people, talking about things that weren't *exactly* legal but . . . well, we were trying to change the world.

The Foundation guys kept asking us for more details about what we'd done in the study – how we'd survived. Sometimes it felt too good, and I didn't deserve it. I apologised for messing up with the pressure pads, and for getting caught.

'Thank God you did,' Dad said, pouring himself a whisky from the bottle that was doing the rounds of the grown-ups. 'It was only when they brought you in that we had a chance. Wahool would never have let me get past those last layers of security if it wasn't for you.'

'You *used* me, Dad! You *used* me!'

He looked stricken. 'I didn't plan to. But I thought you wanted me to . . .'

I nudged him in the shoulder. 'Teasing?'

'Blimey, Peta! Children!'

'But weren't you worried that I wouldn't guess the password?' I asked. This had been bugging me a lot. 'You didn't exactly make it easy.'

He shrugged. 'It was fifty-fifty. If you got it, that was the icing on the cake. But by then, I just wanted them to be distracted while I got the gun off that idiot Max.'

'But I thought . . . by then . . . we were just helping the Marvalians. I thought it was too late for us.'

Dad frowned at me. 'Not if I could help it, love. I wasn't going to let that monster touch my little girl.'

I sighed. 'I didn't get *that* at all.'

He smiled. The nicest smile he'd ever given me. 'I know. You thought it was all over, but you did what I asked you anyway. That's what kept them so mesmerised, honey. I found it distracting myself, to be honest. I'd have got Max a few seconds earlier if I'd been concentrating.'

I noticed Dad had called me 'honey'. He did that a lot now, and I called him 'Daddy' for a joke.

'We're going to need new code words for next time,' I pointed out. 'Those old ones won't work now.'

'Look into my eyes,' he said. 'Your mother would kill me. There is never going to be a next time.'

Yeah, right.

FIFTY-SIX

The Jongleur made it, but only just. The Italian police wanted to arrest Dad for shooting him, Wahool wanted Dad dead, and the people of Marvalia wanted to give him a medal. But Mike Jones was officially dead already, so none of these things could happen.

The days that followed were busy.

Three children without passports somehow found their way to England, where they were all looked after in a hotel on the south coast.

The Marvalian government hired top legal teams to requisition two superyachts and an island off the coast of Italy, several other properties around the world, lots of offshore bank accounts and a very valuable art collection (somewhat damaged).

A lot of rich ex-Marvalians and a well-known arms dealer were sent to jail, awaiting trial for conspiracy to overthrow a legitimate government.

Max and Omar Wahool had to pull out of their top private colleges, because their family's assets had been frozen and they couldn't afford the fees. Max was arrested not long afterwards for a violent attack on a fellow student. His Interface page hasn't been updated for a while. Yasmin, meanwhile, has started going around in public with an unsuitable boy so poor he actually has to work for a living. Mrs Wahool has twice been seen at charity dinners in *creased clothing*. She no longer makes the best-dressed list.

Two famous Marvalian heroes of the revolution returned to their country, where the people held a ticker-tape parade. One was in hospital for a while before returning to the government as the youngest Justice Minister in history, and the other has returned to writing her blog. It's called *Hope Is Blue*.

Epilogue

She talks to me on Interface. She says it is not too bad at her private school, but she misses her friend Luke. She talks too much about Luke, I think. Sometimes I joke that *I* should use crutches. I hope she knows it is a joke. She would miss me too, she says, but as I say . . . we talk on Interface every day. We play live chess. I beat her every time, but she will not give up. She does not give up, Peta Jones. She does not give up, or in. She does not know how.

She asked me about my friend, Mr Johnson. She wanted to understand how a man who was so kind to me could be so unkind also. She has not met so many men like this yet, but I have met many. They are greedy, that is all. They are kind sometimes, but they are greedy all the time. That is why I did not tell Mr Johnson about the outside tunnel. Or the money I saved from playing card tricks on the guards, which I kept in a special belt. It is against my religion to make bets, but I hoped that the money would somehow, one day, save my sister. I am sure God will forgive me. I have given the money to Amina now.

I am like Peta Jones, I think. I do not give up or give in. When I am rich and famous we will return to Marvalia and find my father, if he is still alive. Parissa and her government friends are searching on my behalf, but they have not found him yet.

First, I must study. I live with a good family in the city and I go to an excellent college, where they teach me about art and science and literature. I attend the mosque. My sister is back home in our village, going to school in the daytime and fishing in the evening. She tells me she is not little any more, but that cannot be true.

Every day I say thank you to Peta Jones but she says, *No, I must thank you, Karim. You saved my life. Twice. Many times, in fact.* This is true, but I don't use crutches. I am not sure I can compare with her Psycho Mirror friend.

At the weekends she goes home to her mother and the rich husband-who-is-not-a-husband, and she is happy, I think. But in the summer . . . the summer . . .

In the summer, we will meet up with her father-who-is-not dead. We will go to Florence and discover the works of the great painters. We will eat ice cream, she says, and learn Italian and karate, and jiving, and make plans to find my father. She will beat me at chess. (Ha! She says this, but it is not true. She gets better every day, but she forgets: I get better too.)

She will show me the Ponte Vecchio. I do not know what this is, but when she says the words, they sound beautiful.

ACKNOWLEDGEMENTS

Thank you to my parents, for all the adventures we had as a young family, exploring the world together, and for all your support and encouragement for every story I've written, published and unpublished. And for your help with this book.

As always, thank you to Barry Cunningham, Rachel Hickman, Imogen Cooper, Laura Myers and the team at Chicken House, and to Bella Pearson, editorial genius, who found Peta in this story and encouraged her to shine.

Thank you, too, to Richard Barber for the fun we had considering the London property market, and John Munford for being the fount of all knowledge about the interiors of luxury yachts – though I must assure readers that the design of this one was my own. Also to Tim Rawlins for your help with my security questions, and to Belinda and Katie Lewis, for going beyond the call of duty with details about the Circumvesuviana. And this goes back a long way, but eternal thanks are due to Pia, Saverio and Eleonora Savio for introducing me to Florence as a teenager, and being such generous hosts. Also Petri, Tera, Zetta and Atto Allas: you've been great friends and you inspired Peta's name, and all that followed, so thank you for that.

Simon Singh's books, *The Code Book: The Secret History of Codes and Code-breaking* and *Fermat's Last Theorem* encouraged my interest in maths and codes. They're adventure stories in themselves and I heartily recommend them both.

My stories always end up being about friendship. Thank you to my girlfriends, who make life something to celebrate. The writing sisterhood: Keris, Cat, Keren, Luisa, Suise and

Tamsyn. (Keren, thank you for the title.) The yoga team: Kasia, Clare, Rebecca and Jen. And now, the walking sisterhood: Cynthia, Kim, Nicki, Lucy and Jane.

Emily, Sophie, Freddie and Tom, you are always my inspiration.

Alex, you make life possible. You found the island for me, read the drafts more times than I dare remember, and you are my team. One day, I must show you the Ponte Vecchio.

WHAT YOU CAN DO

This story was partly inspired by my fury and frustration that, nearly 200 years after slavery was abolished, domestic slavery is flourishing in the 21st century. It can happen anywhere. If you suspect abuse, please report it to the police. And if you want to help, check out stopthetraffik.org, who work with Comic Relief. They have resources for schools with several ideas for things you can do. Together, we can make the world a better place.